The Next Big Thing

James Colley

16pt

9781038769701

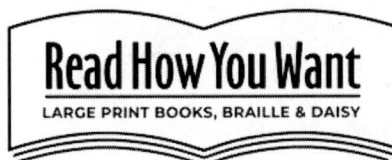

Read How You Want

LARGE PRINT BOOKS, BRAILLE & DAISY

Copyright Page from the Original Book

TABLE OF CONTENTS

Praise for *The Next Big Thing*

'WOW. This book will become an Aussie classic, alongside *The Castle,* Vegemit 1e and Steve Irwin. Run, don't walk to the bookstore. I laughed, I got teary and I cheered for the underdogs in this heartwarming story of overcoming adversity, following your dreams and fighting for what matters to you. Everything is big in *The Next Big Thing* – the humour, the heart and the smile you'll have when you finish reading.' **Rachael Johns**

'James Colley's sparkling wit brings to life this delightful romcom, revealing that at the heart of Australia's absurd obsession with towering prawns, oversized bananas and all things "big" is a passion for a larger-than-life love story. In the quirkiest corner of Australian culture, Colley's charm and warmth spin a tale where "big" laughs lead to "big" love.' **Nakkiah Lui**

'*The Next Big Thing* is absurd and moving, ridiculous and sublime. Its ludicrous plot is grounded in the genuine sweetness of a slow-blooming friends-to-lovers romance, as Norm and Ella weigh up the value of a grand gesture, a Big Thing, against a thousand tiny declarations. *The Next Big Thing* is studded with puns and sparkling dialogue like the night sky over the middle of nowhere. It's soaringly silly and it'll steal your heart.' **Clare Fletcher**

'James Colley is one of the funniest TV writers in Australia. Frankly I'm surprised he had the attention span for a whole book, but by God he's done it!' **Annabel Crabb**

'*The Next Big Thing* is simply adorable. In it, James Colley gently captures the messy, ridiculous, melancholic yet joyful heart of small-town Australia and in doing so pays a well-deserved tribute to one of The Greats. This is a novel with the perfect amount of nostalgia and full of characters you can't help but love.' **Jan Fran**

'Poignant and delightful, *The Next Big Thing* crackles with warmth and wry, gentle humour. A gem.' **First Dog on the Moon**

'The only thing more annoying than seeing James Colley excel at comedy writing is seeing him nail a romantic comedy with so much heart and wit. We get it, James. You can do anything.' **Susie Youssef**

'*The Next Big Thing* is the rarest of things: an Australian novel that leaves you damn happy. Equal parts rom-com and small-town underdog adventure, this is your favourite Australian sitcom in book-form. It's going to make you bark laughing, leave you grinning ear-to-ear ... and might just make you cry too.' **Benjamin Law**

'*The Next Big Thing* combines the joys of a classic love story with a distinctly Australian sense of humour. Filled with affection for reckless, youthful hope and genuinely funny, Colley has written something truly delightful.' **Brydie Lee-Kennedy**

'A completely charming book whose characters leap off the page (and straight into your heart ... via a rickety wheelbarrow).' **Virginia Gay**

James Colley is a comedy writer and producer known for his work as head writer on *Gruen, Gruen Nation, Question Everything* and *The Weekly with Charlie Pickering.*

His writing has been featured in the *Sydney Morning Herald,* the *Guardian, Frankie, Crikey,* the *Big Issue* and *Junkee.*

The Next Big Thing is his debut novel.

For Grace,
who can't even read.

Coffs Harbour started it in 1964 with the Big Banana. Since then an epidemic of elephantiasis has spread across Australia. In NSW a Big Apple has popped up in Batlow, a Big Potato in Robertson, a Big Trout in Adaminaby, a Big Cherry in Young, a Big Gold Digger in Bathurst, a Big Cow near Berry, a Big Strawberry on the New England Tableland and a Big Murray Cod at Wagga. The Sunshine Coast, in Queensland, has had a particularly severe bout of it with a Big Pineapple, Cow, Dinosaur, Egg, Bee, Bottle and Lawnmower. Nearby Kilcoy has a Big Yowie and Rockhampton has a Big Brahman Bull among others. South Australia has a Big Lobster in Robe and a Big Orange in Berri. Victoria has a Big Humpty Dumpty in Mildura, a Big Golf Ball at Spring Valley and a Big Murray Cod at Tocumwal. Tasmania has a Big Teddy Bear and a Big Tasmanian Devil, both not far from Launceston. And at Penguin ... I'll let you guess.

Good Weekend, **4 August 1985**

Prologue

The old dog's deep black eyes flicker with an emotion somewhere between fear and resignation. The garden trolley was out of control. Familiar scents fill his nostrils. Indistinct images bordering on beauty. If this was his last ride, he was going to enjoy it.

The dog is called Puppy, a name he's long since outgrown but one that was never replaced. Pup the Old Dog, they say now. The name rings true. Every day he aches. He holds on only out of love for the young man who, moments ago, carelessly allowed the rusted handle of the garden trolley to slip from his sweaty hand.

Locals watch through shop windows and from wrought-iron seats that threaten to fuse with any exposed flesh. No one moves. Whether it is due to shock, indecision or the macabre desire to see what happens, they are locked fast with only their eyes moving, as though they're trapped inside a portrait hanging over the fireplace in a haunted house.

The wheels of the trolley bounce over the unsealed road that the Norman Council swears they're going to get around to tarring soon. If the old dog had wanted to jump, the option has long since abandoned him. All he can do is look over the rim of the trolley and wonder whether the suddenly wobbling front right wheel will send him crashing into the steel shed with the weathered mural of the young girl dancing on the riverbank, which means certain death, or if it will stay true and he'll be launched through the trees and into the dry riverbed where he'll crash into the rusted chassis of the overturned troopy, and in that way face death. He has no preference.

Overlooking Botany Street, with its runaway trolleys and nihilistic dogs, are two icons of the town of Norman: the Stumbling Elephant Hotel and, behind it, the impressive visage of Vodafone Hill, towering over the dust bowl like *The great wave off Kanagawa,* frozen in time, threatening at any moment to break and crash over the small town.

Halfway up that hill stands another local icon – Norm from Norman, best friend to Pup the Old Dog. He had been pulling the trolley that had brought the old dog into town, when an unfamiliar desire compelled him to climb the hill. He followed the siren's call. He is yet to realise that the handle is no longer in his hand. His mind has wandered off.

Norm has just had a big idea. The biggest idea of his life, in fact. Norm is not used to having ideas, particularly not big ones. The sensation is so strange to him that, for a moment, he wondered if he was experiencing a medical episode. It was as if he had coaxed a butterfly into his hand and now stood frozen, worried that any sudden movement might scare it away.

Norm is allowing himself to dream, and it requires every last drop of his concentration.

Norm is dreaming of a Big Thing.

'I might be a genius,' he says to the old dog who is at this moment bounding past Lucky Duck Pizza and still picking up speed. Norm smiles, an expression so rare that his facial muscles struggle with the burden. It's as if he learned how to smile by reading about it on Wikipedia. His oversized polo hangs off his thin frame, giving him the look of a scarecrow. He brushes aside his wheat-blond fringe and basks in the sunshine. In the future, Norm from Norman will mark this as the third-best moment of his life.

The rumble of a garden trolley reawakens Norm Perkins. He starts to panic. That's all there is to do. His legs are too slow to catch the poor dog. His only option is to bear witness.

But there's one last lifeline for Pup the Old Dog: the dependable incompetence of the Norman Council. The previous summer, Mayor Billy Fitz had sworn on his mother's grave that he had fixed the pothole out the front of the Sunshine Deli. One week later, he sprained his ankle in that exact hole and had to be tended to by his very-much-alive mother. The pothole remained as deep as ever. The mayor claimed he was much too focused on his recovery to do anything about it.

As if gravitationally pulled, the wobbly wheel of the garden trolley falls into that pothole and snaps off. With a horrible piercing screech, the metal frame of the trolley scrapes along the main street, where it slowly grinds to a halt.

Norm races to the site of the crash, takes the old dog in his arms, and tries with all his might to not think about what he almost lost, having already lost so much.

PART ONE

Nothing's Normal in Norman

1

The testicles of Goulburn's now legendary Big Merino hang down so far that they penetrate the roof of the souvenir shop.

The Canberra Times, 19 August 1991

The single pedestal fan inside the Stumbling Elephant Hotel rotated slowly, bestowing its blessing on the patrons. Plates barely contained the Sunday roast, a tradition from another climate, as sacred as church. The meat was doused in gravy because at the Stumbling Elephant all sorrows were drowned. There were a dozen patrons spread out over as many tables, yet no one made a sound. No scraping of cutlery, no idle chatter. Some paused mid-bite, so as to not inhibit the sound of the small, crackling radio on the bar.

Jasper's *Sunday Afternoon Jamboree* on 1228 AM Radio Norman was not typically appointment listening, but this was not a typical jamboree. Indeed, it pushed the very boundaries of what could honestly be classed as a jamboree. Gone was Jasper's usual breathy lilt, his attempt to sound like the hosts on Radio National. Instead his tone was sombre and defeated. According to Jasper, by way of the mayor's office, they had just received official word that, come the end of the month, Delight, a small town about 35 kilometres south-south-east of Norman, would cease to exist.

That announcement in and of itself was not enough to shock the patrons of the Stumbling Elephant, who seemed rather unmoved. They had become used to towns defaulting all around them. According to the government these homesteads were no longer 'viable'. It was selfish to continue living there, considering all the other factors concerning the nation at this time.

Sandy, the publican, kept a map behind the bar of the local area with black crosses marking each lost town. With a movement so routine it lacked any of the appropriate drama, she took her marker and drew a cross over Delight. This was the third cross over a town closer to the city than Norman.

Jasper's weedy voice stammered as he continued to read. 'This means supply runs to Norman will again be reduced—'

A loud groan cut off the rest of the announcement. The bar came alive with cutlery clattering and annoyed chattering. A slow depression seeped up through the floors of the bar as the reality of its patrons' predicament dawned on them. There was no more energy to expend in frustration. Nothing to be done about it, after all. Just another indignity the town must face as it circled the drain.

Norm entered the Stumbling Elephant and looked for Ella, as he did everywhere. He didn't often visit the pub, but the interior was unchanging enough to feel familiar. The same pool table rigged to play without a gold coin, the same old wooden decor with the same sad old townsfolk staring into their drinks, all alone together.

Norm considered climbing Vodafone Hill to text Ella but decided against it. The ordeal of carting the now broken garden trolley weighed down by the dog all the way along the riverbed and back home had sapped his energy reserves dry. Gingerly, he settled into the only seat at the bar that retained most of its cushioning. He had not come in to celebrate. The revelation of the morning had given way to the bitter taste of his least favourite day of the year. It was right that he was here alone. This was the home of misery.

He knew everyone in the bar by name. If pushed, he could quote their home address, mother's maiden name, and just about every other detail he would need to steal their identity.

'Thought I'd be seeing you today,' Sandy said from behind the bar as she poured Norm a dark ale and sat it on top of a coaster that read 'You'll never forget a night at the Elephant'. Her voice was soft and caring, a surprise to anyone who judged her by the biceps that bulged as she poured from the tap or threw you through the front door.

He might have wondered how Sandy remembered but it was obvious enough. Any other day, Norm would only set foot in the Elephant with his head down, headed straight for the town's only ATM. He took his money and he left. He didn't even wait for his receipt. Sandy knew this well, as she checked every one. It was her way of keeping an eye on his dwindling pile of funds. This was the only day of the year that Norm took a seat at the Stumbling Elephant. One drink, a tribute.

She gave him space to wallow for a moment and he was grateful for it. He'd barely cracked nine when he was left alone. It was nearly thirteen years ago now. How was it already thirteen years? How was it only thirteen? He wondered what had possessed his father to name him after this town. And, if his father could see them now, which one would he find more disappointing?

The plight of Norman was the same tale that had played out across the wheat belt. Those who could leave had gone a long time ago. The rest had resigned themselves to going down with the ship. It was Norm's experience in life that awful things happened suddenly. Life changed in an instant and then it was up to you to hold on and ride the aftershocks. But this was different. It was a car crash at painfully low speeds, with no one willing to grab the wheel or so much as tap the brakes.

Norm took another sip and winced involuntarily. It was impossible to separate the town from the memories of his father. One was lost in a moment, the other he was losing slowly. Every memory he had was forged on those streets. If the town was lost, they would be, too.

Through the window of the bar he could see Vodafone Hill, the exact spot where he'd stood earlier that day, lost in a dream. Norm was comfortable in the world of dreams. Growing up, he was called a space cadet. He thought that meant he'd work for NASA one day.

Still, this one idea stuck in his teeth. He wondered if the two sips of dark ale had gone to his head. His left leg began to bounce restlessly against the metal footrest on his stool while he tore at the coaster in his hand. The idea filled his lungs like water. He had to release it or else it would consume him.

Norm had never really felt the pull of destiny, at least not in a positive way. Yet, at this moment, it was as if he was being called to a higher purpose.

It was the town that spoke first. Specifically, it was Rocko, no known last name (unless that was his last name). No one knew for sure but there had never been two Rockos in the Stumbling Elephant at the same time, so differentiation had never been an issue. His smell reached Norm long before his words, intoxicating and thick, a mix of Melbourne Bitter and rollies, strong enough to kill a cat.

'You're in my seat,' Rocko snarled.

'I think you'll find they're all my seats, Rocko,' Sandy interjected, sliding over the moment her spider-sense tingled.

'This one's got my name on it,' Rocko replied, pointing to a crude carving on the underside of the bar where ROCKO had been scratched out with a key.

Sandy smiled. 'You swore to me you didn't write that. You said it was some teenagers and I asked why would teens scrawl ROCKO on the bar and you said, and I quote, "Who can understand kids these days".'

Rocko demurred, mumbling something about how the teens probably knew that this was his seat. Norm didn't want to get distracted and wanted to cause trouble even less, so he jumped out of the seat and offered it to Rocko with a flash of a smile. In return, Rocko generously gifted Norm a hit from his shoulder as he pushed past and sank into a well-worn groove in the padding.

Sandy gave Norm a sympathetic smile but the boy couldn't have cared less about losing his seat. His eyes had shifted to the corner of the bar. The radio announcement had provided a merciful early end to the Sunday session acoustic set, which was a fancy way of referring to Harvey Claystone playing an ill-advised and off-tune cover of Dragon's 'Are You

Old Enough?' on a guitar missing its D-string. Through the stained windows he could see Harvey's silhouette rolling himself another cigarette. The microphone remained in its stand on the abandoned stage.

Looking out at the crowd, Norm wondered if he had happily walked himself onto the gallows and popped his head in a noose. He grasped the microphone stand in his clammy hands and adjusted it to a height more suitable for his gangly frame. He went to speak and the stand crashed back down to bellybutton height. The crash reverberated through the speakers and for the first time the patrons seemed to notice he existed.

Rather than risk another fumble Norm chose to lean awkwardly down to the microphone, somewhat in the shape of a gazelle drinking from the watering hole unaware that it's about to be swallowed whole by a crocodile. Whatever courage he had felt stepping onto the stage had quickly manifested itself into the early signs of a panic attack. His heart was beating so hard he wondered if it could be seen through his chest like he was a cartoon character. The crowd could smell fear. It energised them. At last, there was something to see in Norman.

'Go on then, whistle,' said Big Gavin Walsh, to the laughs of his friends.

'Do you take requests? Piss off!' added regular-sized Eka Ismail, to no response. He sank back in his chair, annoyed.

8

The blinding stage lights limited Norm's view to the first three rows of tables, meaning each voice ripped out of the darkness and felt even more threatening. All in all, Norm would have much rather been driving with the top down on a lovely day in Dallas.

'Is this the quiz?' asked another voice from the void. To Norm, this one seemed kinder, if undeniably thicker.

'Yes is it, Stephen!' called Sandy from behind the bar, as she passed Rocko another can of Melbourne Bitter. 'Question one, what night is the quiz?'

'It's Tuesdays!' said Thick Stephen with delight.

'Correct you are,' Sandy called. 'Question two, what day is it today?'

'Uh, it's Sunday!' said Thick Stephen, absolutely chuffed with himself. He'd never gone two from two in the quiz before and rated himself a real chance at picking up the meat tray.

Sandy turned to Norm and, with the same sweet but firm voice she used on the drunks, told him to either piss or get off the pot.

That was enough to spur some life into Norm. He cleared his throat and spoke in a voice a full octave higher than he'd ever reached before.

'Norman – ahem – Norman is dying.' He paused for what he thought was dramatic effect. 'Nothing grows. Nothing lives. No one stops by anymore.'

'Yeah, that's why we're trying to have a drink,' called Rocko from his stool at the bar, flinging the can of Melbourne Bitter directly at Norm. Lucky for Norm, a lifetime of being bullied had him in a constant state of alarm and as the can appeared through the lights, he managed to deftly duck and let it sail past his right shoulder. The quick reflexes gained him a little bit of respect from the crowd, all except Rocko, of course.

'You owe me a beer,' he called.

'Rocko, behave yourself,' Sandy chided.

'He's being a sooky-la-la,' Rocko replied, a dirty hand thrust out towards Norm.

This was one of the most devastating accusations that any Australian could face. The crowd grumbled in agreement. Norm was losing them fast.

'I'm not a sooky-la-la,' he mumbled. It was too late, the crowd was emboldened now.

'He's having a sook!'

'Since when has this been the Sunday Sook Session?'

'But ... but ... but it is not too late to save the town,' Norm pushed on.

Whatever enthusiasm he had expected was not forthcoming. All Norm received were a few rolled eyes and the scraping sounds of patrons returning to their Sunday roasts.

'Did you hear me? We can save the town! Yay!' Receiving no response, Norm dropped his arms to his side in frustration. 'What, you're just going to sit there, chewing on your dinner and letting Norman die?'

'It's already dead, mate,' Gavin said, his mouth half-full of lamb, bits of gravy spraying across the table. 'No use sooking about it.'

Norm's eyes lowered, his posture softened. He received a small, sympathetic smile from Bettsy Langham, the local florist, at the table in front of him. Kindness radiated from Mrs Langham. Norm could sense that she was about to speak, maybe offer a desperately needed word or two of support, but before she could, her husband Sidney leaned forward, looking at Norm over his half-moon glasses as if the boy were a bug.

'Young man, you simply do not understand the situation of which you speak.' He spoke with the vocal flourish of a Shakespearean actor. Here was a man who truly enjoyed the sound of his own voice. Despite the heat, he was dressed in trousers and a collared shirt, his jowls having descended over time to lock his face in a permanent frown that reminded Norm of an old mastiff. 'Right at this moment, you are standing at a wake telling us that there is still hope for the patient!'

He projected these final words with a flourish, as if expecting the crowd to cheer him on. No cheer came.

'He's a sooky-la-la!' Rocko cried. Now came the applause. Mr Langham scoffed and returned to his meal. Norm looked to Sandy for a life raft.

'You are coming off as a bit of a sooky-la-la, love,' Sandy confirmed. 'Just tell us your little idea and then we can all sit here in miserable peace.'

The crowd applauded again.

'To the rest of you,' Sandy said, commanding the room in a way Norm never could, 'if you can sit through five minutes of Harvey's awful racket, you can give this kid the same courtesy. Sorry Harvey.'

Harvey, having just returned from his cigarette break to find his stage taken and his talent insulted, skulked in the corner, glaring at the usurper.

Norm pushed back his fringe and took a deep breath, aware that it may be his last.

'My plan is uh, radical to say the least but I have thought very hard about it and I ... and I think that radical might just be the way to go. Even if it isn't, heck, isn't it better to at least go out swinging than just sit and wait for death?'

Norm laughed nervously. The stony faces of the crowd didn't budge. He took a sip from the dark ale in his hand, choking it back. Still disgusting but enough to clear his windpipe.

He thought again about his father. Norm imagined him sitting in the crowd, proudly watching his son try to save the town. He lost himself in the bright stage lights, as if looking into heaven itself. Time seemed to hold still. Somehow, amid all the chaos, a perfect calmness engulfed Norm. He exhaled deeply, puffed out his concave chest and spoke.

'I think we should build a—'

At that very moment, Norm became suddenly entranced by the outline of something in the light. His mouth opened in wonder. By the time he saw the red label of the Melbourne Bitter can it was too late to duck.

Awful things happen suddenly.

It hit with a satisfying crunch, spraying Harvey's portable amp in foamy beer. Norm's knees buckled. Electricity crackled. Harvey screamed.

'Phwoar, d'you see that!?' Rocko shouted, jumping from his stool, arms up in triumph.

Thick Stephen sighed deeply, having just realised he wasn't going to win a meat tray. The stage lights flickered. A fire erupted from the back of the amp. And Norm's whole world went dark.

2

Once upon a time, the town of Norman was bisected by a river. Legend has it that the shopkeepers could hop from one side to the other holding a pallet of fresh fruit without worrying about getting their feet wet. Once you passed Langham & Sons Ironmongers, the river would curl and widen as it made its way out of town.

Now that the river had run dry, the fastest way into town was right down its centre taking a left at the rusted-over chassis of the upturned troopy, making sure to slap the number plate for good luck, and straight on until you hit the old painted shed that had nearly ended Pup the Old Dog.

Norm would have rather never shown his face on Botany Street again. The rejection of the night before still stung. The red welt on his forehead stung even harder. His stomach, usually tight with anxiety whenever he was in public, now boiled with anger. He was trying to save these people but they'd rather wallow in misery. He decided, all things considered, to be a petulant child about the whole situation. Dragging his feet, kicking stones, doing everything he could to indicate that he really didn't want to be in town, as if he had a say in the matter.

Norm had woken up that morning on a mattress on the floor of the Batchens' living room. He was in a world of pain. Ella Batchen had been tapping away on her laptop, acting as if there was nothing more fascinating in her life than organising spreadsheets for her father's concreting business.

Norm had pushed back the blankets and noticed he wasn't wearing the same clothes as the night before. Instead, he was dressed in an oversized t-shirt and shorts both bearing the logo of Norman Concreting. The tagline read, 'Where else are you gonna go?' A little cocky, admittedly, but Ella's dad, Mick Batchen, was the only concreter within an hour in any direction so he could afford to be cocky.

'You didn't change me into this, did you?' Norm asked.

Ella closed the laptop and scrunched up her face as if he'd just offered her a bite of a worm. 'Ew. No. Dad carried you home from the pub and hosed you down in the front yard. He said you smelled rank, too. How much did you have?'

This gave birth to a new feeling in the pit of Norm's stomach. Still shame but a different twinge of shame. How nice, he thought, to get to experience all of them at once. Like ordering a beer paddle of humiliation.

'He told you what happened, then,' Norm said, unable to look Ella in the eye.

'Nah, he said I'd have more fun finding that out myself.'

Ella, like her Nanna Doris, simply refused to listen to good gossip without a hot drink to sip on, so that had meant walking up the river to Norman's one and only cafe. The Sunshine Deli was in no sense a deli. It was just a word that sweet old Mr Baylis believed meant 'fancy eatery' and so he went with it. He had a lot of beliefs. His coffee philosophy was one of quantity over quality. The stein he placed in front of customers could attest to that. He called it a latte but what that really meant was that he shook up the Nescafe Blend 43 before serving it. Its colour was about the same as you'd see trickling down the river when it rained (if it ever rained again).

Although Mr Baylis was rarely seen without a broad smile peeking out from under his overgrown moustache, Norm saw the man frown as he emerged from the dead trees at the river's edge, sweating as he pushed Pup the Old Dog, now seated in an old wheelbarrow. With a helpful, albeit a little too forceful, shove from Ella, he was over the lip and cruising. Norm knew word would have gotten around already that he'd humiliated himself the night before. He used to be a harmless oddity. Now, they might well have him committed.

Mr Baylis was an incredibly humble man. His was perhaps the only cafe in country Australia that didn't claim to have the world's greatest vanilla slice. Instead, the hand-painted sign on the glass read 'World's 3rd Greatest Vanilla Slice'. He'd once admitted to Ella that he'd tried a vanilla slice on his honeymoon in Northern Italy that he couldn't in good conscience claim to have beaten. Third felt safe. No one checks who came third.

With great care, Norm slowly manoeuvred the wheelbarrow into the patch of shade cast by the shadow of the old Sunshine Deli sign. Sneaking to an adjacent table, he emptied a pile of napkins out of a small purple clay tray then took the water from the table and poured out just enough to reach the lip of the tray. Delicately he placed it in front of Pup.

With the dog settled, Ella and Norm placed their usual order and sat at their usual table. Moments later they were presented with their steins of coffee. Ella sipped and retched slightly, then added a spoonful of brown sugar from the small, misshapen pot that Mrs Baylis had made herself.

Norm shifted in his seat, trying to hit an angle that blocked the punishing light from roasting him as well. There was another small patch of shade, offered by the rooster-shaped weathervane atop the long since abandoned Maffezzoni Metals warehouse.

The scent of burning scones wafted through the air. Mr Baylis' sense of smell wasn't what it used to be. Nothing about him was what it used to be. At this moment, he was shuffling inside, shaking arms filled with plates from another table. 'Table two needs milk, Mrs. Don't forget to pop the kettle on for the tea,' he said. There was no one inside.

Ella stirred her coffee, leaned in and then recoiled suddenly as her elbow singed on the table frame. 'This had better be worth it,' she said, gritting her teeth as she tried to rub the pain away. 'Spill!'

Norm started to feel shy. It had been a bad idea, a bad mistake, a very bad day. That was the problem – the day. He had been caught up in the emotion of the day. He'd been enchanted by a silly idea as a way of escaping it all and then in a terrible moment the reality of the world came crashing down on him. Awful things happen suddenly. He didn't know how to explain all of that to Ella. The thought made his mouth turn dry. He felt that same pulsing fear that he had felt on the stage in the Stumbling Elephant, as if he only had a few seconds to say something or Ella would brain him with a can of Melbourne Bitter, or lacking that, her gigantic cup of watery coffee.

He realised he hadn't been looking at her for some time now. He'd been silently staring at his hands, fidgeting in his lap. He assumed when he finally met her gaze she'd be annoyed by him, as sick of him as everyone else, but that wasn't true. She was patiently waiting. There was no move to hurry him, no boredom creeping into her brow. She could be rough with him, but she was always kind. He couldn't help but feel a little guilty at that, though. Ella spent her life waiting for Norm.

'I ... I don't...' he struggled.

Ella tilted her head. 'What's with the wheelbarrow?'

'Oh that,' he laughed. And he was off. He told Ella all about the bouncing garden trolley, the long journey dragging it back home and the guilt-ridden triple serving of dog food and ice cream he'd given Pup on return.

'Ice cream isn't good for dogs,' Ella informed him.

'Let him indulge,' Norm said with a wave of his hand, as if the problem was the old dog's summer figure not his digestive tract.

'So,' Ella began in the soft yet direct tone of a hostage negotiator. 'How did you end up on my couch?'

Norm recounted the events of the night before as best he could, save for a couple of details that were lost when the Melbourne Bitter can indented itself in his skull.

Ella was stunned. 'How do you not call me?'

'I didn't know I was going to do it,' Norm said. 'I went there because it was—'

Norm stammered and Ella remembered there were only one day each year that he would willingly set foot in the Stumbling Elephant.

'Oh, Norm,' she said, reaching out for his hand resting on the table, her voice thick with the pain of realising her mistake.

He shook his head. 'It's fine. It's a silly tradition. Part of me is glad he didn't witness it, really.'

Norm let out a small laugh but Ella didn't.

'I should have been there for you.'

Norm could tell she was looking at him with those wide brown eyes, but he couldn't meet her gaze. He stared down at his hands in his lap, where he was tearing a napkin into small pieces.

'Death sucks,' Ella said.

'Death sucks,' Norm nodded.

'It should be illegal.'

'I think it is. Causing it at least. It's hard to punish the victims.'

'But it's wild, isn't it? Like, mortality is wild. We're all going to die and it hardly ever comes up. It should lead off the news every night.'

Norm laughed. 'Okay, so how do you see this working? Every night – *every night* – they play the news theme and the anchor starts by saying, "Good evening, you and everyone you know is going to die. Now here's Janine with the weather."'

'I don't reckon you'd go straight to the weather.'

'You'd better hurry, Janine's gonna die.'

'Never liked Janine anyways.'

All of a sudden they were both cackling, and Norm could feel a warmth cascading through his entire body. He met Ella's eyes and could have sworn he saw them sparkle.

'Come on then, what happened, Cadbury? Had a glass and a half of beer and triggered a complete psychological meltdown?'

'Kinda, yeah. I was thinking about Dad and how much he loved this town and how he always said it had saved him and I wondered what he would do to save it. You know him, he wanted everything to be big and bold so I had a big and bold idea. I thought the town would love it. But they were all mean to me and made me feel bad and they wouldn't even listen.'

Ella scoffed. 'You are such a sooky la-la.'

Norm was aghast. 'I am not a sooky la-la. Would people *please* stop calling me a sooky la-la?'

'Or what, you'll have a sook about it?'

'No,' Norm mumbled, aware that he was sooking at this very moment.

'So, what inspired all of this? Were you drunk?'

'I only had like two sips of beer.'

Ella whistled. 'Bloody hell, you were white girl wasted.'

The air hung still for a beat. Pup the Old Dog snapped at a fly.

'So?' Ella asked, her eyebrows raised.

Norm leaned in, confused. 'So?'

'What's the idea!?'

'Oh.' Norm exhaled deeply and shook his head. 'Forget about it. It was a silly idea. The emotion of the day, you know? Doesn't matter, anyway.'

He reached out to grab another napkin from the table, but Ella caught his wrist.

'Norm,' she smiled sweetly, without loosening her grip. 'If you don't tell me, I am going to kill you.'

She threw his arm back.

'When you put it like that,' Norm smiled, rubbing his wrist. He braced himself for yet more humiliation. 'A big thing.'

Ella snorted.

'Not like that,' Norm said. 'Get your mind out of the gutter.'

'What? You said you want a big thing and a person isn't supposed to think of—'

'I don't mean a big ... that ... I mean a Big Thing. One of the Big Things. I don't think there is a grouping term for them. No one ever really thought about it before now, I guess. They're the Big Things, you know, like the wonders of the world but off a highway in Humpty Doo or whatever. A Big Thing!'

Norm performed a useless gesture of raising his hand above his head to indicate something was very tall and Ella finally managed to catch his meaning. She paused for what felt like an age to Norm.

He tried to read her expression, usually so open to him. She gave away nothing. Her lips pursed as if she were a sommelier, tasting the idea for the first time. Her brown eyes looked through him. At what, he couldn't tell. He looked away, scared to be caught staring. He focused on the table, on his hands, on anything else other than the delicate face he knew so well.

'I think we should do it,' Ella said.

'What?'

'Let's do it. You and me. Let's save the town.'

Norm's eyes lit up. The bleak mood that had engulfed him all morning seemed to slide off his shoulders and onto the ground. They shared a smile. It was a perfect moment that couldn't even be dampened by the profane curses of Mr Baylis pulling charcoal husks from his oven.

3

The Big Pavlova is the work of Goulburn businessman Mr Peter Jackson-Calway who has developed an industrial site in Marulan for his pavlova, cheesecake and chocolate factory...

'And nearly everybody thinks it's great,' Mr Jackson-Calway said.

The Canberra Times, 18 September 1984

Mick Batchen was out of his depth, but there was nothing unusual about that. He had spent most of his life with his head completely underwater, only treating himself to a gasp of air when his schedule would allow it.

He was badly outnumbered already with three kids and only his mother-in-law, Doris, providing support. Widow-in-law? Was there a word for whatever their relationship was now?

It was a handful to say the very least. But still, when his only daughter returned from primary school with poor Tony's kid expecting a feed, Mick just smiled and pulled up a chair. After all, what was a little more chaos?

At least Ella had someone. Mick knew how to talk to the boys, or not talk to the boys. He could line them up in front of the wheelie bin with a bat in hand and bowl half-trackers. He was still learning how to be a single father, but he'd been talking cricket all of his life. There was always a lesson to be learned about reading your conditions, the benefits of patience, and how you can do absolutely everything right and still end up on the long, lonely walk back to the pavilion.

But how was he supposed to talk to Ella?

He was already out of ideas. In a few years she would be a teenager. It was scary to even begin to comprehend. They needed a quiet moment, but when had this lot ever been quiet?

He'd taken the kids down to the river to try and wear them out, but it was a lost cause. Gary was screaming and splashing about in the knee-high water, trying to bait his Nanna into chasing after him. Zeke was roaming the bank with a nerf gun and was in turn was being chased by an overly excited golden lab puppy. A puppy? Where on Earth did they find a puppy? Bloody hell.

Mick was drowning alright. He hung his head down and settled into the camping chair. He thought about the thermos full of instant coffee sitting in the picnic basket but decided it wasn't worth the effort of standing up. He closed his eyes and let the sound of the river, the screaming kids and the excited barks all turn into white noise. His tranquillity was short-lived, as a nerf dart connected with the very top of his head and ricocheted into his lap.

'Enough!' he cried with an almighty roar.

And for a moment, peace reigned throughout the land.

They gathered by the river's edge and distributed the devon sandwiches, bags of chips and cut-up cucumbers and carrots. Usually, Mick was the type to eat in silence, only intervening when the conversation got too loud or was likely to start a fight – so only fifteen or sixteen times a meal. But this felt like a chance to impart some wisdom to the thin and pale young boy who had wandered out of a Dickensian novel onto his picnic blanket.

'Do you know where the modern world began, Norm?' he asked.

Norm, all of nine years old, simply did not have a satisfactory answer to that question. He looked at Ella. She rolled her eyes. Mick pretended not to see the attitude as he pushed on.

'Have you ever heard of Göbekli Tepe?'

Norm shook his head and with a voice more suited to a cartoon mouse explained that he didn't own any video games and that was why the other kids at school didn't want to hang out with him. Ella helpfully added that it wasn't the only reason. Mick decided to let that through to the keeper.

'It's a proper dry place. Nothing there, hey? During the day, it feels like you've stepped into a fan-forced oven. Pasty fella like you would turn as red as a lobster. Burnt to a crisp, you'd be.' He held up a bit of crust as he said this to illustrate the point. Norm watched on, completely mesmerised. 'But at night it was quiet, cold, no signs of life. Only the weary traveller, lost on their way somewhere else. Passing through with no regard for where they were standing. Until one day – CRASH!'

Mick clapped and Norm jumped, spraying a packet of light and tangy into the air.

'Easy, eff you,' Nanna Doris cried.

'A bolt of lightning strikes the rock and suddenly there's this sizzling crater in the ground.'

Ella and Zeke were both mouthing along but Mick took some satisfaction from seeing that Gary was on the edge of his seat. 'Who sent the lightning?' he asked.

Mick hadn't been expecting that question and it threw him off his rhythm. 'Uh, I don't know, son. God.'

'Is God real?' Ella asked, crunching on a cucumber.

'I ... uh ... I don't know. The point is—'

'How could God have sent the lightning if you don't know if he's real?' Ella said, clearly enjoying this far too much.

'Well, he did then,' said Mick, trying to get back to his point.

'Why?'

'He was smiting someone?'

'What's mighty mean?' Gary asked.

'Not mighty, smiting.'

'It's when you're bad so God hits you with lightning and you go *pfshhhh* and explode everywhere,' Zeke added helpfully.

'I'm gonna smite you,' Ella said, elbowing Zeke.

'I'll smite you first. I'll double-smite you.'

'I'll might your bum-bum,' Gary shouted, overflowing with excitement.

'No one is smiting anyone's bum-bum,' Mick said, raising his voice to regain control of the room.

'Wish someone would smite me,' Nanna Doris muttered.

'So anyway, there's this smoking crater in the ground, right. And when the people—'

'Which people?' Ella interjected but Mick wasn't being thrown off course again.

'When they came across it ... whoever they were ... they noticed this dust on the inside.'

'Deadly! Dust!' Gary added.

'Proper deadly, Gary. As you might know, Norm, limestone is made of what we call calcite aragonite,'

Mick continued, taking a finger of red dirt from the ground and holding it up like a precious relic.

'Boring,' Gary said. Ella cackled and Mick shot her a warning look. She straightened and spoke in an overly proper voice.

'Come on, Gary, there's nothing more exciting than calciowhatsitsface.' Mick snorted and there was silence. He sat for a moment while everyone remembered who was in charge of this family. All the while, Norm looked on, his big curious eyes wide open and awaiting more.

'If you take this limestone dust and you heat it, you add sand, you mix it. Do you know what you get?'

'No!' Gary answered, his enthusiasm more than making up for his lack of useful information.

'Concrete,' Zeke said, the boredom dripping from his voice.

'Cement,' his father said.

'Same thing.'

Mick's voice burst in rage, pinning Zeke to the ground.

'They're not the same thing, Zeke. You know damned well that they're not the same thing.' Mick turned with a smile back to Norm. 'For the first time now, humanity had this magical material. What they had in their hands was going to change the world as we know it forever. They had discovered something that would outlast us all. When everything else crumbles, this will be known as the Concrete Age, like the Bronze and Iron before it.'

'It was in their hands?' Ella asked.

'Metaphorically, Ella,' her father replied.

'Okay, because that would be gross and go all hard and then they'd have rock arms.'

'You see,' Mick said, desperate to power through his story, 'when you lay down cement that says to the world that this is your place. Here is where I will stay. This is where you can reach me now. This is home. And if people know where to find you, they know where to trade with you. They come from all over the known world and they bring to you everything they have found. Suddenly, trade, commerce, society, all of these wonderful things are born. And where are they born? On top of cement.'

'I don't know, I reckon your great-great-great-grand-father or whatever might take some issue with that,' Ella interjected. This chastened Mick for a moment, as he realised his error.

'You know what I mean,' he said, trying to save face.

'Did us mob have concrete?' Gary asked.

'Cement,' Mick corrected.

'We didn't need it, bub,' Nanna Doris interjected, giving the little fella a kiss on the cheek. 'We don't need no slab of cement to say, "Here's who I am and where I'm from." That's a load of phooey.'

Ella, Gary and Zeke all burst into laughter. Norm, too, though his eyes darted nervously back to Mick.

'Phooey! Phooey! Phooey!' The mad kids were all chanting, banging their hands together.

'Oh, stuff yas all then,' Mick said, rising up from his camping chair and walking to the car. Wisdom could wait for another time.

4

Pup was thoughtfully deposited in the shadow of a tree at the base of Vodafone Hill. Ella could see him watching her from far below as his wise old eyes took in what was surely a very odd sight.

Sweat was pouring down Norm's face, soaking through his already stained oversized polo, as Ella's knees dug into his shoulders. One hand was tightly gripping Norm's wavy blond hair while the other reached as far into the sky as she could manage, desperately clutching her phone.

'Anything?' Norm pleaded.

'Quit your whining. He might be busy.'

Zeke had moved into the city to study town planning at the University of Melbourne, and Ella had an inkling he would be able to offer the directionless pair a clue on how to get started. They'd never had to build an iconic structure before. Norm tried to build a doghouse once, but the roof had collapsed. Anyway, Pup was perfectly happy sleeping at the foot of his bed.

Vodafone Hill received its nickname because it was the only spot in Norman where you could get mobile reception. If anyone in the town had to send a text, an email, or post a photo on social media they'd have to begin the long climb to the top of the hill. It really added to the drama of Facebook arguments. You knew someone had to be really pissed if they were willing to embark on a hike just to reply. It was an intimidatingly steep climb to get to the top and always a source of great amusement for Norm and Ella to watch locals stumble out of the Elephant at the bottom of the hill and try and climb up the face to attempt to send a text they'd surely regret in the morning. Sometimes they'd spend a Friday evening sitting in the branches of the tree Pup was under at this moment, taking bets on whether or not the next contestant would make it to the top of the hill.

There was a gentler way up around the back of the hill but that took too long and was generally understood to be for losers, and thus rarely if ever used. Climbing the hill was a point of pride for the residents of Norman. The tallest members of the town bragged about getting three bars of reception from up top. Gavin Walsh claimed to have once streamed an entire quarter of footy until his arm got tired and, since the Bombers were getting flogged anyway, he headed home.

'Still nothing?' Norm whimpered. Ella could feel him wavering and knew his slender frame could not support her for long.

'Maybe I've got to go higher,' Ella replied.

'My shoulders – your knees.'

'Oh, don't be a sooky la-la,' Ella interjected, pushing off Norm's head and lifting her foot onto his shoulder in an attempt to stand like a circus acrobat.

Norm opened his mouth to object, or simply scream in pain, but his jaw was pinned to his chest. At last, there was a loud ping and Ella leapt to the ground, landing with impossible grace.

She unlocked her phone and furrowed her brow.

'What? What did he say?' Norm asked, swaying slightly as his world seemed to come back into focus.

Ella read the message aloud. Not only had Zeke failed to give them any advice, there was no sign he had read Ella's text at all. It was as if he had seen her name flash up on his screen and composed his entire message without bothering to read it. She might well have said that she was trapped at the bottom of a well with two broken legs and he would have answered the exact same way.

Smella! How's Norman? The Deli burned down yet? Can you send me some gingerbread, a couple of the Anzac bikkies and ask Nan if Patty has made up any rosella jam. Love ya.

She wasn't a sister, she was a grocery delivery service. Ella wanted to stomp her feet in frustration. Her brother was bad enough, but the delight that Norm took in it all was even worse. It gave him such satisfaction to hear Zeke long for Norman. Whenever he returned they'd talk about how much her brother missed every little inch of the town. Norm took this as an endorsement of his thesis that leaving was always a mistake. But Norm's self-satisfied smile quickly disappeared as Ella dug her knee into his back.

'Hold still, I'm going to tell the dickhead he's getting nothing.'

'Ow, ow, ow! Wait, wait!' Norm cried.

Ella stopped climbing him for a moment. 'What?'

'Maybe there's someone else we could ask?'

She looked at him sceptically. Norman wasn't exactly flush with large art installation experts.

'Mayor Fitz! Like, we're going to need his help at some point. And who is more invested in saving the town than the mayor?'

'Billy Fitz!? Pff. I'll believe that when I see it.'

'Well, we might as well try going legit. If it doesn't work then we'll consider our options.'

Ella doubted Billy Fitz could find his way out of a wet paper bag, but she couldn't help but be struck by Norm's excitement. Usually, the slightest setback or hint of trouble down the road would be enough to scare him off.

'Fine! But Zeke is still a dickhead. Now, hold still. I have to let him know.'

There was some interesting intel to be gleaned from Vodafone Hill. From her vantage point atop Norm's rapidly compressing spine, Ella could see a moving van parked on the Pattersons' property. If she squinted, she could even make out what seemed to be the tiny, sweaty form of Edwin Patterson as he lost an argument over whether moving the credenza was a one-man job.

'No way,' Norm spat. Not about the credenza, of which he had no opinion. He couldn't fathom that the Pattersons, who had lived in Norman for generations, would ever pack up and leave. Ella prickled. There was the old Norm again. Too comfortable being comfortable. Unable to comprehend that someone, somewhere could want more from their life. Leaving Norman had never crossed his mind so for someone else to do it was unfathomable, bordering on a personal attack. It was as if they were saying that his entire worldview was wrong.

Easing off Norm's back, Ella grabbed two discarded Lucky Duck pizza boxes off the ground. Lucky Duck was a Norman institution not because it was good pizza but because it was the only pizza. Takeaway choices were few and far between. There was Pete's Chinese, which included a dine-in section that was an absolute must for birthday dinners, and the Stumbling Elephant would do takeaway but you had to wash your plate and return it the next day or Sandy would hunt you down and take it back herself. But Lucky Duck pizzas did have one advantage above the competition. There was no better way to get down the steep climb of Vodafone Hill than sliding on one of their pizza boxes. Eka, who ran Lucky Duck, would always leave a pile of boxes on top of the hill both for the benefit of the local community and because each box had their phone number emblazoned on the front and this was the only spot where you could call to order delivery. That was never much good to Ella, who had to pass Lucky Duck to get to the hill in the first place, but that was part of the charm of Norman.

Norm and Ella bumped along, bouncing on the flattened pizza boxes as they softly slid to the bottom of the hill. At least, Ella did. Norm banked off a rock and came tumbling down the hill in a great crash, which Ella found very funny until the gawky, tumbling wrecking ball knocked her off her box and landed right on top of her. For a moment, time held. Ella felt the surprising heft of Norm's body on top of her, their faces only inches apart. She could feel his chest rise and contract in panicked breaths. She could feel her own heart thud in time.

Then, Ella recalled the look on Norm's face as he lost control. It was the kind of panic you'd expect from a baby bird that has just leapt from the nest only to realise its small wings weren't ready yet. She erupted in laughter. Norm was horrified, mistaking the noise for the sounds of serious injury. He cursed his pointy frame and called out her name in a panic. The look of concern on his face caused another shotgun burst of laughter from Ella, whose red face and cackle made

Norm laugh, too. They paused for a moment, perfectly happy at the bottom of Vodafone Hill.

From under his tree, Pup the Old Dog let out a little bark. Ella snapped back to her senses and pushed Norm off her. 'Ew, you got cheese on me,' she said. 'You're supposed to flip the box over, genius.'

Norm slowly returned to his feet, gave Pup a pat on the head and flicked on the radio at the old dog's feet. The receiver was only strong enough to pick up one station, 1228 AM Radio Norman, recorded in the lounge room of Jasper's home right at the edge of Botany Street. He'd converted the room to function as a studio and looked out into the window as he broadcast, often commenting on who was going about their shopping or whether someone's haircut was a mistake. The station had a 100 per cent market share of the town listenership, with up to ten people often tuning in at once. And who could blame them when the station broadcast scintillating talkback conversations like today's effort, 'Where is a place that you've seen a bird when you didn't expect to see a bird?' So far, no one had called in, and by the lack of activity around Vodafone Hill it didn't look like anyone was racing to contribute.

Still lying on the grass, Ella watched her friend then turned her gaze up towards the night sky. Norman might be dead during the day but every night the sky would put on the most spectacular of shows. She had spent hours as a girl making up her own patterns in the sky and assigning great cosmic meaning to them all. A small cluster of stars might be a sugar glider and signify the need to take off and trust yourself. Sparse, dull stars peeking from behind a cloud might be the sign of the elephant and signify that she should spray Zeke in the face with the hose. It was all a complicated stellar ballet.

Over the years, though, the stars had faded for Ella. She thought of Gary, her little brother with the oldest of old man names, somewhere in London at this very moment under those same stars. Or, different stars, she supposed, if he could see the stars at all. God, how she'd love to be in a place with lights so bright they blocked out the night sky. How odd, she thought, to be faced with the majesty of the cosmos and yet hunger to hide it all away.

Ella blamed the town. There was no drama in Norman. All their problems were depressingly mundane. The only dark secret in the town was that Bettsy Langham, who ran the florist, was hooking up with Daisy Peach who worked at the council, and everyone knew that except for Mr Langham. He was a grumpy old prick anyway, Ella thought. She hoped Mrs Langham was happy.

Ella remembered the night before. She had been listening to 1228 AM Radio Norman when the announcement came over that Delight was being abandoned. She could read the tea leaves. Ella had known instantly what that meant for Norman.

It was currently graduation season, and Ella's social media feeds were full of former classmates celebrating finishing degrees and plotting trips around the world. The lack of reception throughout Norman had frozen her feed on the same obnoxious posts. Cap and gown, white teeth, glasses of champagne. Ella wanted that, too. She wanted a piece of paper that could definitively say that she had done at least one thing with her life. It was long past due that she did something that wasn't for her brothers, her family or for Norm.

Never someone to do what she was told, Ella decided she would leave Norman before she and everyone else was kicked out. And so, she had finally sent her application to the University of Melbourne. When the summer was over, she would be studying the stars for real. Or at least, enrolling in a first-year physics course with kids years younger than her and with much more life experience.

It was a decision she had made in a heartbeat and at a glacial pace. The rest of their cohort had left three years earlier, but she and Norm had stayed behind. He hadn't wanted to leave and it wasn't the right time to leave him. She told herself she'd give it one more year and then be on her way. But the tethers were too strong. The weight of her family responsibility. The thought of being another person in Norm's life who abandoned him. It was all too much. So, Ella stayed, year after year.

Now, she had no choice. The town was dying. She had to go.

She would tell Norm eventually. He would probably notice if she just wasn't around anymore, though slipping away in the night and skipping the whole drama was a tempting option. The news would break his heart. There was no avoiding that. But there was also no need to do that just yet. Anyway, she didn't even know if she was actually leaving or if some university administrator would send back a form letter in a week snuffing out her dreams once and for all.

And so, presented with Norm's hare-brained scheme to build a big thing, Ella had made another split-second decision: she had decided to support her friend. And why not chase Norm's dream? If it worked, he would have a huge souvenir to remember her by when she left. If it didn't, well, at least they'd get to have one last perfect summer together.

Ella watched Norm lift the wheelbarrow with the old dog and slowly make his way down Botany Street. She picked up her bike, hopped on and started to follow her best friend through the streets of Norman.

5

The home of Australia's only cow race, the Compass Cup, now has its own landmark right in the main street ... The cow is made of fibreglass and according to one local, 'is one and a half times bigger than a big cow!'

Organisers have plans to eventually make the cow 'moo' for the price of 20 cents.

Victor Harbour Times, 6 February 1985

Norm had been late to start at the school. For much of his early life, he had lived mostly in the cab of his dad's truck. There were lessons broadcast over the radio and they'd listen together. Norm remembered one particular day scribbling in a notebook in his lap as his dad proudly called out every answer to the primary school maths quiz, then when the lesson was over, they pulled into a servo with a roadhouse attached for banana milkshakes that they would later regret as they re-emerged on the bumpy road in the 40-degree heat. It was the fourth-best moment of Norm's life.

Then, it came to an end. At the start of Year 4, Norm had been told it was time for him to attend regular school. To stay behind when his dad had to travel and try and get a semblance of stability in his life again. He stood on the porch and watched as his old man, water welling in his eyes, reversed the truck, honked his horn twice, and took off alone.

What counted as a school in Norman was the pavilion underneath the generously named grandstand at the Norman Oval Cricket Ground, which had been deemed a more essential priority than a school during the town's construction. Each day, students of all ages would be crammed into the hall and would be slow-cooked until they graduated or were tender, whichever came first. After the opening address, junior students would be shifted to the Away dressing room while seniors had reign of the much more comfortable Home dressing room. The top of the grandstand was given to the English and Arts students, with the hopes that the majestic vista of the oval would inspire the next great works to come from Norman. The goal of this facility, other than to provide adequate space for Norman's First XI to sit in shame and think about how they'd disappointed everyone, was to provide free babysitting. Any education was incidental.

This suited Norm perfectly. To him, school was a place to kill time until his dad rumbled back into town with a truck filled with fresh supplies. If the rain had picked up and the river overflowed, it could be days before he could cross. Norm hated the rain. He had read once that the human nose can detect rain in the air with the same sensitivity that a shark detects blood. He wasn't sure if that was true, but he did know that when he sensed the rain coming, he would fall into a deep depression that wouldn't lift until the clouds parted.

Norm had learned to live alone but he never learned to enjoy it. The noises at night frightened him. The house groaned like a weary ghost. Something clicked, something rolled. He spent the nights wide awake, yearning to hear heavy tyres tearing at the gravel as the truck eased back home, and afraid that he might hear something else entirely.

In those early, lonely days, Norm had found an escape through a collection of second-hand books kept in the back of the pavilion in a bookshelf made of cinderblocks and uneven scrap wood. In this makeshift setup, Norm had stumbled across a collection of science-fiction books, all from an author named Rayburn Fink who had written in the wake of the Second World War. The pages were yellowed and had to be handled delicately, lest they crumble to dust in his hand. They were ugly and tattered. Bent from being read and re-read. Left behind by everyone else for that very reason.

The covers looked like adventure books. Astronauts with ray guns and horrible green monsters with three eyes growling from the dark of a cave. Or a spaceship captain tied to a metal table being forced to answer questions for a squid wearing a crown. Proper pulp.

Yet, in them, Norm found something that spoke to him. Rayburn Fink understood that everything promised came with a great cost. He knew that a world with great opportunity also invited great terror. He wrote things like 'a human being is a machine designed to feel embarrassment' and 'life is the crime and life is the sentence', and of course, 'awful things happen suddenly'. These books did nothing to alleviate Norm's great anxieties about the world. If anything, they were greatly heightened. But Fink's words did whisper to him that maybe he wasn't alone.

Norm would even sneak down on weekends, when his dad was out of town, to retreat to his corner, hide from the bitter heat, and spend the morning fighting cyborgs in a distant galaxy. The groundskeeper, Mr Gilbert, had told Norm he was allowed to stay inside as long as he liked, provided he didn't interrupt the concentration of the cricket team, who needed to focus on new and innovative ways to get hit plumb in front. Norm had nodded knowingly, though he didn't really understand. Still, staying invisible was his superpower.

One Sunday morning, however, Norm wasn't given the chance to retreat to his corner of the pavilion. He didn't even make it through the front door. And yet, Norm from Norman would remember that morning as the second-best moment of his life.

It began in a burst of delight. Fresh flowers lined the pavilion fence, erupting in pinks and yellows that seemed to awake Norm from some internal slumber. His heart swelled at the very sight, for he could not remember ever seeing colours so bright and vivacious. The sound of laughter cascaded across the paddock.

Not just laughter but music. A small band had set up beside the pavilion, led by a trumpet playing a jaunty melody that called Norm down the hill and onto the ground.

It was a fete! The usually small and dour crowd had been replaced by a flurry of activity the likes of which hadn't been seen since Mick Batchen's 135 not out, an achievement immortalised by a mural on the pavilion wall of a steely-eyed and well-built batsman leaning down in a forward defensive shot. Underneath, Mick Batchen had even laid and signed a fresh slab of concrete like it was the Mann's Chinese Theatre and wrote 135* with a flourish of pride. The match score hadn't been included. The Norman XI lost by an innings and 68 runs.

Now, stalls had been erected all along the ground, aside from a patch of dirt in the centre of the oval laughably roped off so as to not damage the entirely grass-free pitch. One of the older kids called it Brazilian cricket. It would be a number of years before Norm understood that joke and even then he wasn't entirely sure he got it. If he did, he didn't like it.

The smell of blueberry muffins wafted through the air and Norm could feel himself practically floating over to a stall packed with an impossible number of treats and pastries, each glistening as if begging him to reach out and take them all. Norm reached his small hand up towards an almond croissant that was hanging tantalisingly close to the edge of the table, his mouth already salivating.

'Don't even think about it,' cautioned the man behind the stall, his moustache flaring over his curled upper lip, his eyes narrowed as they watched Norm suspiciously. The boy shrank behind his backpack as if it were a shield that could protect him from dragon's breath. The man leaned over the top of the counter to survey his prey, only to recoil as an elbow hit him with some force in the ribs.

'Arthur, let him have it.'

A kindly woman was now standing by Norm's side, the type of person who radiated joy from her mere existence, plump and rosy, with curly brown hair and a blue apron that matched the moustachioed man's own fetching number. Arthur was immediately exasperated. 'It's a fundraiser, Maria. How am I supposed to raise funds if you keep giving away my food for free?'

His concerns were shushed away with no further debate, and the next thing Norm knew he was being handed that almond croissant with a bonus vanilla slice on a little cardboard tray. He had the worrying feeling that seizing that tray would lead to a lot more trouble than it was necessarily worth but his stomach won out, and with a grateful smile he took it with both hands.

As he turned and happily stumbled away, the crumbs already accruing on his cheeks, Norm heard the kind woman, her voice now distinctly less sweet, admonishing her partner.

'Don't you think today is tough enough for the boy, Arthur?'

The comment washed over Norm, absolutely lost in the flurry of activity surrounding him. All around him kids were being pulled this way and that, stalls were filled with cellophane-wrapped hampers and the kinds of crafts that tested the limits of the phrase 'it's the thought that counts'.

Norm stood at a stall displaying colourful knitted blankets, not exactly a heavy seller as Norman's autumn rarely dipped below 35 degrees, along with a series of handmade cards decorated with ornate crepe paper flowers. He chewed on his croissant, a pleasant warmth slowly growing in his stomach. He would often put off eating as late as he could in the mornings. There was a kind of hunger that sat dormant in your stomach until the first bite of food roused it with a vicious anger. The longer Norm could stave it off, the less he would need to eat to get through the day. His thinking was that if he saved as much food as possible in the pantry, then one day his dad might not need to leave for more supplies. If only he wasn't such a burden, he would never need to be left alone again.

Slowly, ever so slowly, the pieces came together in Norm's mind. This wasn't a fundraiser for the cricket club or a harvest celebration. It was Mother's Day, a holiday that Norm's father had protected him from every year with some kind of elaborate distraction. One year a pirate map trapped inside a glass bottle somehow managed to wash up in their front yard. Another year, Norm had woken to find an alpaca in the living room. The year after that, it had suddenly become very important that, as father and son, they try to tunnel to the centre of the Earth from their backyard. But this year, his dad was on the road and Norm was all alone.

A presence at Norm's side shook him out of his daydream. He jumped, fearing that perhaps Arthur had returned for the vanilla slice, and in the process Norm sent a cascade of croissant crumbs into the air, dousing himself in buttery flakes. It was in that moment, when he was as humiliated and delicious as he'd ever been, that Norm met Ella.

She was leaning on his shoulder, a gesture so familiar, though she'd never spoken a word to him. To most, you would attribute this to her youth – still too young to know awkwardness or fear. But the answer for Ella was something different entirely. Nanna Doris liked to say that Ella arrived fully formed, that something in her eyes said she'd been here before and wasn't too impressed to find herself back again.

'Sucks, doesn't it?' she said, shoving a handful of fairy floss in her mouth and pointing the opening of the bag towards Norm, who was too frozen to respond.

She looked at him with those large brown eyes he would soon know so well. It wasn't as if she was waiting for a response but rather as if she were reading him without needing one. Norm had the uncomfortable feeling of being noticed in a way he'd never been noticed before.

'You lost your mum, too, didn't you?'

This wasn't entirely true. At least, not in the sense that Norm felt Ella had meant it. But he was scared that the wrong answer might scare this person away and he would be once again relegated to invisibility. So instead, he said nothing and nodded his head.

'Everyone says it gets easier but they're lying. I don't get that. When I lie, it's bad. When they do it, it's for my own good. Makes no sense.'

She thrust the fairy floss bag into his side again. Norm reached in and pulled out an overflowing handful. Embarrassed by his own apparent greed, he tried to destroy the evidence by shoving the whole fist of floss down his throat at once. The result was Norm very nearly choking on his own fist. When his eyes stopped watering, he saw Ella observing him with great intent, like someone would a bug in a jar.

'I like you,' she said. 'You're proper strange.'

It was the sweetest sound Norm had ever heard. He wanted to reply but what was there to say? Even if he knew, there was no way he could regain enough control over his body to form the words. He was dumbstruck. He was in awe.

As would become their tradition, Ella carried the conversation for them both.

'Funny that we would run into each other on this day of all days. It must be fate.' A brilliant, shimmering smile erupted across her face, the likes of which Norm had never seen. With a friendly elbow in his ribs, she cackled. 'It must be fate! Ha! Get it?'

It took Norm more than a second to follow her fete joke, but when the pieces finally fell into place the ripple of laughter rising in his throat shocked him so greatly that he snorted, a great bubble of snot erupting from his nose and bursting like chewing gum. In shock and shame he gasped and froze, his ghostly complexion turning siren red.

This incredible eruption caused an equal but more dignified eruption in Ella, who burst into uncontrollable laughter. Norm, of course, had been laughed at before. But this was different. She wasn't laughing at him in derision. She was finding him joyful. No one had ever found him joyful before.

'It must be fate!' he repeated. These were the first words he'd said to her so far, and they were her own words repeated back.

Still, Ella smiled.

'Yeah, you're weird as. We're gonna be best friends,' Ella said, reaching down and taking the vanilla slice from Norm's cardboard tray then skipping off happily.

This was devastating for Norm. Not the loss of the vanilla slice, which he had hardly remembered existed. What hurt him most was hearing that they were going to be friends. After all, he was already in love.

6

Farnham was coming through the speakers, singing about paradise. Sandy whistled along in the empty bar as she scraped half-eaten food into the bin and hosed down the plates.

The sound of laughter from outside caught her attention. It was far from a common noise in Norman. Joy in general was discouraged. If you were happy, you didn't know enough. Drying a plate with the towel in her hands, Sandy surreptitiously approached the window, slowly as if she might scare away what was on the other side.

At the base of Vodafone Hill she could see Norm and Ella, clambering over one another. One word came to mind to describe them: frolicking. It had been years since anyone had frolicked in Norman. Perhaps it had been made illegal. Billy must have cracked down on frolicking like that mayor from *Footloose* who outlawed dancing for some reason.

Sandy watched on from the window, not wishing to disturb the scene. Their joy was contagious, and she felt herself smile. That, too, had been a while.

She pulled back from the window to give them a touch of privacy. Though, she knew in her heart there was no chance of finding that in this town. You couldn't sneeze here without creating a scandal that would be whispered about over coffee at the Sunshine Deli.

The strange thing about such a small town was the sense of responsibility and ownership over these kids who, it saddened her to think, might not know her as anything other than the weird lady who ran the bar. Norm wouldn't remember the weeks she'd spent trying to find a relative who could take him in. He wouldn't remember the room she'd made up for him in the back of the Elephant, the one he refused to enter. And he'd have no idea about the degree of deception and outright fraud she'd had to commit to keep the authorities from taking him away. To him and Ella, she was nothing more than Sandy from the Stumbling Elephant. But she knew them. She had seen them both overcome unthinkable obstacles, grow into themselves, and grow towards each other.

Little Norman was so different from his father. So, so different. There was none of that brash confidence. Tony was a man compelled to be 10 per cent louder than anyone else in the room. He brought energy everywhere he went, whether it was appropriate or not. He loved people. Sandy had often wondered how he passed those long hours in the truck alone, ferrying supplies back and forth. May God have mercy on anyone unlucky enough to find themselves on the same radio channel as him.

That was the Tony she liked to remember. Full of love, so annoyingly proud of his family that he had to show you a stack of new photos every time you saw him. For whatever it was worth, it comforted her to know that he did experience true happiness for a while.

The bell on the door rang and Rocko stumbled into the bar. Sandy couldn't remember having ever before felt thankful to see him, but she could feel herself about to fall into a memory and relished the opportunity to focus her mind on playing bartender for a while.

As she opened a can Sandy allowed her eyes to drift towards the window once again. Norm and Ella were gone. She closed her eyes in a silent prayer.

Don't leave it unsaid.

She opened her eyes to find Rocko staring at her over his beer.

'Did you just drop one? *Pff,* you dog. No worries, I did, too.'

7

Coffs Harbour, on the NSW north coast, has been declared a banana republic. A newly risen El Presidente made a proclamation to this effect before nearly 500 cheering onlookers at the nine-metre concrete Big Banana, three kilometres north of the city yesterday.

Complete with scout cars and jungle troops, district farmer and media personality, Mr Gary Nehl, declared himself the new republic's Top Banana ... He promised an era of glorious instability and declared himself available to be corrupted for money – or for tourism promotion purposes.

The Canberra Times, 14 May 1979

The Norman Council Chambers didn't inspire a lot of confidence in the abilities of those who gathered within. Were you to ask the people of Norman what they expected from their local council, their demands would have been simple: keep the grass cut and take the bins out. A level of civic duty approaching the responsibilities you would give a thirteen-year-old who wanted to earn a little pocket money. That's a wise level to keep council expectations. Still, if you were to observe the Norman Council Chambers, the dilapidated granny flat that sat at the end of Botany Street surrounded by knee-high grass with rubbish strewn about its entrance, you couldn't help but feel the council were failing to reach even those simple goals. The only sign that this was a government building at all was a corflute pegged into the ground advertising the 'Norman Do Nothing Society' with the catchy tagline, 'Solving today's problems, tomorrow, or the next day!' The sign had been put up by a disgruntled town member some months before. The council had decreed that it was to be removed but hadn't got around to it.

Ella shot Norm a sceptical look.

'What have we got to lose?' he replied. They had no momentum, no resources and, as for dignity, that hadn't been seen since he'd dropped it on the stage of the Stumbling Elephant. At least he wasn't the first person to lose their dignity there. It was, after all, the same spot where Simon Glassner thought he'd won big in Keno and decided to quit on the spot by getting on stage, bending over and dropping his trousers right over his boss's Sunday roast. That led to one of the biggest scandals Norman had ever seen, when Sandy was forced to admit she had been recording old draws and replaying them.

As they knocked on the door, they could hear the distinct sound of rustling and movement coming from inside.

A gruff voice called out, 'One second!'

There were more sounds of frantic movement and a large thud. Then, the sound of a throat clearing, which seemed to trigger a large coughing fit.

Ella and Norm shared a confused look. Finally, they were greeted by the same voice, this time affecting a high-pitched, cheery demeanour. 'Come in!'

They opened the door and Ella let out an involuntary, 'Oh, yuck.'

The cramped space was overrun with papers and discarded food wrappers. The shelves were a mix of old farming almanacs, thick volumes of local regulations and a healthy mix of empty and half-empty beer bottles. As Norm stepped inside, some unknown substance grabbed a hold of his shoe, requiring a great deal of physical effort to dislodge and even more mental fortitude to not worry about what it might have been.

An undersized desk sat at the entrance, a chair welded to its frame with a metal bar. Norm recognised it as one of the school chairs from the pavilion. Squeezed into it was a large man with an infant's face. In fact, he looked like the kind of baby that family friends call 'interesting' in a lacklustre attempt to spare its parents' feelings. What remained of his hair was strewn about in all directions, his cheeks were swollen and puffy and his eyes bloodshot. Norm had the distinct impression this man had just woken up and clipped a tie to the stained singlet barely covering his stomach.

'How may I help you today?' he asked, feigning professionalism.

'Uhh, we wanted to see the mayor,' Ella said.

'Do you have an appointment?'

Norm and Ella looked at each other.

'Oh, no,' Norm said. 'Sorry, I didn't know we needed one.'

'Do you think you could squeeze us in?' Ella asked. 'Or is it just balls-to-the-wall here?'

The man sniffed, failing to appreciate Ella's joke. 'Well, the mayor is very busy but I'll see what we can do.' He reached over and opened a large yellowed book sitting on the corner of the desk and flicked through the pages, looking concerned. Tutting to himself, he mumbled, 'Maybe next Thursday, though that's pretty packed. Perhaps in the next fiscal quarter.'

Ella leaned over his hunched form and saw that the pages were blank. She snorted with frustration. 'We know it's you, Billy,' Ella replied.

Billy sputtered. Ella swept the book off the table, revealing a poster underneath with a much younger, sleeker-looking Billy and the campaign slogan 'Billy Fitz: Norman's Only Choice'. It wasn't an inspirational slogan or even an attack but rather a fact. The townsfolk used to say it didn't matter if Billy ran unopposed, he'd serve as his own opposition. To Ella, it captured something telling about Norman: everyone could see the mess but no one wanted to grab a broom.

Billy gave them both a broad smile, less charming than it was yellow. With a kind of quiet dignity he said, 'One moment please,' then stood, lifting the desk-and-chair set along with him. Carefully and thoughtfully, he pried the desk off his body, made his way around the piles of trash and walked, head held high, into a back room, slamming the door shut behind him. The council chambers shook and, from beside them, a single murphy bed fell from the wall, slamming into the ground with a thud. Norm looked to Ella for answers. Ella returned that look with her own that said 'how the hell am I supposed to know?'

An intercom buzzed on the overloaded bookshelf. Norm leaned down and pressed the button. 'Hello?'

'The mayor will see you now,' came the distorted voice from the other end of the line.

'One second,' Ella said, holding Norm back. She picked up an empty beer bottle and ducked out the door. Norm heard a smash and Ella returned, holding the broken bottle in her hand as an improvised weapon. 'Just in case,' she shrugged.

At least the back room had a gleam of professionalism. There were no empty beer bottles and no rubbish on the floor. A framed photograph of a young Queen Elizabeth II leaned against the back wall, in the corner hung a weathered Australian flag

60

on a small piece of dowel. Norm swore it was missing a star but decided not to dwell on it. A large pine desk dominated the space, adorned with a nameplate that read:

> *Mayor William L. Fitz, mayor.*
> *Mayor of Norman.*

Billy sat confidently behind the desk now dressed in a shirt that was almost entirely ironed. 'Welcome, constituents,' he said, his voice suddenly an octave deeper.

He rose to shake their hands. Ella quickly tucked the broken bottle behind her back.

'Please, take a seat.' He indicated towards a pair of wicker chairs. 'Now, what can I do for you today?'

'Err, well, you see,' Norm began, feeling the sweat start to coalesce on his back. Now, at the moment of truth, his nerve was faltering once again.

'We have a proposal that we think can save the town,' Ella interjected.

'Oh, do you now?' The mayor's voice was patronising, as if a small child had just told him they were going to blast off to the moon.

Ella refused to be spoken down to by a man whose bed folded into the wall. 'Yes, and I think, as your constituents, our concerns are worthy of your professional attention and consideration.'

Mayor Fitz scoffed then, realising this might not be optically ideal, tried to alter his scoff into a clearing of the throat as he sat up to pay attention.

'Of course. As you know, it has been a tough few years for Norman and we would be happy to consider any and all proposals that may lead to the betterment of life for our citizens. Unfortunately, at this time, it is not going to happen. Thank you for your consideration. Please, take a souvenir pen.'

He gestured towards a glass jar at the edge of his desk filled with ballpoint pens. Norm picked one up and examined it. There was nothing to indicate it was actually a souvenir. He seemed to be offering them a standard ballpoint pen for their trouble.

'You haven't heard our plan yet,' Norm said, placing the pen back in the jar.

'No, I find it easier to reject plans before I hear them. Saves me the worry of staying up all night and wondering what might have been.'

'It's a good idea,' Ella pushed.

'I'm sure it is,' Billy rebounded.

'You'd really like it,' Norm volleyed.

'I'm sure I would,' Billy answered.

'It's named after you,' Ella spat.

'I'm sure—' Billy paused, looked conspiratorially around the room and leaned forward over the desk. 'What would be named after me?'

Norm was just as wide-eyed as the mayor. 'Go on, Ella,' he said. 'You tell him.'

'Oh, it's your idea,' Ella offered.

'But we're a team,' Norm rebutted.

'You're too modest,' Ella prodded.

'Look, maybe we—' Billy began, but before he could take a breath Ella had interrupted him.

'It'll be called the Mayor William L. Fitz Centre.'

'Great name,' Norm added.

'It is a brilliant name,' Ella agreed.

'Mm,' Billy said, his interest waning fast. 'And what would happen inside said centre?'

'It's a tourist resource hub,' Ella said.

'Yes,' Norm agreed. 'That's the idea that I had and also that we had.'

'We don't have tourists,' Billy said.

'We don't have a tourist resource hub,' Norm replied.

'Well, that makes sense,' the mayor said, scratching his chin in a way seemingly designed to resemble thoughtful consideration. In reality, it gave off more of an 'undiagnosed skin infection' vibe. 'And what kind of resources would you find in this tourist resource hub?'

Norm and Ella looked at each other.

'Jams,' Norm stammered, smiling weakly.

'Jams?'

'You know, strawberry, raspberry, a bit of marmalade perhaps?'

'All sources of local produce!' Ella added, sending a look to Norm that was more of a death threat. 'It will be a hub of all the best products made by the people of Norman.'

'Well, that's a bit of a problem since the people of Norman aren't producing much of anything right now,' the mayor responded.

'That's not all,' Ella interjected, attempting to distract him. 'There will be guides to the cultural history of the area.'

The mayor laughed. 'I don't see how—' he stopped himself. Ella clearly wasn't amused by this offhand dismissal. Smelling his own social cancellation in the air, he decided to quickly change tactics. '—we could go wrong by informing people of the history of this land but with that being said, why would they come here to discover it in the first place?'

'There would be a public bathroom,' Norm added.

Ella gave him a confused look. Norm leaned in her ear and whispered, 'Sorry, I need to pee.'

'Great idea. Come on down and piss on Norman,' the mayor mocked. 'Look, kids. It's a great idea and I love to see young people engaged with their community. One person really can make a difference. And with the two of you, that's a double difference. But there's no point investing in our tourist resources when we don't have tourists. Between the three of us, there's no reason for anyone to come to Norman anymore. We'd might as well put a *Wrong Way Go Back* sign underneath the one that says *Welcome to Norman.*'

'Then we give them a reason,' Norm said, shooting a look at Ella. It was time to go back to Plan A. 'We need to build something. Something that can capture the imagination of the people of Norman. We have to build a Big Thing.'

Norm sat forward expectantly. The mayor mimicked his pose, not realising the sentence had ended.

'A big what?' he asked.

Ella tried to jump in but Billy waved her away.

'Alright, kids. I think I have listened long enough. You have some wonderful ideas and like I said, I appreciate you doing what you can for the town of Norman. As for capturing the town's imagination, well, good luck with that. I'll believe it when I see it. I am not too certain there is an imagination left to capture.'

He leaned back in his chair and clamped all ten of his sausage fingers onto the edge of the desk, rapping them against the wood in a short wave, enjoying the tension in the room, relishing the moment like he would right before crushing a bug.

'Unfortunately, we live in the real world. Look around you. Kids, the town is out of money. We haven't got a pot to piss in. Why do you think I had to fire Daisy? It's too late. The town isn't dying. The town is dead. It just doesn't know it yet.' These words seemed to cause him physical pain to say. His bloodshot eyes were watering as he looked across the table at them.

'You know what I would do if I was a young couple?'

'What?' Norm asked.

'We're not dating,' Ella mumbled.

'Leave. It's too late for the rest of us. You can still go somewhere and live happily ever after together.'

'We're not together,' Ella mumbled again.

'Really? Whatever.' The Mayor's expression turned suddenly grim. 'You need to get out of here before it's too late. Don't go down with the ship. Don't die for this town, don't die with this town.'

Usually, this would be enough to make Norm hang his head and skulk out the door. He was easily knocked off his course. In all honesty, he wasn't certain he had a course. It was probably more accurate to say he was always a little lost at sea and easily capsized. But something inside Norm told him today was not an ordinary day.

There was a rage bubbling inside of Norm from Norman like he had never felt before. His jaw clenched. His back stiffened and his chest, whatever chest there was, puffed out. On an ordinary day, when consumed by any overwhelming emotion, Norm from Norman's throat would close over. The words would sit inside him with no escape. Not today. Today they ripped out of him with the force of a machine gun.

'You are letting it die! This town is dying on your watch and you aren't lifting a finger. Why? You're too lazy? You're too stupid? No, you know what I think it is? You just don't care. It's easier to just let things go to hell so that's what you're doing. This town is dying because you are crushing its windpipe under your heel.'

Norm was heaving. From the corner of his eye he could see Ella watching him, speechless. He didn't dare meet her gaze. Norm braced himself for the mayor to return serve or, if words failed, simply lunge over the table and grab him by the throat.

And for a moment it looked as if Billy Fitz was considering doing just that. Then, as quickly as the thought seemed to cross his mind, it was gone again and his pearly-yellow smile had returned.

'Well, thank you for your time. I always enjoy hearing from my constituents.'

There was nothing more to say. They left the office, heads hung low. Norm felt sick to his stomach. All the bravado he'd had a moment before was gone. He fell to his knees in the long grass outside the granny flat. He put his head to the ground and broke down.

Before Ella could move, another figure appeared through the long grass. Pup the Old Dog lay beside Norm. He curled his body against the heaving boy, the weight and warmth as familiar to Norm as a childhood blanket. And he stayed there, looking as though he would wait with him until the end of the world.

8

Norm still lived in his father's home. The papers were in his name but he'd never taken ownership over it. It was as if he were preserving a historical relic rather than living in a home. There were vinyl floors with an impossibly ugly grey-green pattern designed to keep anyone on the downhill slide of an acid trip entertained for hours. Thick curtains that, to Ella's memory, had never been opened even on the most beautiful, sunshine-filled days. But she had to give it to Norm, he knew how to keep a kitchen clean. This was out of character. Norm's oversized polos had enough stains that they could serve as an abstract painting detailing the history of every sausage roll he'd ever bought. The cleanliness of the kitchen was more a testament to the fact that Norm had the same meal every morning, two eggs he scrambled and microwaved, while dinner was a bowl filled with microwaved rice, a tin of canned tuna and a dash of soy sauce on special occasions. The living room had an old, busted television connected to an ancient DVD player.

Perhaps the only part of the house that was noticeably Norm's was the precariously stacked piles of DVDs he'd picked up in the local charity shop bin. Everyone else may have given up on the format but not Norm. Part of it was pretension, part of it was reliability in a town where internet connections were shaky at the best of times, and the rest was the desire to hold something real, to look over the artwork, read every word, appreciate the thing that someone had made, rather than scroll on to the next show. He liked to say that one day he'd be found crushed underneath them all. Ella was pretty sure it was a joke. It sounded like a joke.

Norm hadn't spoken on the walk home. Neither had Ella. They let 1228 AM Radio Norman do the talking for them. Jasper's track selection was always a little without rhyme or reason and this afternoon's offering was no exception. The Andrews Sisters singing 'Don't Sit Under the Apple Tree' was followed up by Regurgitator's hit 'I Will Lick Your Arsehole', much to the shock of Jasper himself, who promised listeners to follow up with something 'a little more family friendly' and technically delivered by playing all five minutes of 'La Marseillaise'. Ella had laughed and looked over to Norm, but his head was still down as he pushed along Pup's wheelbarrow.

It was only appropriate that Norm's house would be the first you passed on the road into Norman. It was equally appropriate that if you were to ever leave, you'd have to go through him.

Norm kept his father's weather-beaten boots by the front door, as if at any moment he might emerge, slip them on and wander down to the newsagency for his Sunday paper. As he walked through the door, Norm gave them a little nod. Borderline imperceptible, like he was afraid Ella would catch him nodding to a boot and roast him for it. She never would, though. Not in a million years. Not that. Everything else he did was a different story.

Ella collapsed on the beaten-up couch where she had spent a large percentage of her life watching some boring film or another. Pup curled up beside her, needing a little more help now getting onto the couch than he once did. Norm busied himself perusing his leaning tower of obsolescence. The Friday Night Feature had been a staple of her life for as long as she could remember. They didn't even need to call Lucky Duck Pizza anymore. Their routine was so encased in the stone that these days Reggie Piper would just arrive at their door with a large pepperoni. Ella would kick and moan about how boring it was to always keep to the same routine but in truth, this was where she felt completely safe.

But it couldn't last. It wouldn't last. She had already signed its death warrant. 'Norm,' she said softly, almost as if she was hoping he wouldn't hear her. If she said anything more the illusion would shatter. Their perfect world would be lost. Maybe he hadn't heard. Maybe this could wait.

'What?' Norm replied, more than a little annoyance in his voice. Of course he'd heard. He was always listening. Ella worried for a moment that he had heard her thoughts but quickly realised his frustration came from an expectation that he would be chastised for taking too long to pick a movie. To be fair, he was taking too long.

She settled back into the couch and allowed Norm to go about his work. There were cracks in the walls she hadn't noticed before. A light fixture was dangling out of its socket from where a younger Norm had stood on top of a stool straining to change the bulb. Now, he could probably touch the ceiling flat-footed.

Even in its prime, there was no way this home would feature in *Better Homes and Gardens.* The polite way to describe it was sparse. Functional, maybe. This was a home put together by a man who spent most of his life on the road. Flat-packed furniture so poorly built Ella could practically smell the beers he drank during construction. A square bookshelf that leaned at a 35-degree angle, transforming it into a jaunty rhombus. A TV stand missing its cabinet doors. Not so much as a picture on the wall.

Try though she might, her memories of Norm's father were fleeting. Her memories were of his absence. Of Norm left on their doorstep like a stray cat, time spent staring jealously at a packet of Arnott's Assorted Creams and complaining to her dad that they always boxed up the good food for Norm (a memory that made her cringe now), the boy watching the rain run down the front window, looking for headlights in the darkness.

'What's it going to be?' she asked.

Norm grumbled. 'Don't rush me.'

'Alright, Stroppy,' Ella shot back. 'I meant the Big Thing. What's it going to be?'

He turned back and flashed her a broad smile. 'It's a surprise.'

Ella found this answer to be as charming as it was annoying, and it was very annoying.

'Tell me,' she demanded.

'No way,' Norm spat back.

Ella pouted and leaned towards Norm still sitting cross-legged at his DVD pile. 'You wouldn't keep anything from me, would you?'

Norm was suddenly flustered, which in turn flustered Ella. This was not how Ella had intended to change the vibe in the room. She decided the best course of action was to ignore it, whatever it was, and press ahead.

'Just tell me. Come on, we're supposed to be in this together.'

Norm looked around conspiratorially. 'You have to keep this a secret,' he said, standing up and moving towards Ella. He leaned in and whispered right into her ear. It was so intimate, so very un-Norm. He smelled like home. A bit of rain, a bit of charcoal. Warm breath that made the hairs on the back of her neck rise. Ella found herself so entranced by the feeling that it took her a few seconds to process what he had actually said.

Norm flashed a confident smirk that Ella wasn't sure she'd ever seen before and returned to his natural home at the bottom of a pile of DVDs. She took a pillow from the couch and threw it with as much force as she could muster at the back of his head. Unfortunately, her aim wasn't quite what she had hoped it would be and it only ended up knocking the tower of DVD cases to the ground.

'Oi, those were alphabetical!' Norm objected.

Ella was quietly thrilled that she both had his attention and annoyed him, but made sure not to show any of this satisfaction.

'What do you mean you don't know?'

'I ... don't know. I mean, I do know. I mean that I don't know. You know?'

Ella stood up and crossed her arms, leaning over Norm.

'Do I look like I'm laughing?'

Norm squinted as if he was really trying to work it out. 'Hard to say. You look angry but you always look angry. It could be gassy. Is it gassy?'

Ella started to laugh and tried to suppress it, but it was no use. Instead, she reloaded. Reaching under the now napping Pup, she pulled out a second pillow and cocked her arm back. Norm, manly till the last, squealed and collapsed on the floor as if he'd just seen a brown bear.

Ella gave him a hard kick in the ribs.

'I'm so mad at you!'

'You sure?' Norm wheezed, now sprawled out on the ground. He slowly got to his feet and handed Ella a peace offering of three DVDs. A golden rule of their friendship was that he could choose the shortlist, but she was choosing the movie. It gave them both just enough wriggle room to actually decide on a film, while retaining the ability to blame the other if it ended up being a bore. The pattern was simple: one rom-com, one mindless action film, one wildcard. Horror was strictly forbidden. They were both self-confessed fraidy-cats, plus the wounds hadn't completely healed from the time Norm had tricked Ella into believing the film *The Babadook* ended with a children's choir singing this haunting song:

> *Here comes the Babadook*
> *He'll make you feel Baba-crook*
> *You will have a Baba-sook*
> *When you see the Babadook*

Harmless, until teenage Ella found herself bluffing about having seen the movie to some older kids. She recited the song, complete with a spooky dance, in front of them all.

So, to avoid arguments, they settled on the three-film system. The rom-com was for Norm, a softie at heart. The action film was for Ella, a jock at heart. The wildcard was for Pup, whom they had both decided had arthouse sensibilities.

Norm sat on the edge of the couch and gave Pup a scratch between the ears. The old dog put on his best acting display trying to feign that he was still asleep while slowly turning his torso in a bald-faced play for a belly scratch.

'Here's the problem,' Norm said. 'The concept is good. The plan is great. But every actual idea is bad.'

'Try me,' Ella said.

'Oh, where to start ... the Big Wheat.'

'Not there. Don't start there.'

'The Big Silo.'

'Already big.'

'The Big Crab.'

'There's already a Big Crab and the only crabs in Norman belong to Reggie Piper.'

'Gross.'

'He is gross. It has to be something Norman-y. What's Norman-y?'

'Nothing. The Big Nothing.'

Ella clapped her hands together. 'The Big Nothing. That's it! And look at that, we've already got it. Job done. Go us!'

'Maybe there's a famous Norman. Greg?'

'Yuck. You know we'd have to make it nude. No thanks.'

'There's Norman Lindsay. We could do The Big Magic Pudding.'

'You could go to hell. Come one, come all, witness the Big Racist Dessert. That would draw a crowd, actually. This country.' Ella snorted. 'Maybe we go with Tiddalick, place the frog right at the end of the river, then when someone asks what happened to the water, we'd have a good answer.'

They were running out of steam.

'You see what I mean?' Norm said. 'Any single idea is bad but the concept in general is good. So, let's sell the concept first and come up with the details later. That way, everyone can imagine whatever they want it to be. Let them believe in it first, then they can see it.'

'I don't know if Norman is capable of believing in anything anymore,' Ella said. Norm paused for a second scratching at the light stubble on his chin. Fluff, really.

'They're capable of belief. Everyone is capable of belief. No one is born without it. It's taken from us.

Bit by bit, if you're lucky. All at once if you're not. Awful things happen suddenly. Then, before you know it, you don't believe anymore. You don't know how to believe anymore. So, we need to show them the way. We don't need to build the Big Thing yet, we just need to make them believe it's going to happen. As soon as it's real, it becomes possible.'

Ella watched him in quiet awe. How was this the same person who froze in panic if you asked what he wanted for dinner?

'Norm,' she said, putting her hand on his shoulder.

He looked up as if seeing her for the first time. He always looked at her that way. Ella felt herself at a crossroads. She had two choices at this moment and taking either one would change the path of her life forever.

A knock at the door meant she would never get the chance to take either.

'The pizza,' she said.

That was enough to shatter Pup's Oscar-worthy sleeping act. A youthfulness returned to the old dog as he sprang from the couch and raced towards the door, Norm in hot pursuit.

The pizza soon disposed of, Ella rested her head on Norm's shoulder as *Starship Troopers* played for what had to be the fortieth time. Norm chewed obnoxiously on the last piece of garlic bread, which Ella noted he made no effort to offer around.

'You know,' he said between romantically garlic-infused chews, 'I've never actually seen a Big Thing.'

Ella pulled back and shot him an incredulous look.

She stomped to the other end of the room as she tried to resist the urge to boot him in the ribs again, worried that this time she might not let up.

'What did I say?' Norm said. 'I'm sorry, okay?'

Ella folded her arms and frowned. 'What for?'

Norm, having not thought this far ahead, gawped like a goldfish suffering in the fresh air.

'Norm, you're a smart guy, yeah?'

He didn't answer. A smart guy knows a trap when he sees one.

'Sit down,' Ella said, pulling a chair out from a dining table that was only ever used for table-top gaming.

'Are you going to kill me?' he asked.

'One day, yes. But not right now.' Ella let out the kind of sigh that says *I'm not just tired today, I've been tired my whole life.*

'Now, answer this question. Why are we doing this?'

'I dunno,' he shrugged.

Ella could have shot steam from her ears.

'Why do you do this, Norm? I was so proud of you. I was – I was in awe of you. Then I find out you haven't thought this through. You're just drifting where the wind takes you like always and – and – you're screwing with me.'

Norm was smiling from cheek to cheek.

Ella was more furious than ever. 'You dog. You absolute dog.'

She grabbed a catalogue from his junk mail pile and hit Norm over the head with it.

'No, no, please go on. You were talking about being in awe of me?'

Ella flushed bright red. Luckily, Norm didn't seem to notice.

'I was thinking about the money. There's no money in the ground anymore. If we can't support ourselves and we have nothing to send out, we need to have some way of bringing people in. The reason I like the Big Things is because they're silly, like Norman, but they're also built with pride, like Norman.

'The Norman that we grew up in was proud. We grew things, or made things, or built things. I thought maybe if we built something, we could remind people of that. We'd help them hold on for a little while. Just until we get back on our feet.'

The night wore on and they left Pup sleeping on the couch and retired to the back porch. The night was lit by thousands of stars performing just for these two. At once, they felt perfectly alone together.

They spoke long into the evening, as they always did. They talked about the Big Thing, and what it should be. They talked about the stars, and how small they both felt. They talked about aliens, and whether they'd ever come to visit. They packed a cone and sparked a lighter. They filled the night air with smoke. They talked about the night, and how it felt to lie alone. They talked about dreams. They talked about everything except the things that mattered most. Best not to disturb the peace.

'You know the oldest pyramid is less than five thousand years old?' Ella said. 'They call them ancient! My mob have been here ten times as long as that. I don't think people get that. I think they learn the numbers but they can't actually fathom that amount of time. It's an abstract number, unreal people. But every minute of their lives was felt just the same as every minute of ours. They looked at these same stars and they dreamed, just like us.'

'You sound like your dad,' Norm replied.

'I'll flog you,' Ella said.

'Now you really sound like him.'

Norm laughed and the smoke caused him to cough, a red-hot fire burning in his throat. They both agreed he deserved it.

Slowly, ever so slowly, Ella pried herself out of the folding chair and stepped off the porch. These were the nights she wanted to sit in forever. It was never easy to leave. Norm sat on the porch and watched her go. She wondered what might be going on in his mind. She quieted the thought before it caused any problems.

Then, she turned. Her heels scraping against the pebbles of the driveway.

'Have you really never seen a Big Thing?'

Norm shrugged. 'Dad was always on deadline. We'd drive right by – and then he started leaving me behind and I've barely left the town since.'

'Well, it's time for that to change.'

Ella walked away, a secret smile on her face. Norm's voice called back through the darkness. 'Ella, wait!'

She turned again. He was still on the porch, the moonlight dancing upon his face, framing him in a soft glow.

'Were you really proud of me?'

Ella's round cheeks reddened, whether from embarrassment or annoyance even she could not tell. She looked into those large, kind eyes, sparking under the light of the moon. 'Of course not,' she said, and let the night take her away.

9

The Big Banana tourist centre at Coffs Harbour is
  for sale.
Auctioneers expect it to sell for nearly $1 million.

The Canberra Times,   21 November 1980

Billy caught his half-opaque reflection in the glass wall
of the office and smiled. The bowtie made him look
sleek and professional. You couldn't tell it was pre-tied.
Even if you could, that just spoke to the kind of man
he was: formal but in a hurry. William L. Fitz was
swimming with the sharks now. His hair was slicked
back, his suit crisp, he looked – he looked like a child
competing in a spelling bee. Billy did a quick
calculation in his head. What would be worse – to
wear the bowtie or to risk being caught halfway
through taking it off?

The black leather Eames chair groaned as Billy shifted
to try and see down the hallway. It was the most
expensive spot he'd ever had the pleasure of placing
his arse. His fine posterior belonged in this class of
comfort. He'd be damned if he was going to let it
pass. The coast was clear.

Screw it, he thought, pulling the elastic from around
his collar and slipping the bowtie into his jacket
pocket. Sweat poured down his brow. The room was

kept at a perfectly optimal 22 degrees, at great expense. Sweating was an insult. It projected weakness. You can't be cool and calculated if you look hot and wet. The watch on his wrist buzzed. On its screen a notification asked if he was performing High Intensity Interval Training. Billy needed to calm down. He took a cloth from his pocket and wiped his forehead.

A tall man with chiselled features appeared in the hallway, his dark brow focused on a phone in his hand. Billy sat back in his seat. Now, there was a worthy opponent. Billy's eyes followed as the mystery man walked past the meeting room and continued down the hallway.

He sank back into the chair and turned his eyes to the ceiling, hoping well-supported L1 and L2 vertebrae might help him achieve a kind of enlightenment. Too often towns like Norman and companies like The Marshall Group existed in opposition. They were the boogeyman, the grim reaper.

Fear clouded any potential opportunities. Billy knew better than that. When brown snakes mate in the long grass they're surprisingly tender, passionate. Side-by-side they sit, tails ever so gently touching. Ferocious predators turned into gentle lovers. That was the relationship he wanted to seek.

He could understand why people would fear this firm. Maybe they were the grim reaper, in a sense. Or a vulture was closer. Vultures were part of the ecosystem. Vultures heralded the coming of death, yes, but for the business of survival. The Marshall Group had a similar reputation. They arrived as towns were abandoned, took over farms that had supported families for generations and pumped the soil for whatever mineral worth still remained. They drained the last drops of blood from the body and used it to fund beautiful things like the chair that Billy sat in at that very moment.

But it is not the vulture's fault that death approaches. Perhaps by feeding it, Billy could pave the way for his own future. At great personal risk he had organised soil testing under the guise of plans for a new reticulated watering system. It came back with one word that would change the town's future forever. Cobalt.

An essential part of modern technology, particularly renewables, cobalt was one of the rarest metals on Earth. It could not be synthesised easily, it had to be found in nature. Until now, the overwhelmingly largest source of cobalt had been in the Democratic Republic of the Congo. The slow collapse of the global order had made mining, extraction and shipping routes from this location prohibitively expensive. Australia had managed to produce only three tonnes of the mineral in the last financial year, yet that was still enough to make it one of the world's top exporters. If there was cobalt under Norman, no matter how small in quantity, it would be gold to a rapidly transforming world. Billy corrected himself: it would be much, much more valuable than gold. If he owned the properties that held the cobalt, then he would have the power.

Opportunistic, perhaps, but evil? Surely not. He hadn't caused the drought. He hadn't salted the fields. He didn't kill the town. Yes, he might have marinated the corpse a little bit and delivered it to the vulture, but that would be the best result for everyone. The town was already gone. They were just too stubborn to know it. The ones smart enough to jump ship now would get their own cut of the profits. Billy had visions of Fredo, peacefully looking out on Lake Tahoe.

The sound of the door opening brought him back into the office. A woman in thick black glasses entered and offered Billy her hand. She introduced herself as Allison but did not provide her title. He guessed her age around early thirties but nothing about her attire gave away whether he was speaking to the intern or the CEO. Her last name might have been Marshall for all he knew.

With horror, Billy Fitz saw the cloth he'd wiped his brow with was still sitting on the table. It wasn't a cloth at all. It was his bowtie. His eyes moved to Allison. She'd clocked it, too, and was now looking back at him in confusion or perhaps judgement.

'That's not mine,' Billy said and immediately regretted the short-lived lie.

Allison pursed her lips ever so slightly then returned her expression to neutral, taking a seat opposite Billy and placing a folio down on the desk.

The sleek, professional man reappeared in the doorway. Billy straightened up subconsciously.

'Can I get you a coffee?' he asked.

He looked to Billy who shook his head. The man disappeared again. Allison clicked her pen and looked up at Billy.

'How can we help you today, Mr Fitz?' she asked. Her eyes had drifted down to her notes to check his name. Billy felt the pang of his own unimportance. It was time to give her the old William L. Fitz razzle-dazzle.

'Have you ever watched two brown snakes mating?'

This time, Allison made no effort to hide her expression of confusion bordering on disgust.

'No, I haven't,' she replied.

Billy realised this was the wrong tactic and tried to land gracefully before swiftly changing course.

'You really must. It's a sight to be seen,' he said, then coughed awkwardly. 'Anyway, I am here today with a proposal. Something I think might be mutually beneficial.'

He slid a coffee-stained manila folder across the table.

10

Ella's midnight walks had become an essential part of her secret routine. She couldn't help but enjoy having a hidden second life that only began when the sun went down. Here, she was a grand scientist studying the stars. Here, she had dreams and ambitions – she existed for herself. The moonlight danced off the abandoned chassis of the cars that had never quite made it across the once raging floodwaters. She tapped the number plate of the upturned troopy and pulled herself up over the bank of the dried riverbed. She had been lost in thought, a million miles away, moving by muscle memory.

Ella looked up just in time to see a car with its headlights off, thundering towards her. Where had she been? She should have heard the rumbling, spluttering sound of the engine cut through the night air, yet it had snuck up on her like a memory.

Ella slid back down the front of the riverbank, scraping her elbows and knees in the process. She looked over the lip of the bank to see a baby-blue Torana, more at home at Bathurst than Norman, tearing through the spot where Ella had been standing only seconds before. Ella's heart was racing. She knew that car. Everyone in Norman knew it. That was Mayor Billy Fitz's pride and joy, the only thing he loved nearly as much as his reflection. He mustn't have seen her.

He mustn't have wanted to be seen. Why else would he be racing through the night with his headlights off?

The only solace Ella could find as she inhaled deeply and pulled herself back onto the bank was that, wherever he'd been, the town of Norman was probably safer for not having him around.

As she reached the cusp of Botany Street, she took another moment to pause and try to absorb every detail. The moon hung directly over Vodafone Hill and the town shone like a painting. She remembered so clearly a night just like this one, sitting on the back porch, as Gary told her he was moving to London. She couldn't speak, couldn't even look him in the eye. Not for days. The family said it was unbearable sadness, that she couldn't bear to say goodbye to her little brother. Only Ella knew the truth: she was sick with jealousy. He was so free. He was a boy, he was the youngest, he didn't have to help run the household. She felt as if Gary had cut ahead of her in line, that she had been forgotten by fate. All this time she had told herself that, when she finally had the opportunity to leave, she would grab it by the throat.

Slowly, purposefully, she dragged her tired body up the main street and ascended Vodafone Hill. Without Norm here to use as a stepladder, Ella had to be a little more resourceful in her attempt to get a spoonful of reception. She cupped her phone in her hands and like a wedding guest throwing rice into the air she propelled it upwards into the night sky. The grey rectangle shimmered in the stars for a moment and came crashing back down. Ella caught sight of it at the last minute and gently caught it back in both her hands. Nothing yet. She tried again, really putting her back into the fling. This time, the phone spiralled down with such force Ella was afraid to get right underneath it. She stepped aside and the phone implanted itself into the dirt.

Ella picked it up and cursed herself. A large crack had appeared in the corner of her screen, worming from one diagonal to the other. This had been one hell of a night. It wasn't over, either. Ella retrieved her phone and opened her emails. She saw it but she could not believe it. There, sitting at the top of the page, was one new unread email with the simple subject line: Enrolment Offer.

She could hardly breathe. She screamed a scream that floated off into the sky in all directions. She jumped up and down on the spot. Feverishly, she opened the email, scared that it might be a mistake, or spam, or a delusion conjured by her bleeding brain as she lay across Billy Fitz's bonnet. But it was there. It was real. She took a screenshot, texted it to Zeke, and flung the phone back into the sky to help the message on its way. This time when it came back down she caught the phone with glee and sank into the ground.

She read and reread the email. It was a late-round offer. Someone must have pulled out. She'd been ready for her life to change but not so fast. In three weeks, she would be standing in a hall at the University of Melbourne, scribbling her name onto course enrolment forms. In three weeks, a whole new life would begin.

For an hour she sat there and watched the lights go out around Norman. Beautiful Norman. To know she was leaving, to know for sure, made the town shine all that little bit brighter. And deep in the distance, at the very edge of town, she saw Norm's light. Still on.

Sandy was sweeping the front porch of the Stumbling Elephant. Either that or delivering a stark warning to the last patrons too drunk to take the hint that it was time for bed. Ella took a pizza box to the bottom of the hill.

As she passed, Sandy gave her a nod and a smile. That was the extent of their relationship. Friendly from afar. She had flashes of memory of Sandy from when she was young, very young, but she couldn't place them in space or time. That smile tingled something in the back of her brain. But Sandy kept her distance, so Ella did the same.

She was also taking cues from her father. He would go to great lengths to avoid the Stumbling Elephant, a bizarre habit as the man was built to spend his afternoons planted in front of the pub telly. He had

92

seemed shaken the past couple of days, a little slow to react, lost in his mind somewhere. Ella had put it down to the discomfort that surely came from having to carry your daughter's semi-conscious friend to your car, hose him down and dress him. But maybe it was less about Norm himself and more about where he'd been found.

Ella turned on her heels and walked back towards Sandy, who had put her head down and resumed her sweeping duties. She felt as if she might be violating some great family pact but she didn't really care. It was all Zeke's fault, anyway.

'Hey.'

Sandy stopped sweeping. Her eyes studied Ella as if trying to discern if this were a trick or a hallucination. Slowly, she nodded in return. Ella took this as her invitation to continue. The energy inside her was so great that her words came out in one rapid burst.

'So, I know you probably don't care or whatever, and that's fine, but I have to tell someone and I can't tell Norm and my brother isn't answering his phone, but it's good news and I never get good news. I have to tell someone and you're the only someone around because everyone else in this town is asleep because they're boring. So I have to tell you, even if you don't care, because I care and I can't keep it in, so here it is.

'I got into university and I am going soon and it actually happened and I didn't think I ever would, and I didn't think I would ever leave here but I am and I will, and I know you don't care but this is really, really big for me.'

Ella gasped for air, only to feel it shot back out of her lungs as Sandy engulfed her in the tightest embrace she'd felt in her entire life. Ella could feel her ribs threatening to crack from love.

'Of course I care. Oh, my girl, of course I care.'

Sandy had her off the ground, an impressive feat when Ella must have been at least ten centimetres taller. She breathed in Sandy's scent and was taken away by visions of coffee tables and laughter, her home alive with joy, biscuits snuck under the tablecloth. A bank of memories that had been left dormant for years. Finally touching the earth again after some time, Ella was shocked to see that Sandy had tears in her eyes.

Sandy put her arms on Ella's shoulders, the tears now freely flowing down her face. 'Your mum would be so proud of you.'

Ella hugged her again, tighter this time. They sat together on that porch for some time. They spoke about everything, except Ella's dad. But it was Sandy's thoughts on Norm that played on Ella's mind the whole walk home, and again as she lay in bed that evening.

'The way I see it, he's got two choices,' Sandy said. 'Either be happy together or miserable alone.'

11

On the epic road trip across our continent, a stop at Kimba was a must. In more recent times, the Big Galah's not been much to write home about. She is looking a little embarrassed. Never has this pink monument to one of our iconic bush birds looked so forlorn.

7News Australia, 17 September 2021

He'd spotted Rona Patterson through the window and performed an inelegant spin to avoid being detected. His back to the brick wall, Billy pulled the sample from his jacket. He didn't know why he felt compelled to keep it with him. It was far from normal for a mayor to be carrying a little canister of soil with him everywhere he went. He didn't find it calming, it evoked a great anger in him. That anger drove him.

He shook the vial. The soil was packed too tightly to move, making it an ultimately unsatisfying dramatic gesture. This was the land worked by his father, his grandfather, and generations before. The street was named after his grandfather, the church was where his parents were married, and the cemetery behind was where most of the family now resided. His grandfather, was one notable exception, having asked to be committed to the ground where he had worked every day of his life. Billy snorted at the thought.

Striving to be fertiliser, a pathetic existence. The old man had it easy. Billy had been cheated. The land that was bountiful for his father and his father's father and so on had turned fallow for him. He had been promised that if he worked the land, tilled the soil, put in the hours cultivating the crops, he would be rewarded, he would be sustained and he would receive the kind of life gifted to his ancestors. No easy existence, sure, but a noble one and a sustainable one. That had been a lie. Yet this vial in his hand would see that he would get his reward. The land would provide for him.

The sound of too many windchimes signalled the door opening. Billy tucked the vial back into his jacket pocket and tried to look preoccupied with a give-way sign on the street corner. In truth, it probably was not a necessary sign. He couldn't remember a time when two cars had last met on the side streets of Norman. He watched Rona's dress billow as she walked away. He counted to three and slipped inside the store.

An array of aromas attacked his senses, incense burning so thick his eyes stung. Michelle had done well transforming what was once a newsagency into a gateway to the occult. Slowly, she had gathered the necessary accoutrements of the mystic. An aquamarine headband held together her wild, brown curly hair. Her voice had even acquired a slight vibrato, as if she was speaking to you from behind a curtain that separated our world from the supernatural realm. With the town on the brink of collapse, hers was one of the only businesses still booming. The more spiritually inclined people of Norman looked to her for a window into the future and perhaps a bath bomb.

'All good?' Billy asked, brushing aside a bead curtain to spy Michelle, still at her desk, tarot cards laid out in front of her atop a purple velvet cloth with golden frayed edges.

'She was having second thoughts. So, she came to me for a reading to make sure she was doing the right thing.' Michelle extended her arms over the cards with a flourish. 'Wouldn't you know it? They told her to seek new opportunities.'

A devilish grin extended across Billy's face. 'Oh did they now?'

He sat down and grabbed her hands by the wrists.

'You are a brilliant woman, Michelle.'

'Oh, don't thank me, thank the stars,' she said. Then, reconsidering the thought, she shook her head, causing her resin jewellery to rattle. 'You know what, thank me a little.'

Billy took this as his cue to cover her arms in kisses while her giggles filled the room. On the edge of losing himself to passionate fervour, Billy retreated, his face red with excitement.

'Tell me again.' Michelle took Billy's fingers in her own and slowly blew hot air onto his wrist. A tingle rippled all the way down his arm. He leaned across the table, putting his lips against her ear.

'Champagne on the plane, of course, and a limo to pick us up.'

'A limo?'

'Only the finest,' Billy said, punctuating the thought by kissing her hand. 'Then oysters and more champagne as we watch the sun go down over Brunswick Heads, and a five-course dinner cooked to perfection by one of those celebrity chefs they have there. Then martinis under the starlight as we toast our new life.'

Michelle shook her hair and let out a primal growl of excitement. 'Mullumbimby. God, I cannot wait to be somewhere that appreciates my gifts. I wish we could go tonight. Just take off and run.'

'Me too, babe. Me too,' Billy said, taking his hand back and cracking his knuckles. 'Okay, okay, who is next?'

Michelle raised her hand to her head and looked to the sky. The crystals on the table began to rattle and for a moment, Billy felt a chill run down his spine. His tension only eased when a fold in the velvet cover revealed Michelle's foot bouncing on the table leg.

'Bettsy Langham came in yesterday. Told me Sidney has been really worried about money.'

Billy raised an eyebrow. 'Oh, is he now?'

'I wouldn't worry about it,' Michelle said, with a wave of her hand. 'According to the cards there's a great windfall coming her way.'

Michelle leaned over the table, suddenly serious. 'Have you heard any more about the shut-down?'

'Nothing yet,' Billy said, playing with a flame from one of Michelle's many burning candles. He ran his tongue across the inside of his mouth as he pondered the one strange happening of his week. 'Some kids stopped by the other day. A young couple with some *plan to save the town.*'

Billy smirked, then, feeling the burn of the flame on his fingers, he pulled his hand away, shaking it in the air.

'Ella and Norm,' Michelle replied.

Billy's jaw flew open. His voice dropped to a low whisper. 'How did you know that?'

'There aren't a lot of young couples in Norman, Bill.'

Billy nodded. 'Yes, well, I'm not actually sure they were a couple – or at least, they didn't know they were – who knows. Anyway, I think I deterred them,' he said, then bit on this fleshy part of his palm between his thumb and finger as he wondered if he had sufficiently deterred them. The meeting hadn't ended on the best of terms, after all. A momentary panic hit Billy that Michelle might be able to read his thoughts. He quickly tried to think of something that might be more appealing to her, perhaps about how annoying it was to try and find underwear that fit his prodigious genitals.

'It's just really difficult sometimes,' Billy mumbled.

'Don't worry about them,' Michelle said, her large red nails digging into his wrist in a way that Billy found equally intimidating and erotic. 'We get this deal done and we're on the road before anyone knows what hit them.'

12

Never had a small pile of dirt caused such a commotion. It was all the customers of the Sunshine Deli would talk about. All morning, residents of Norman were making their way up Botany Street, around the Stumbling Elephant and to the base of Vodafone Hill to have a look for themselves. There was no mistaking it. That was a pile of dirt, alright. A pile of dirt on a large blue tarp. Next to it, a collection of metal piping arranged in a little pyramid, a concrete block preventing the structure from collapsing. To complete the display, a series of plastic cones had been placed around the two piles and a wooden stake pegged into the ground with a very official-looking piece of paper in a plastic sleeve stuck in with a single nail.

NORMAN'S BIG THING PROJECT
AUTHORISED PERSONNEL ONLY

This small declaration was a pulse of electricity for a town starved of drama. There were whispered conversations about where it had all come from, who had given it approval, what the Big Thing was going to be and who was behind the whole operation. Thick Stephen declared that the piles could not have possibly been constructed by man and that they showed clear signs of alien interference. He was mostly ignored, though Reggie Piper showed some interest.

Only Jasper knew the full story and he wasn't about to reveal the truth. He understood the magic spell being weaved, and that dreams required champions were they to ever come true. He felt the weight of responsibility to do whatever he could to keep that dream alive.

Jasper had been manning the console of 1228 AM Radio Norman, injecting the stillness of the night with the sharp tones of his favourite aria from *La Traviata.* With no activity on the request line, he was taking his own requests. Usually, at this time of night, the streets were empty. The final drunk had stumbled home. The already sleepy town had finally succumbed. Such was Jasper's surprise, considering this, to see young Norm Perkins pushing a wheelbarrow of dirt up the main strip. It was a steep climb and an evidently heavy barrow.

Jasper was entranced, watching the struggle of the boy as if he were seeing the stations of the cross. There were points where the boy's entire form slipped under the handles of the barrow, the young Perkins nearly horizontal as he pushed with all his force to gain another metre up the sharp incline. Sweat poured down his face, his oversized polo clinging to his chest as he worked. Then, he turned the corner at the top of the street and slowly disappeared into the night. Jasper shook his head and wondered for a moment if his medication had been hitting a little too hard.

Then, young Norm was back, passing rapidly down the street, the barrow bouncing along the pockmarked road as he raced as fast as his unusual gait would allow.

Again, Jasper believed this would be the end of the incident. Silence prevailed once more and he realised the station had been broadcasting dead air for some minutes now. He had settled into a Chopin concerto, a cup of tea in his hand, when the boy re-emerged, like Sisyphus, condemned to repeat his actions, to push the boulder once more up the hill.

Through the night, this pattern repeated itself. Each time, Jasper was convinced the young fella could not possibly make it to the other end of the street. But such was the sheer force of will of the Perkins kid, Jasper found himself proven wrong time after time.

Not once had Norm looked in his direction or, indeed, anywhere but the road ahead and the wheelbarrow in his hands. When enough dirt had been piled, something like twelve or fourteen barrows by Jasper's count, the boy returned with metal piping. His tired arms wouldn't allow him to carry more than three at a time, and even then he would struggle, taking long pauses to catch his breath before forcing himself to move again.

Jasper, not wishing to break the concentration of the young man but determined to help nonetheless, left a bottle of cool water on the sidewalk, the way hydration stations were set up for marathon runners.

After looking upon it cautiously at first, as if it may have been a trap, Norm stopped and greedily emptied the bottle, save for the last few drops which he poured over his already very sweaty dirty-blond hair. Jasper slowly opened his window, taking care to make just enough noise to alert but not frighten the boy. He looked as if he wanted to run but lacked the energy. Instead, he stared at Jasper like a deer caught in the headlights.

'How can I help?' Jasper asked.

A smile appeared on the Norm's face as he pushed his fringe away from his eyes. Perhaps he had assessed this old man would not be much help with the physical labour, but Jasper was still surprised when he didn't request food or water but instead requested a song. Jasper told him he'd be happy to oblige.

At some point, the job had been completed and the boy did not return again. Jasper stayed awake for an hour longer, wondering if this seemingly magical figure would re-emerge one last time.

Now, as morning broke, he watched the excited residents unknowingly re-creating Norm's long journey as they approached the hill.

Something was happening in Norman. It had been so long since he could say such a thing. So, that morning, he decided to play into the myth. After all, it was for the good of the town. His tactic was to speak of the display as a foregone conclusion, something that anyone paying attention would have already seen coming. Momentum was so rare in Norman and Jasper would not allow it to cease.

'Well, a little bird told me construction has already begun on Norman's Big Thing. The planning is all a bit hush-hush as we know, cannot spoil the surprise for everyone, but it did have me wondering, what would you choose to be Norman's Big Thing? Text in or come knock on my window. We'll be talking about this all morning so get your suggestions in. Right now, here's a big thing himself, it's The Boss.'

Jasper sat back, satisfied. He was a little disappointed that the CD he thought contained 'Thunder Road' turned out to be the theme from *The Love Boat,* but otherwise it had been a perfect tease. Not only would it keep the town talking, but to contribute they'd have to pass by Vodafone Hill and see it for themselves. There was a little bit of mischief in the air, and Jasper loved it. The hair on his arm tingled with excitement.

13

It had been a while since the old paddock-basher had seen a real road. Norm made a note to repent a few things before they hit the highway. He leaned forward and fiddled with the radio knob. Ella, though reversing down his driveway at pace, still managed to playfully slap away his hand with remarkable accuracy. Norm looked over at Ella with the same look of delight he always did.

To say that Norm loved Ella is simply not correct. It's wrong on the level of magnitude. Technically speaking, Uluru is a rock, Niagara Falls flows and the Big Prawn is a statue of a prawn, but were you to simply state this fact you would miss everything that makes the subject remarkable.

And it's wrong in tense. Norm loves Ella. But if there is one quality which Norm has perfected up until this point it is survival and Norm understands that, while he may indeed love Ella, he needs her much, much more than that. As such, Norm understands that were he ever to vocalise that love, Ella might well go away. A life without Ella is unfathomable. A life in which he quietly suffers, never actively pursuing what he wants deep in his soul ... well, that's a standard weekday. Nothing ventured, nothing lost. One small sacrifice and Ella stays in his life forever.

Norm persisted with the radio knob and soon heard the soothing sounds of 1228 AM Radio Norman's station ident, Jasper not holding down the strings quite hard enough as he strummed a heavily distorted electric guitar.

These were the moments when Norm missed his dad the most. He knew there were little gaps in his knowledge that, to any other kid, might be a rite of passage. The lessons that went untaught throughout his adolescence. It was easy enough to look up a shaving tutorial, but relationship advice seemed strictly the domain of the world's angriest dorks.

Norm had a plan, though. He'd been over it in his mind a thousand times. It was brilliantly simple: don't be yourself. For one beautiful moment in this car with Ella, Norm Perkins wasn't going to be shy and deferential. He wouldn't be scared of his own shadow. He was going to be the kind of person who knows what he wants and makes it happen.

Norm felt his mouth go dry as Jasper introduced the track. His hands felt numb. He had the impatience of a man who realised his real life was waiting to begin. Either his heart was working overtime or in complete failure.

'Really?' Ella complained. 'The signal won't even reach the end of the street.'

Norm turned up the volume.

'We have a very special request, and I have to say it took some digging but here at Radio Norman we are very loyal to our listeners, particularly the ones who I find outside my window in the early hours of the morning. So, here is a classic little Australian track from an outfit called The Triffids. This is "Wide Open Road" on 1228 AM Radio Norman.'

Ella looked at Norm in disbelief. It was her favourite song. She shook her head and smiled, pulled onto the road then looked back at Norm as if seeing him for the first time.

The only way the moment could have been more perfect was if Jasper had managed to play 'Wide Open Road'. Instead, the radio crackled with the unmistakable sound of the theme from *Sesame Street.* Norm groaned.

Ella, though, perfect Ella, laughed and sang along. At his moment of despair, she filled the world with joy. She seemed to glow when she smiled, and Norm could feel his heart thumping against his chest, aching to be heard, demanding it.

Yet, nothing. Try as he might, he could not speak. The moment passed. The radio lost signal. They drove in silence. The coward dies a thousand deaths.

He thought about the yellowed Rayburn Fink book in his bag. It was called *The Transmit of Venus,* a story about a boy summoned to Venus to receive a message from the heart of the universe. The message was to reveal the true purpose of humanity. Once there, the boy discovers that the invitation was sent to him by accident. But before he can be discovered and sent back to Earth, he sneaks into the celestial palace to hear the transmission. The book ends with the boy discovering that human beings were specifically designed to be the only creatures capable of feeling shame. God (who is a speaking character in the final third of the book) admits to the boy (who by that point is revealed to be Rayburn Fink himself) that he did not do a very good job creating the universe. So, as a form of self-punishment, the divine being had created self-aware creatures as a way for the universe to feel shame and misery at how poorly it had been constructed. Every prayer thereby was a reminder that God had fallen asleep on the job. Norm thought it was a fun read when he was little, but now there were entire sections that made him cry.

***

Pup the Old Dog had his head out the window, gums flapping in the breeze as they drove. In the front seat, Norm had his head in the same position, eyes filled with wonder, mouth full of bugs. There are times on the long road out of town where you'll crest a hill and swear that you've just driven into a painting. Impossibly colourful, eerily still, perfect in every way. Drought be damned, this was beautiful country.

Ella could sense a change in Norm. He tended to walk heavy on the Earth. Even that morning, he seemed troubled. By what, Ella could only guess. Then, over the last hour, it was as if that weight had been lifted. They had broken away from Norman and he was suddenly free. She could only imagine what it felt like for Norm to see this with fresh eyes. She used to beg him to hit the road but he'd fight the idea every step of the way. Everything he needed was in Norman, he'd say. Seeing him now, fully entranced by the world around him, she couldn't help but think of the sweetest words in the English language: *I told you so.*

Her phone buzzed. They must have hit a patch of reception. Ella reached into her pocket and pulled out the phone. Norm snatched it out of her hand.

'Hey!' she cried.

'You're driving,' he said.

Ella made a noise that translated to something in the region of 'you are such a frustrating nerd' and made a show of keeping her hands at ten and two so she could be as safe as possible while hitting a stunning 60 kilometres an hour on a lifeless country road.

'It's Zeke. Want me to read it?'

Ella's blood ran cold. She shook her head, trying to seem dispassionate, willing Norm not to ask any more questions. She glanced over at him nervously and caught him holding the phone to his eye like a Victorian-era detective, examining the fresh crack.

'What have you done to this?' he asked.

Ella shrugged. 'Dropped it.'

She kept her eyes on the road, not daring to look at Norm.

They crossed the winding, dry riverbed once more. There were flood warning signs that felt somehow sarcastic. Cracks in the earth made it hard to believe that water had ever flowed here. The only sign of these once glorious and dangerous flood rapids were abandoned shopping trolleys and the hollowed remains of rusted-over cars, the remnants of misguided acts of courage. Ella slowly passed. Not a word was spoken. They watched the shells with a morbid curiosity. It was like passing through an elephant's graveyard.

'Oh my god,' Norm whispered under his breath, and Ella's attention turned again to the road ahead. They were now entering Woolcutter. Ten years ago, it had been as vibrant and full of life as Norman. A cricketing rival, home of the only petrol station for 30 kilometres in every direction, and the best ice cream money could buy. Five years ago, it had been abandoned, deemed no longer viable. The residents had been shipped out. Now, Ella and Norm drove through a ghost town. Empty streets, boarded-up buildings falling into disrepair, the carcass of a town Ella had once loved. They didn't speak. There was no need. They both knew what the other was thinking. This is what awaits Norman if they fail.

The empty streets and crumbling facades conjured in Ella's mind images of the earliest photography, when the technology was still new and required hours to capture a single image. In those pictures, the towering grey buildings stood proudly but there was no sign of human life. People's lives moved too quickly to be captured. They were reduced to a faint grey haze against the permanent backdrop of the city. Somewhere in that almost imperceptible cloud, lovers may have held hands for the first time, friends said their last goodbyes, or a careless man in a rush to do something that seemed altogether very important at the time may have been hit by a wagon. There was no way to know. These moments were lost to time. All that remained were the buildings.

Ella heard her father's words in her head once more: *we live in the Concrete Age.*

There was movement in the distance. A truck was stalled at the side of the road, black smoke billowing from its engine. They could just make out the shape of three people sitting on the road, resting in its shadow.

'Is that the Pattersons' truck?' Ella asked.

Edwin Patterson was a large man with a thick and unkempt goatee, wearing a singlet that showed off a shoulder tattoo of a rattlesnake that once belonged to a much younger man, and a beer belly that was a new addition. He would look quite intimidating were it not for the big, broad smile that filled his face at all times and the hairclips lovingly placed on his head in an attempt to keep bored little Anthony from having a tantrum while they waited. Rona Patterson was, as always, dressed in beautiful colours. Thin and tall, taller than Edwin, Rona's dark skin had survived better in the heat than Edwin's, who had already turned a very painful red. Her features were sharp and it would be easy to assume a certain meanness of character but anyone paying attention would see the glint of mischief behind her eyes, the kind of glint that tells a young person that she isn't one of the other grownups. They were a beautiful couple, and Anthony was beautiful too, six years old and dressed in a wizard's hat and cape on a 40-degree day.

If the joy with which Mr Patterson jumped to his feet was anything to go by, they'd been waiting there a long time. They piled into the car. The Pattersons squeezed into the back, Ella at the wheel, Pup on Norm's lap, curled up in a way that had been a lot more comfortable when he was fifteen kilograms lighter.

'We really do appreciate this,' Edwin said, little Anthony's ribs sticking into his side. 'I was starting to worry no one went down this road anymore.'

They drove on, the fields slowly turning green again. Signs of life returned to the roadside. The Pattersons had packed plenty of snacks for the trip and were happy to share them as a way of thanking their rescuers. Ella started to politely decline but Norm snatched a fistful of muesli bars before she could get a word out. He chewed thoughtfully on one while looking out the window.

'So, why are you leaving Norman?' he asked.

Ella shot him a look but stayed silent.

Edwin shuffled in his seat.

'It was just the right time for us,' Rona answered. 'What with Anthony here getting bigger and the town the way it is—'

'Plenty of room in the town, though,' Norm said, with an obnoxiousness that only comes with innocence, the ability to trample entirely unaware into someone else's business.

'That's true,' Rona said, biting her lip. Ella saw Rona glance at her husband for help. She let out a long exhale. 'We received an offer and it uh—'

Ella checked the rear-view mirror. Edwin was distracted, looking out the window at an unusually large cow.

'Big heifer,' he said to himself, softly.

'What was the offer?' Norm asked, his mouth half-full of muesli bar, honeyed oats spraying across the car as he spoke.

'Oh, just, a reasonable valuation,' Rona said, valiantly batting him away again. Ella coughed. For a moment, silence reigned.

'So, someone is moving in, then?' Norm said, taking another bite of his muesli bar. 'Who are they? We should get to know them.'

Ella saw Rona turn to her husband for support, only to find his attention still captured by the cow. In Edwin's defence, it was really very large and if you'd seen it scamper across the paddock you, too, would have been caught in the lava-lamp-like rhythm with which it bounced.

'It's not ... we aren't able to discuss it. It's a contract thing. They make you sign a non-disclosure agreement, you know?'

Ella shuffled beside Norm. Something about that struck her as odd but she couldn't put her finger on it. She glanced at Norm, her brow furrowed. He imitated the look but it was impossible to tell if he was also troubled or just being his usual annoying self.

With Norm distracted, Rona took her opportunity to give Anthony a hard poke in the ribs and he burst into tears.

'Oh, oh you poor dear, what happened?' she said, grabbing him in her arms.

Norm slunk into his seat as far as Pup would allow. Perhaps he really was troubled. Ella could understand why he would be. The Pattersons could not see a future in Norman. The town was destined to become like Woolcutter, a husk on the road, a curiosity for anyone passing, if they ever did.

Towns like these once stood in defiance of the elements. Its survival was not a certainty, it was an idea. That idea had to be carried. Now, the world was contracting again. People were huddling in fear. Norm and Ella were fighting to save Norman but they were fighting alone.

***

The motel room stank of cigarettes. Ella briefly thought about knocking on Norm's door. He'd spent dinner with the Pattersons mostly silent, fiddling with his hands in his lap, eyes downturned. A cab was called and the Pattersons had said goodnight, though it was really goodbye. Depressed, Ella and Norm had retired to their separate rooms.

Ella checked her phone again. The photo of Zeke proudly posing in front of a room full of flatpack furniture boxes. She typed out a quick reply.

Can't wait to see what it looks like when you're done building it for me!

Ella deleted the messages. There was something else playing on her mind, too. The non-disclosure agreement Rona had mentioned. Surely that was unusual for a simple real estate transaction. Of course, there was every chance Rona had just been grasping for any answer that would shut Norm up for a bit. Lord knows Ella had been guilty of that in the past.

She lay on the bed, feeling every spring in the small of her back, and stared at the yellow stained ceiling. She was deeply tired, yet sleep refused to welcome her. The memory of a morning a few months earlier was playing on her mind.

The final days of spring. Ella on the branch of the old tree, her legs dangling as she listened to the rhythmic sounds of Nanna Doris pulling a sheet off the clothesline, snapping it in half, swearing and popping it in the basket. 1228 AM Radio Norman played soft jazz and for a moment the world was still.

'I'm scared, Nanna,' she said.

Nanna Doris dropped another sheet into her basket. 'I would be, too. Sitting there making an old woman do all the work. I'd be scared my nanna was gonna flog me the second she was done.'

Ella laughed and pulled herself down from the tree. She took up her place on the opposite corner of the clothesline and started hanging clothes.

'Now, you tell me what's troubling you,' Nanna Doris said. 'And don't you leave out any good gossip. You know I've got to have something to tell the ladies.'

The words began spilling out of Ella and they wouldn't stop. She started with telling her grandmother that she'd been thinking of applying to university, about her life feeling stagnant, her fears that she had been left on the starter's blocks and now it was too late to catch up. But soon, she was talking about loss.

Loss of Norm, loss of the town, and the fear that she couldn't reach out and grab a new life without the one she loved so dearly crumbling in her hands.

Usually, when Ella unleashed whatever was troubling her, she would be assured by some kind words, a hug, a cup of tea and some treat that Nanna Doris had been hiding from the boys. Today was different. Her nanna seemed terse, as if she was also troubled by something Ella couldn't quite understand.

Nanna Doris picked up the laundry basket and thrust it into Ella's hands. 'I've made plans to see Patty this morning and you're coming along,' she commanded. 'You're driving.'

So much of Ella's childhood was spent hiding from her brothers at Patty Lu's house. She would sit with Nanna Doris having early-afternoon cocktails, heckling the characters on *The Bold and the Beautiful* and sneaking outside for cigarettes. That part Ella was banned from telling her father about. Patty Lu had a bottle of Febreze at her doorstep that she'd practically douse Ella in before she'd be allowed to leave, in case any trace smells remained.

This time was different. Nanna Doris directed Ella past Patty Lu's house with the lavender still growing in open rebellion against the drought. Instead, she was taken down a dirt road and into a corner of town she never much visited.

With cold realisation Ella understood where she was being taken. The flecked yellow sideboards of the church house stood out against the dirt. Norman wasn't a place for Sunday Service – too few believers, too little to believe in. The church house was there for special occasions, happy and sad. But it had been a long, long time since it had seen a happy one.

'Keep going,' Nanna Doris said, keeping Ella attached to reality. The last time she'd been here ... she couldn't bear the thought. They passed the church house and Ella heard a sharp whistle, the calling card of Patty Lu. There was nothing she enjoyed more than making you jump in public with one of her patented sharp blasts. She was seated in a green folding chair with an esky by her side, a can in her hand.

Ella stopped the car and took a long, deep breath. Her head felt heavy. Her heart even more so. The world fragmented around her. Blue sky, red dirt, tree husk, concrete, broken gate, fallen fencepost, Patty, Nanna.

With a groan, Nanna Doris lifted herself out of the hatchback and pulled more folding chairs from the boot, handing one to Ella. Slowly, they made their way towards Patty. Ella knew what was coming and tried her best to prepare herself. Slowly, her eyes traced down to her mother's grave. The tombstone was simple. Unremarkable was the cruel word that sprang to Ella's mind. A concrete slab, handmade, surely by her father. There was no poetry in the inscription. Only dates and a few words.

Jennifer Batchen
Beloved mother of Zeke, Ella and Baby

Tears welled up in Ella's eyes and she choked. She felt as if she was on fire. The family home worked under the simple understanding that what you do not remember cannot hurt you. There were no pictures of Ella's mother, and no one ever said her name – it was as if she had disappeared into the ether. Yet here was concrete evidence that she had existed, and she was missed.

Patty gave Ella's leg a reassuring rub and patted the seat. Nanna Doris put one arm around her granddaughter's shoulder. Ella saw that she was holding back tears of her own. She couldn't remember ever seeing Nanna Doris cry.

'Why are we here?' Ella asked.

Her grandmother took a white handkerchief out of her pocket and wiped her eyes.

'Loss isn't something that happened in the past, my love. Every day, my daughter is lost. Without her, I am lost. We have to carry this hurt. We don't get a say in that part, I'm sorry to tell you. But we also have to carry our love. We get to carry it.'

Ella could feel the tears flowing down her face.

'Sorry, I'm sorry,' she said.

Nanna Doris wiped her eyes and kissed her forehead.

'My child, I owe you an apology. I thought it was for the best that ... that ... it doesn't matter what I thought.'

Patty had been sitting stern-faced, looking straight ahead, but now that the dam had burst she couldn't help but join in.

'Your Nanna won't say this because she thinks it's not her place, but I know it's not my place and I'm old enough and ugly enough that I'm happy to barge on in anyway. Your father believes the best thing for you kids is to not think about it. To get on with life. That's a load of phooey. If you try to hide from pain, it comes looking for you.'

She took a long pause and sipped her drink.

'You have to greet it as a friend. Pain is a kindness. It is a reminder of what is important. God help you if it ever goes away.'

Nanna Doris smiled kindly at Ella, her hands on her granddaughter's knees. 'You know what your mother would say right now? She'd say, "Quit sooking, you lot."'

Ella laughed, brushed back her long black hair and settled into her seat. 'So, what do I do?' she asked.

Nanna Doris tilted her head towards the concrete slab. 'You talk to your mother, dear. Doesn't have to be anything big. You tell her what's going on in your life. You keep her a part of your life. Talk to her.'

Patty reached down into her esky and handed Ella and Nanna Doris each a gin-and-tonic premix can. Nanna Doris opened hers with a satisfying crack.

'It's easy, kiddo. Watch me,' she said, settling back into her chair and taking a long swig. 'Oh, Pet, you've got to hear this. You know Bettsy at the florist? Well, they can't grow anything, can they? So, that ham-faced bloke—' she started clicking her fingers trying to remember.

'Sidney.'

'Sidney. Crap city, worse bloke. Anyway, he wants them to pack up. But we all know how much Bettsy loves her daisies.'

Patty Lu snorted, and they were off. They talked about Mr Baylis going to sleep with the oven on and nearly burning down the deli. They talked about Nelson, Patty's husband, who was also buried somewhere in the cemetery. It hadn't been a happy marriage. A few cans in and Patty declared she needed to go water his flowers. They laughed.

They took a moment to wander around the other stones, Ella looking for last names she recognised, taking the time to do the quick maths of birth and death dates and mourning appropriately. Patty pointed out where she was intending to spend eternity, to the left side of Nelson. He always liked to sleep on the left, she explained. Taking that spot would forever bother him. She was already looking forward to their first argument in heaven.

They passed the stone for Maria Baylis, impressively large. Half-dried flowers said that Mr Baylis had been recently. At the edge, Ella found the grave of Norm's father. The stone was small and simple. Name and dates carved in concrete. There was a handprint pressed into the slab covering the grave. Norm's hand, small, trying to comprehend the unimaginable. She looked for his mother's grave but couldn't find it. His father's headstone stood alone.

14

Glenrowan boasts an enormous several-metre tall Ned Kelly statue in armour which is but the draw card to the animated models that lie beyond ... And somewhere, amongst the sound effects and gun smoke, and the racks of Ned Kelly t-shirts there is a stirring like a feeling of the Ned Kelly spirit. But perhaps it is just excessive marketing. No one is really sure which.

The Canberra Times, **18 March 1990**

Norm didn't know at what point in their journey he'd dozed off. The warmth crossing his face slowly welcomed him back to consciousness. He curled tighter into the passenger seat, fighting the waking world.

Through a squint Norm caught a glimpse of a barrel of a rifle, pointed directly through the window. He cringed and pushed back into the seat, waiting for the shot. To his right he heard Ella squeal. Then the squeal turned into a cackle. Norm opened his eyes and saw that he was cringing at a statue. That rifle was resting in the arms of the Big Ned Kelly.

He should have been embarrassed, as he so often was, but that would have to wait. He was in awe.

'Good morning,' Ella said. 'And it gets even better.'

She nudged two paper bags resting by his legs. Norm reached down and opened one, revealing a bacon-and-egg roll. He ferociously bit into it, the pain in his stomach forgotten. There's a school of thought that hunger is the most universal of all emotions. Gifts such as hearing or sight are not known to everyone but there isn't a creature on the earth that does not know hunger. Norm ate as if he had been lost at sea. Ella had to elbow him to come up for air and hand her the other bag. In the back seat, Pup chewed on an extra piece of bacon with decidedly more sophistication and decorum than his owner.

'So, what do you think?' Ella asked.

'I don't like the lettuce. People try to get all fancy with these things. They add all this aioli and hollandaise sauce or whatever. I'm not here to be gourmet. Just give me a bit of bacon, an egg and some barbecue sauce, thank you very much,' Norm replied.

Ella gestured towards the Big Ned Kelly, standing over them. 'I meant the gigantic thing we travelled for days to see in person.'

'Sorry, my stomach took the wheel. Come on, let's say g'day to Ned.'

Ned dominated the landscape. He stood on a street corner in front of an old newsagency, the roof of which barely reached his hip. His legs were thick as tree trunks and ascended into the sky. His long, army-green overcoat hung down to his knees. Of course there was also the iconic helmet, robotically scanning the road into the town as if at any moment he might see signs of troopers and have to take to the hills. But the part that caught Norm's eye were the hands holding the rifle that had startled him awake moments before. Oddly, the hands were the most delicately crafted part of the statue. One hand held the stock, finger resting over the trigger, while the other gripped the barrel.

From all the descriptions he had heard, Norm expected Ned to be resolute, defiant and intimidating. And to be sure, there was certainly something non-human about his stance. But these were the hands of a scared boy. They gripped the barrel in white-knuckled terror. Norm could practically feel them tremble. It was then a revelation dawned on him. Norm was not standing at the place of Ned's greatest victory but rather the beginning of the end. Glenrowan was where he was captured. According to the plaque he would have been twenty-five years old when his luck had finally run out.

Norm imagined finding Ned, not a legend then, just a young man, shaken and bleeding, sheltered under a window of the newsagency, broken glass around him, bullets ripping through the air, and telling him that someday there would be a six-metre fibreglass statue of himself just outside. Would Ned laugh or cry? Norm could hear the hacking coughs of laughter followed by a spit of blood, as if the cruelty of it all had finally overwhelmed him.

***

Ella laughed as she watched Norm skip down the Glenrowan streets. The sight of Ned had completely energised him. A joy that had been lost for the past few days seemed to return to his face. He twisted and turned through the streets with Pup doing his best to slowly follow, barking in excitement. Norm spun in the middle of the street and turned back to Ella, lifting his arms in triumph.

'Look!'

'At what?' she said, sarcastically copying his gesture. The town was dead. There might have even been a tumbleweed blowing down the street if they could only muster a breeze.

'Oh, it's just early,' Norm said. 'See what Ned has built.'

The town had undeniably shaped its entire identity around Ned. There were separate businesses that seemed to be built around selling essentially the same merchandise with either cartoonish images of the Big Ned Kelly or a photo of the man himself. The park had a Ned Kelly helmet kids could look through, the Glenrowan Hotel had life-sized figurines looking down from the balcony as if ready to fire upon the police, were they to arrive. There were motels, cafes, a tourist centre and even a place going by the name of Ned's Burger House. Ella imagined Ned trying to force a cheeseburger through the eye-hole of his famous iron mask.

She left Norm to gloat in the streets and wandered into one of the merchandise stores. The walls were filled with Ned Kelly paraphernalia. Shirts, hats, keyrings, mudguards, iron signs built for man caves, doormats casually threatening solicitors with murder, everything a Ned Kelly fan could want. Each item was emblazoned with a powerful or sarcastic slogan, the ideology of which changed from shirt to shirt. 'Don't tread on me', one of them read as Ned pointed two guns at the imagined shirt viewer, while another said 'F**k off, we're full'. Ella quietly hid those ones with what she imagined was the blessing of the Irish immigrant bushranger. The most popular slogan by far was Ned's famous catchphrase 'Such is Life', the nineteenth-century equivalent of 'shit happens'.

Then, as if it were calling her across the room, a single beam of light caught Ella's eye. She traced the dust particles dancing along it to a bargain bin hidden in the far corner of the shop.

Inside the bin she found a pile of folded shirts, dust collecting on top. She brushed it away to reveal the standard over-the-top faux-metal-album stylised Ned Kelly graphic but instead of 'Such is Life', in the same large block text these shirts featured a slightly varied proclamation, 'Sushi Life'.

Ella had never felt her hand go to her wallet so quickly. She moved like a cowboy drawing her six-shooter the moment the clock struck noon.

Her enthusiasm wasn't enough to speed up the shop owner, who was much more interested in the blender infomercial playing on the small TV she'd set up behind the counter. With a huff that seemed to say 'how annoying that you should want to give me money for goods' she slowly lumbered to the register and lifted up the t-shirts with a disapproving look.

'Oh, darl, you don't want these ones,' she told Ella. 'The bloody woman at the supplier couldn't hear me over the dog races. I'll get you a proper one.'

'No!' Ella snapped.

The shopkeeper was surprised. Ella tried to laugh it off.

'I mean, these are perfect. I love it. And the price is right,' she smiled.

The shopkeeper shrugged and pulled out a thin plastic bag, opening it wide with a practised flick of the wrist.

'Oh, don't worry, we'll wear them right away,' Ella said.

'Whatever,' the shopkeeper answered, her powers of customer service now completely diminished.

Ella bounded outside to Norm and flung a shirt towards him. He swiped at the air nowhere near the actual trajectory of the shirt, which slapped onto his face, nearly pushing him off the raised deck of the storefront.

A muffled curse later, he examined the shirt and let out an undignified squeal of delight. 'Oh my god, Ella!'

'I know, right,' she said.

Norm pulled his shirt over his head in a mad rush.

Ella couldn't help but notice a surprising amount of definition in Norm's chest. Possibly the result of having so little body fat he could pass as a Halloween decoration. Or maybe carrying Pup around all these years was finally paying off. She caught herself staring and looked down, kicking at the dirt. Norm thankfully hadn't noticed and instead was completely entranced by his new shirt.

'Is this the kind of thing we're supposed to be selling in Norman?' Ella asked, spinning a hat stand that held a series of trucker caps with a Ned helmet and guns crossed like swords.

'Sure, who cares?' Norm retorted, surprising Ella with his frankness. 'We're not looking to lift the culture. This is the culture. If we can't change it, why not lean into it? I don't care if someone gets in their car and drives away with a shirt that says "Nothing's Normal In Norman" if it means the rest of the town gets to exist.'

Ella was suspicious. 'Have you been thinking of shirt slogans this whole time?'

Norm pretended not to hear the question and moved on, well into his sermon now. 'We need to be brutal about this. We're creating a spectacle here. We aren't looking to bring in friends, we're looking to squeeze every last cent out of the tourists. They come to gawk at us, we swipe their wallets while they stare. It's us or them, really. It's them or Norman. Anyway, if someone wants to spend their money on this kind of tat then it's a good sign that we shouldn't feel bad about charging them.'

'That's a pretty convenient way to divorce yourself of all responsibilities,' Ella noted.

'Sushi life,' Norm retorted, and Ella snorted with laughter.

***

Norm felt that pang in his stomach he felt whenever he thought his dad wouldn't approve of something. If you do a good thing out of spite, is it still a good thing or is it forever tainted? What else matters but the result, right?

Ella had a point, annoyingly. Norm didn't hate the Big Things lovers. He was one. The sight of Woolcutter had lit a fire in his belly, or more accurately poured petrol on the fire that had always been burning. He always said he would do anything to help the town survive. It would be naive to think that it would be easy or pretty.

There was pride, too. Norm remembered the faces of the Stumbling Elephant patrons laughing at him. He remembered the mayor dismissing him so casually. He was tired of being underestimated. He wanted to be the one to save the town. Him. Norm from Norman.

If he had to get his hands dirty for that, so be it. Rayburn Fink once wrote that empathy was invented by God so that man would fear his own brutality. Norm had always been proud of his ability for empathy. He liked putting himself in other people's shoes, if only for the brief respite from being himself. But maybe the time for that had passed. Maybe the thing holding Norman back was that no one wanted to get their hands dirty. Norm looked up at the masked bushranger still towering over him and gave him a small nod.

He sat down on the wooden logs used to demarcate the parking spaces and Ella joined him.

'Do you think you'll ever leave?' she asked, her voice light.

He looked up at her confused. 'What, you're bored already? We just got here.'

'Not here,' she said. 'Norman, I mean. Home. Could you see yourself ever leaving?'

'We left. That's how we got here,' he mumbled, kicking at a bit of tall grass. Pup settled at his feet and Norm dropped him a scrap of biltong.

Ella bumped his shoulder playfully but forcefully. 'Why are you being deliberately frustrating?'

'Oh, you don't like when the shoe is on the other foot, do you?'

Ella laughed. 'I'm being serious. I am! I've never really understood why you stayed. Even now, I don't understand why you're fighting so hard for this town that has never really offered you much of anything.'

Norm nodded slowly and shifted on the uncomfortable wooden post. 'Dad's still alive there. The people in Norman know him. They tell me things. Stupid little things like that neither of us really liked tomatoes but we both love zucchini. I like that. I want to know his story.'

'Zucchinis are bad. You're wrong. So is your dad. You have being wrong in common.'

Norm laughed. He wasn't really thinking about zucchinis, though, or his dad. All that was on his mind was Ella leaning against him, the bare skin on their arms touching, her hand close enough to hold.

'Do you ever think about your own story?' Ella asked, her voice hovering just above a whisper.

'I don't think I have much of a story yet,' he said. 'Maybe this could be the start of it. Or the end of it. Who knows, really? I don't think we get to decide.'

Inside Norm, a battle was raging. His heart screamed for him to say something. *Don't die another death,* it called to him. *Please, please, don't die another death.*

And for once, his body obeyed. Norm spun and slid a leg over the post so that they could face each other. He looked deep into Ella's eyes. 'What do you want?' he asked.

'Could go another bacon-and-egg roll.' They were so close that Norm could feel her breath on his neck, their noses inches from touching. Norm sat in the silence, refusing to let her evade the question.

'I don't know,' she admitted, lowering her head to his shoulder. 'I don't know. I want too much. I want everything. I want to take every path and experience everything, but if I choose one I can't go down another. I'm scared I won't take any. I'm scared it's already too late.'

She shifted in place again, turning away from Norm as she said almost to herself, 'There are some paths we don't come back from.'

They leaned into each other. There were no words, just silent comfort. Norm softly, nervously, stroked her back as she looked over his shoulder.

Norm's eyes rested on Ned Kelly, still watching over them with his rifle drawn. His heart was thumping. He wondered if Ella could feel it through his chest. At that moment, she pulled back and held Norm's shoulders in her hands. Her eyes grew wide. Norm searched them, desperate to see any sign calling him forward.

'I've got it,' Ella shouted with glee, right into Norm's shocked face.

All he could stammer was a, 'You ... what?'

'The Big Thing,' she said, jumping to her feet. Norm felt disappointment rush over him. He tried to swallow it before Ella could see.

'What about it?'

'I know what it should be.'

136

PART TWO

Sushi Life

Here we are at, well, it's a bloody travesty of a sham of a farce of a joke. Look at this. It's the once magnificent, once beautiful Big Prawn of Ballina reduced to decrepitude, to decay, to being a shell of what it was. I thought things were bad when I saw the Big Oyster of Taree turned into a car yard but by golly, by jingo, this is just not good enough, people. I mean, when someone is travelling between say Grafton to Byron on the Pacific Highway, one of the more comforting sights of travel is knowing that you're going to be passing The Big Prawn in all its crustacean beauty, but look at it now. What a shame. Puts me in the mind of Shelley's Ozymandias. "Look on my works, ye mighty, and despair." Well, the good folk of Ballina, look on this. This is a bloody – this is a sham, this is a farce, this is a joke. I've got to turn the camera off. This is too upsetting.

Reaction to finding a penis graffitied onto the Big Prawn Transcript from YouTube video 'The Decline and Fall of the Big Prawn' uploaded by user MrAgm65, 23 November 2012

1

Mick had been lying in what some would consider his natural habitat, the recliner in front of the telly. The Test match had slowed down. No movement in the pitch, established partnership at the crease, spinners going to work at both ends. Mick was drifting somewhere between awake and asleep. Light enough that he'd be woken by any credible LBW appeal, deep enough that no one would bother him. The dream.

Out the back he could hear Doris bringing in the sheets. He ignored the gnaw in his stomach as he remembered that he'd been asked to do that. This was his day of rest, after all. A lot of days lately had been his days of rest. Anyway, Ella was out there with her and they seemed to be having a nice enough time. He let himself sink a little closer to sleep.

Somewhere in the distance he heard Ella's voice. She was excited. She was telling her grandmother that she had applied for university. She could be living with Zeke by the time the summer was over. Mick kept his eyes closed. He let his heart ache a little. His baby girl was leaving home. That was it, then. He'd be stuck in the grandstand. If that. He called Zeke now and then, but he never knew what to say. They'd share a few results from the weekend and then Mick would seize up. It was hard to shake the feeling that he was always interrupting something more important. His kids were busy living their own lives now. Then there was Gary. He hardly heard from Gary. An email now and then asking for money. Second-hand reports from Zeke or Ella. That was it.

He heard the screen door open and acted as if he'd just awoken. He pasted a smile on his face and greeted his daughter. He told himself to react positively when she told him. Show her that he was excited. Fight it and you lose her, he reminded himself. This was good. She should live her life. This was good. It was good.

But there was no announcement. All she said was that she was spending the day with Doris and Patty and wanted the keys. Mick obliged. Soon, they were gone and the house was quiet again. LBW shout. Outside off. Not a chance. Mick fell asleep.

***

Months passed and he still hadn't officially been told anything. Maybe he wasn't supposed to know. Maybe Ella wanted to escape him. God, he hoped not. He wasn't a bad dad. Not an evil dad, at least. He tried his best. But maybe that just wasn't good enough. Ella wasn't around. She had borrowed his car again and headed off with Norm. Doris said they'd be gone for a few days. Doris always knew things that he didn't.

Mick wanted to do something to show his daughter that he supported her. That was important. He had let Zeke wander away with barely a word. He shared a hug with Gary at the departures terminal and that was it. He let them walk out of his life. He was never good at goodbyes. He would have to learn to be better. He could take the initiative. He'd show his daughter that he knew she was leaving and it was okay.

A celebration was in order, he thought. That was proper. Give her something to remember. Mick dug up the paints from the shed and made up a sign and stuck it underneath the one that said 'Welcome to Norman'. It wasn't pretty but it got the point across. That was the easy bit. The next step would be much harder.

The phrase 'cap-in-hand' came to mind, though Mick did not own a cap. Still, to find himself at the door of the Stumbling Elephant was not something he would have imagined a week ago. He didn't come by here too often. The last time was to pick up and hose off the kid. Even then, it was purely transactional. Sandy had the good sense to leave him on the front porch rather than force an interaction.

The way she reacted, he might as well have been a ghost. In a sense, he was one, he supposed. When Jen died, so did their friendship. His fault. Always his fault. It was too much. He couldn't look at Sandy without thinking about Jen. He couldn't think about her anymore. So, he shut it off. Excoriated the wound.

But there was no way to hide, not really. Jen had left a ticking time bomb. His little girl, growing every day to look more and more like her. She had her mother's eyes and her mother's look of absolute disdain and boredom whenever he yammered on and on about one thing or another. It had been there from the very first days.

At least the Stumbling Elephant hadn't changed. Everything here was stuck in time. Even Rocko hadn't changed. Mick was fairly certain he had been wearing the same hi-vis polo ten years ago. Definitely smelled that way.

'You've got a lot of guts coming here after what you pulled,' Sandy said, keeping eye contact with Mick while pouring a drink. It wasn't as aggressive an opening as it seemed. If anything, it was a peace offering. The line came from Lando Calrissian greeting Han Solo as he entered Cloud City. Though, as Mick remembered it, that meeting didn't end too well for Han.

'G'day Sandy,' he said, settling into the chair next to Rocko, whose head was down on the counter.

Sandy placed a glass down beside his head and Rocko stirred. Mick waved his hand.

'No thanks, I'm—'

'This is for me,' she said, taking a sip. 'Now, why have you decided to darken my doorstep?'

Mick gulped. 'Maybe I will take that drink.'

'Why not? You're paying for this one, too.'

Mick cursed himself for not thinking of a game plan. What explanation was there, anyway? If there's one thing he knew about Sandy, it was that you couldn't bullshit her. Best to be upfront.

'Which do you want first?' he asked. 'The apology or asking for the favour?'

'Oh, there's a favour, is there?' she replied, as if she didn't know. He could tell she wanted to see him squirm a little. The good news was she was certainly getting her money's worth.

'It's for Ella. I want to throw her a party.'

Sandy softened. He'd said the magic words. She smiled a little but clearly wasn't happy about it. She slammed his drink down.

'Take this, you prick.'

'The apology?'

'Save it.'

Mick smiled. Sandy held up her palm.

'You're still gonna say it. I'm just choosing when. I'll let you know.'

He told her about the university application and tried to hide his hurt when Sandy revealed Ella had spoken to her. In fact, Sandy knew the application had been accepted. Ella hadn't said a word. He wondered if maybe he had already lost her. This last step was just a formality.

Talking to Sandy was good. Real good. Mick had forgotten how much he'd missed her friendship. Any friendship, really. If he'd had his way, he'd have gripped his daughter in his arms and cried, 'Please don't leave. Please, God, don't leave.' But that was not an option. That was not fair to do. He had already given her too many burdens to carry in her young life. He would not be another.

But this was no time to wallow. They had a party to organise.

2

The Big Potato has just been crowned Australia's worst Big Thing. You heard it right. Not the best. The worst. For a minute there I had to concentrate to make sure it was actually a potato.

Look at that. There's so much to not love.

David Campbell and Ally Langdon, *The Today Show,* **8 July 2022**

They had added a new colour to the weather chart. A vibrant lilac that translated to 'inhospitable for human life'. On the days when the sun was particularly oppressive and their shirts stuck to their skin, Norm and Ella liked to say it felt pretty purple outside. This morning was downright ultraviolet.

The slow trip home was made even slower by the need to stop by the side of the road every hour or so to keep the old car, and old dog, from overheating. Without any trees to shield them from the heat, the trio crouched in the shadow of the car as they waited. Norm couldn't help but imagine his father, rattling down these same roads. Somewhere in his mind he always imagined his dad out here, making his way back home.

They pushed on as the sun held high. Windows down, the car fan cranked to its limit. The empty country repeated and repeated. The same old story was being told everywhere. Burnt-out fields, dry creek beds, abandoned stores, boarded-up outposts, the crumbling remnants of lives left behind.

Norm was lost in time. He was stuck in a moment, outside the Big Ned, when he could have sworn Ella looked at him with ... what was it? Passion? Desire? Surely not. But why not? There was something in her eyes. And what if it was real?

As they drove, they spoke about the Big Thing. The goal, Ella said, was to generate controversy, not wonder. People will be intrigued by an oddity but they'll have to see an outrage for themselves. Australia was a nation of larrikins until someone stepped out of line. Then, they had to be crushed. She told him that if they pushed the right buttons, they could have grey nomads driving across the country just for the chance to be appalled in person. Norm listened, nodded his head, and smiled. *She believes in me,* he thought. *She believes in us.* Happiness had long been a stranger to Norm, yet here it was, rapping at his door, begging to come in.

'It must be fate,' he whispered to himself. Norm was scared, his heart was thumping. The coward would not die today.

Norman was somewhere over the horizon, Vodafone Hill towering over the flat terrain, and for the first time Norm did not want to see it. Something had changed on this drive, in this car, and he wanted it to last forever. He couldn't shake the feeling that it was still too delicate. That if they reached the town, it would shatter into a million pieces and disappear.

***

The car rumbled to a stop at the side of the road. The trio climbed out of their seats and took shelter in the shade once more. Ella unfurled a picnic blanket. The heat was oppressive, yet they sat close. Everything was quiet, as if it were waiting for them. The sky felt so low. Soon, they would be back in Norman. This was the last stop. Something inside Ella whispered that she had to tell him now or it would be too late.

In an instant, it was as if night had fallen inside of her. She could feel the wind rushing through her heart. Ella had played this moment in her mind a hundred times, a hundred different ways. She thought of Norm's hands fidgeting the way they do when he panicked. She thought of his lips curling in pain. She had imagined his hurt so vividly. Only now did she realise that her heart would break, too.

She took his hand and interlocked her fingers in his. He looked at her with the look of a man emerging from a dream, his ocean blue eyes so gentle and kind.

The whole world slowed like the moments before a car crash. She was hardly aware of the tears falling from her eyes until she saw them disappear into the earth, instantly erased by the heat.

When she spoke, it was from a distance, as if witnessing another person controlling her body by remote. 'I'm leaving, Norm,' this other Ella said. 'I got into uni. I'm moving to the city.'

He did not move. Not one inch.

'How long?' he asked, like a patient receiving a terminal diagnosis.

This time, she could not meet his eye. She spoke to the gravel, she spoke to her shoes, she bounced the words off the pitch hoping to lessen their impact. 'Ten days,' she said.

Time of death.

'Sushi life,' he mumbled.

Ella didn't know what she had been expecting, some grand reaction, screams or tears or something to show he understood what she'd said. Anything was better than this – Norm catatonic, his expression unchanged, lost somewhere between shock and disbelief. Slowly, he looked down at his hand, still interlocked in her own.

'I should have told you,' Ella said, hoping to find the words to fill the vacuum that had just opened between them. 'I should have said something sooner but ... but...'

She didn't know how to finish that sentence. She didn't know what she could possibly say, so she reached out to hold him. He pulled back instinctually. A small gesture, barely noticeable, yet to Ella, completely heartbreaking.

'I have to try. You understand, don't you?'

He looked up after a long while and, with the simplest gesture, shattered her into a thousand pieces. With a soft hand, he caressed Ella's face, raising her chin to look deep into her watering eyes.

'I am so proud of you,' he said.

He pulled her close and again they wrapped their arms around one another. Ella cried harder, lost in a sea of relief and sadness. Grateful and grieving.

When they separated, it was into a different world. The unspoken sadness cloaked them both.

They returned to the car and lumbered along the empty road. It felt like a funeral procession. The radio crackled and returned from the dead. 1228 AM Radio Norman was back within range. Jasper was playing 'Wide Open Road'. Actually playing it. Ella cried. She couldn't help it. There was too much to hold in. Shamefully, she stole a glance to her left. She saw the tears running down Norm's face and she wished she had never looked.

The entrance into Norman was marked by a surprisingly ornate sign, delicate metal framework and beautifully hand-painted lettering. The dry, windless years meant that the painting was slightly faded but otherwise well preserved. Wildflowers bloomed around the words 'Welcome to Norman' while underneath, in cursive script, were the words 'Born, 1913'. What had attracted Ella's attention, however, was a sign attached to the metal posts underneath. A long piece of cardboard, painted in a much cruder hand, the final letters squashed to fit.

Congratulations, Ella!

She pulled over and looked to Norm. Had he known all along? But before she could ask, he had loosened the seatbelt and stepped out of the car. The back door opened and Pup lowered himself onto the ground, staying, as always, one step behind Norm.

Ella restarted the engine and called through the window.

'I don't know what this is,' Ella said. 'I swear. I thought ... I thought maybe you did it. Norm, please—'

He stopped, his shoulders slumped. He leaned down into the car window.

'I ... I thought I saw something.' He inhaled deeply. His nostrils flaring. 'I thought I saw it in your eyes. I thought for a moment that you could have wanted me. I believed it, too. It was the nicest thing I've ever thought about myself – that I could be wanted by you.'

He smiled a painful smile. 'Goodbye, Ella,' he said.

Then Norm from Norman turned and walked away.

Ella didn't call after him.

She drove on in stunned silence. Another sign appeared, a red arrow, tied to a burned-out tree. A few metres along, another arrow, then a third and fourth. Then, the mysterious signwriter seemed to lose all patience, as the next card read like this:

Out of cards – meet at the Eleph.

She followed the arrows like a condemned man walks to the gallows.

The banister of the Stumbling Elephant porch had been decked out in green and red crepe paper streamers. A balloon was tied to each post of the entry stairs.

She eased the car to a stop and broke down on the steering wheel, howling with a pain that she could not fathom. A different kind of grief.

The doors burst open. There, in the wake, stood Thick Stephen. He pointed to Ella and made a noise as if he'd just seen a ghost.

'Hey, you're the one the surprise party is for,' he said. He turned and wandered back inside, calling loudly, 'Guys, the girl is here. Get ready to surprise her!'

3

Zeke's handprint would be visible between Norm's shoulder blades for days. It looked like it took all Norm's strength to not fall face-first into the grill. Ella watched him give a cordial smile and turn back to the barbecue before anyone could see his eyes start to water.

Ella's legs dangled from the porch as she sipped on a vodka cruiser. Gary sat next to her enjoying his own, much to her annoyance. As far as her dad was concerned this was her first drink, enjoyed legally on the afternoon of her eighteenth birthday. Yet the boys, the golden boys, were allowed to try one each as a rite of passage. She had already shamed Gary for calling it a girl's drink, even though she agreed with him. She couldn't help but feel for Norm, enlisted in these bullshit rituals even though it was clear to all and sundry that he was a deer on ice. He had already been pelted with tennis ball bouncers before having his left arm slow half-trackers dispatched all around his own backyard. Now, the boy who lived off cereal and microwaved eggs was forced to operate the barbecue under the watchful eye of both her dad and Zeke. She smiled to herself as Norm lifted a chop off the heat only to drop it back down in panic as her dad said through a half-cough that it needed a bit more time.

It was strangely unnatural to see Norm in a position like this. Meek though he may be, he did not perform for people. It was as if he understood that he was incapable of hiding so he refused to try. In another world, a better world, Norm would have been left alone to spend a decade at the top of a mountain, looking out to the horizon and pondering. He would be forgotten by society and allowed to simply exist until one day, when he would slowly re-emerge and gift the world the theory of calculus. He would then return up to the hill to live out the rest of his life in peace.

'He loves you, hey?' Gary announced between greedy bites of sausage, tomato sauce smeared all over his face. He said it with the kind of joy that can only come from a youngest sibling, knowing that they're speaking out of turn, and that even so, they aren't wrong.

'Shut up,' Ella snapped back. She felt a wave of embarrassment flow through her. It felt like hot air on the back of her neck.

Ella had good enough instincts to know that fighting back too hard would let her brother know he'd hit a soft spot. Showing weakness invited more attacks. Distraction was the wiser course of action. She held up her paper plate and gestured it towards the barbecue advisory committee.

'Pretty deadly of dad to chuck this on,' she said.

Gary replied with a mouth full of food, a habit he never dropped. 'Dad didn't do it.' Bits of sausage and bread sprayed the dead grass under the porch. 'This was Norm. He made the plan, he sent the invites, he even gave Dad the shopping list. He loves you. Norm loves Smella.'

His point proven, Gary stood up and tried to sneak a second drink from the esky, distracting Nanna Doris with a comment about how beautiful her hair looked that afternoon. A noble but ultimately unsuccessful effort.

The night wore on and the family were replaced by school friends. Zeke had been allowed to stay at the party under condition of death if he told anyone what he saw that night.

Ella watched Norm as he moved alone across the party, squeezing past the impromptu dance floor on his back deck, making a brief stop at the snack table to fill a plate, and collapsing into a picnic chair to watch the bonfire. She'd been avoiding Norm, the voice of her brother doing damage as it echoed in her ears. Knowing he had done this for her was touching but it came with a weight. Everything was all of a sudden so meaningful. No longer a celebration, this was a grand gesture. How much of this train of thought was inspired by cruisers, she did not know. Either way, the battle was raging in her own head and she thought it would be wrong to punish Norm for it. She took a seat next to him. He reached over and handed her a terribly rolled joint.

'You have to let me do these,' she said.

'Couldn't find you,' he mumbled.

Ella picked up a discarded paper plate and placed it on her lap, repairing Norm's terrible handiwork. The song changed and the crowd cheered. It all felt so far away.

'You know how they jump-start cars with those two little cables with the crocodile jaw bits? I reckon if they did that once to my brain it could really sort me out,' Norm said, his eyes on the fire as it danced so freely.

'I think you just invented electroshock therapy,' Ella replied. 'Besides, I like your brain the way it is.'

Norm's eyes stayed on the fire. He did not speak. Ella handed the joint to Norm, their hands touching for a moment too long. She pulled hers away as if she'd touched a hot plate. She hoped he hadn't noticed. She knew he did. Ella turned to Norm, beautiful Norm, and saw a million ways her life could unfold. She saw her brothers. She saw her town. She saw a perfectly comfortable existence. Comfortable.

'You mean everything to me,' she said, and she meant it. It was no hollow platitude. It was no consolation prize. The way Norm looked at her, he knew it, too.

'It's not that I don't care about you. I do.'

Norm shot her a look, furrowed brow, twisted mouth, full of doubt. Ella was dead serious. 'I do. I need you too much.'

He turned back to the fire and exhaled smoke. Ella sat for a moment watching him, scared that in trying to preserve something, she had just destroyed it. A call came from the dance floor and she looked up. She turned back to Norm. She wanted to cry. Instead she walked inside to dance the night away.

4

In Victoria ... the latest tourist bait is an 8-metre-tall egg with a 5-metre chook perched on it.

The Canberra Times, 27 January 1989

Sandy wrung the mop dry, dipped it back in the bucket and resumed her thankless task. Overnight the blood had caked on the wooden floors and was now resisting any attempts to remove it. At least it hadn't been spilled in anger. This small puddle was the result of a bet between Thick Stephen and the other stragglers, too drunk to know the night was over. They had bet that Stephen could not kiss the carved wooden elephant glued above the door.

The elephant had been carved by her grandfather, modelled after one he had seen during the war. Sandy had never seen an elephant herself and didn't suppose she'd ever get the chance. The thought of taking two days off to drive to the zoo and see an emaciated version of the beast did nothing but depress her. Though, she would like to see the meerkats. They were nature's perpetually anxious gossips. She understood them.

It was Sandy's great regret that she had never properly left Norman. Never really had the chance.

There was always work to be done at the bar. Perhaps that's why the kid's little speech had resonated with her so deeply. He was far from a great orator. He couldn't hold court like his old man. The poor thing could barely hold eye contact with another human being. But he still had a dream. It had been a long time since anyone had spoken of dreams in this place.

Sandy had escaped once. Shelby, Jen and her, for two glorious weeks before the world came crashing in around them. She was seventeen and as the sun rose on the first day of Year 11 she was already gunning it down the highway in her dad's paddock-basher, the girls screaming in delight as if they'd just busted out of prison.

The first hundred kilometres were white-knuckled terror. Constantly checking her rear-view mirror expecting to see the sweaty bastard gunning down the highway ready to drag her back and flay her himself. They drove all the way to the coast that day, sleeping in the car curled up together with the backseat down and blankets spread across the boot. The next morning she woke up long after the sun had risen. They swam in the ocean and sat on the beach with a carton of chips until the sun went down. They spoke of how they would stay there forever, change their names and carve out new lives by the seaside. They dreamed of waking every morning to lives free from exams, their families and the sad old town that never changed. The sea was always changing, no two sunrises alike. It was the second-best moment of

Sandy's entire life, and worth every bit of the flogging she received for it when she came back home.

Now, the girls were both gone, one way or another. Sandy had been left behind. One day, whoever was left in Norman would put her out the back next to her dad. They would mourn the loss of the pub more than the woman who served them every day, listened to their stories and cleaned up after their mess.

The wooden elephant's trunk was raised to accord with an old superstition that said it would bring good luck. Sandy scoffed at the thought as she scrubbed hard, the blood finally starting to give way.

She had started by admonishing the crowd gathered around the bleeding Stephen, saying he had too few brain cells left to invite more head trauma into his life, only to be told that the bet was his idea. A smiling, bloody-mouthed Stephen on the floor confirmed the fact. He later admitted to Sandy that he was hustling them, that he kissed the elephant every time he bet on the Keno for good luck.

The curse of the bartender was to remember the nights everyone else forgot. In the harsh morning light, every table told a story. Sandy examined the scene like a forensic detective. There were two glasses on the table of the corner booth, a wedge of lemon in each. This was the watchtower from which Patty and Doris could safely gossip. The pair had thought they were pulling a fast one on Sandy ordering only tonic water, as if she didn't see the flask, as if there was any doubt the old women were rolling drunk.

She gathered the pint glasses, left half empty as Ella had entered. For a breath, Sandy could've sworn she was looking at Jen. Ella had looked surprised when the crowd cheered. She'd hugged her father, she smiled shyly as he gushed about her in a speech that threatened to never end. But there was a sadness behind Ella's eyes.

Sandy had waited for Norm but he never appeared. She could choke that boy. He, too, was like his mother, in the worst possible way.

There was another problem eating away at Sandy. Why did they come to her bar? This party could have been a backyard barbecue and a full esky. But no, Mick had decided to waltz through the door like the past twenty years hadn't happened. It was as if he believed ignoring the past would drive it away. Throughout Ella's surprise party, Sandy caught him looking for her. That was his tell. His eyes followed her as she moved around the bar, shifting whenever she turned, like a schoolboy with a crush.

Slowly, something had become clear to Sandy. He was scared, and he was lonely. Years ago, Mick had excommunicated himself. Now, he was scared that he didn't fit anymore. At any moment, she could turn him away. It would be well within her rights. Justified, even. But she said nothing. Not yet. She would neither condemn him nor grant him a pardon. He could sit in purgatory for a while.

The only thing that had mattered on this particular night was the girl. Fragile though she seemed, she handled herself with the utmost decorum. Friendly to the locals, answering the same questions time and again about where she was going, what she'd be studying, and whether Norm would be going, too. Slowly, she had extracted herself to the safety of the speakeasy set up by her grandmother and Patty in the corner booth. They had stayed long into the night. By Sandy's measure, they must have gone through two and a half bottles of pure tonic water with a small wedge of lemon. The last few rounds, she had spiked the drinks herself, knowing that the old women's flask must surely be out. They made no acknowledgement that their ruse had been discovered. Instead, they had stumbled out the door only a few minutes behind Mick, who himself had been nursing one drink for hours. Rocko was a good distraction but he was a long way from merriment.

They had shared a moment at the door, a moment that Sandy relived in the empty bar in the harsh light of the new day. It was a look he had given her before, a long, long time ago. You don't forget a look like that, the one that says you should come with me. Maybe she imagined it. It didn't matter anyway. Didn't happen. Couldn't happen. He was just a sad old man and she was just a sad old woman. Nothing to be done about that.

***

The clean-up had lasted into the night. It had just passed midnight by the time Sandy finally locked up. Botany Street was quiet. Everyone had gone home. All except one. Sandy knew where Ella would be, back atop the hill, the stars wrapped around her shoulders.

Sandy figured that the poor girl would have spoken enough for the evening, but still she made her way to join Ella. Without exchanging a word, Sandy sat down beside her.

Perhaps it was the blanket of night or the emotion of the evening; it may have even been the thought of Mick and the path they never walked. Whatever it was, sitting up there in silence next to Ella, Sandy felt a sadness slowly grow inside of her.

Here was this girl, surrounded by love. Clumsy, crude, inarticulate love. Love in all its imperfections. And somewhere in the darkness, on the other side of town, there was a boy who had none. The world was not knocking at his door. Soon, there would be no one waiting for him, save for an old dog. She didn't need to wonder how that felt. Sandy knew that all too well.

'What if I'm making a mistake?' Ella had asked, curling into Sandy, who put an arm around the girl and held her as if she was her own.

'Then, good,' Sandy had said. 'What's the point of being young if you're not going to make any mistakes? Your mother and I made plenty.'

Ella's brow furrowed as if she was lost in thought. Sandy realised the poor girl must not remember those days at all. There used to be photos of the two of them all over the house, but Mick would have taken them down. The friendship that was so fundamental to Sandy's life was for Ella another moment lost in the haze of childhood.

When Ella asked about her mother, Sandy felt as if she was talking about another life, a better one, that she had left somewhere along the way and could never find again.

'I wish I'd always had you,' Ella said. 'I wish you'd always been around. I hate Dad for keeping you away. Why would he do that? Why!?'

Over the years, Sandy had rationalised the thought on his behalf. He didn't want to replace their mother. If there was a gaping hole in their lives, that was because someone great was gone. They were supposed to feel the absence. They could not paper over it. To him, the pain was a tribute.

She said none of this to Ella. Instead, she asked her to be kind to her father. She did not have to forgive but rather to understand that he was an imperfect man trying to survive the impossible. He had dedicated himself to her and her brothers. Not everyone would do that. Not all parents are capable of sacrifice.

Ella was silent for a while. And then she asked, 'How did Norm's mother die?'

On any other night, Sandy would have said it wasn't her place to tell. But she'd been caught off guard. How could Ella not know? She must have heard. Yet here she was, hugging her knees to her chest, nose a little snotty, eyes a little sunken, cheeks a little red, looking out over the town and asking.

There were some memories Sandy couldn't escape. More and more they piled onto her shoulders, weighing her down. You're not supposed to remember pain, or so she'd read, but maybe they were only talking about the physical kind. What was life if not a collection of moments too painful to forget. Perhaps at the end of days, you would receive a report card that read 'I survived the following...'

Shelby never forgot the smell of the ocean. Life had tied them down. She'd found Tony, Jen had Mick. The girls with the world at their feet were now the women with the world on their shoulders. Tony would be on the road for weeks at a time. It was hard to tell whether this was a relief or a curse. Probably both. Then, along came Norm, and what had been a simmering sadness became a crisis.

She'd begged Sandy to go back to the water. She wanted them to join hands and jump. Together they'd flee Norman and snatch the lives they should have been living all along. Sandy wouldn't hear of it. She told her friend to wait, to hold on just a little bit longer.

It was no hollow promise. Sandy truly believed that if you were good enough, kind enough and worked hard, then happiness would find you. By the time Jen was gone, Shelby knew she couldn't believe in that anymore.

Sandy sat for a long time. She let the night air fill the silence. How to explain it in a way Ella might understand? It was an impossible task. So, she led with the truth.

'Not all parents are capable of sacrifice.' Sandy let out a long, deep breath and felt the darkness in her soul. 'Shelby didn't die. She just left.'

5

The coward dies, the coward dies, the coward dies again.

Ella was leaving. Ella was gone. She had walked out of Norm's life and he had done nothing. He had given her no reason to stay. She couldn't stay, of course. Not for him. That was the way of life. No one stayed forever.

Awful things happen suddenly.

She had asked him why he stayed in Norman. Was it an invitation that he had missed? Had she offered her hand? Not possible. Of course she hadn't. How to explain that moment, though? Her hand around his waist. Her brown eyes willing him forward. A delusion probably. A dying brain conjuring up one last fantasy as a gift to its owner. That was more believable.

He had asked. At least he had asked. But he couldn't think about it anymore. He also couldn't stop. His brain retraced his steps like a tongue returns to a cut on the roof of the mouth.

She had asked him why he stayed. He couldn't answer. Or, more correctly, he could answer but didn't. The truth was too pathetic.

It had taken years to stop himself from believing that one day his father would come rolling down the highway. He'd stood and watched as the coffin was lowered into the ground and yet still he believed one night he would hear the rumble and the nightmare would at last be over. It wouldn't happen. He was gone.

But his mother really was out there. At least, he hadn't received any notice of her death. Though, Norm couldn't be sure what he would receive. He pictured someone arriving at his door with a scroll held together by a black ribbon or a folded flag. Even then, what good would he be? He couldn't pick her out of a line-up. Growing up, he used to watch the background of news reports and wonder if she would ever wander past the camera and he would know. It was the same logic by which he held on that she was still alive somewhere. If it wasn't true, he would know. Since he had no way of finding her, he had held hope that maybe one day she would return here. She would arrive back in Norman having missed him too greatly, having been in a coma for twenty years or swept up on some incredible adventure that simply could not be abandoned, for the very fate of the known universe hung in the balance. It was better than having to admit that she knew he was here and every day she made the choice to leave him here.

Years ago, when they'd first met at the fete, Ella had assumed that his mother had died. He hadn't corrected her. He had felt ashamed of that choice, made in a split second, confirmed by silence. The fear, however, prevailed. If Ella had found out the truth, then she would know that the person who brought Norm into the world had looked into his soul and found him wanting. Why, then, would she waste her time on such an unloveable creature? Norm huffed. In the end, the result was the same. It had just taken her longer to work it out.

Smoke tastes different at 10am. The rising heat of the morning mixes with the burning in the lungs and a special kind of satisfaction emerges with the knowledge that you have decided to waste another day.

Norm heard once that the reason people like spicy foods is that it kills their tastebuds, releasing a flood of feel-good chemicals to compensate. That was what he was doing, setting fire to the potential of another day, and in return receiving a brief respite from the thoughts echoing in his head.

It was Ella who taught him how to roll, a skill she acquired from her brother. Zeke had to explain that the patch of tall, spiky plants in the corner of Norm's garden weren't, as Norm thought, pine trees. To this day, Ella would announce that she felt like a smoke by singing 'It's Beginning to Look a Lot Like Christmas'. Norm whistled it to himself as he packed away the grinder and papers, wondering if there was any part of his life, even the simplest gesture, that hadn't been coloured by Ella.

He worked his way back into bed, the blinds fighting hard to let in only a trace of light from the outside world. Pup curled up at his feet, perfectly content to stay inside as long as possible.

Over the radio, Jasper announced another town had defaulted. Burnley Lake, named after a body of water that no longer existed. Norm had never visited, now he never would.

The last vestiges of fight had left his system. What was the point, anyway? Precisely what would he be saving? Norman without Ella wasn't Norman. It would be easier to fade away, to let the dirt reclaim the town. He let sleep take him again.

***

Norm awoke to sounds coming from his kitchen. A fearful chill ran down his spine. Was he being robbed? Surely not. He had a clever security method of never owning anything worth stealing. Slowly, he approached the kitchen, pausing along the way to pick up the closest thing to a weapon he could find, a plastic stick used to launch tennis balls. The ball was still attached. It had been a long time since Pup had been able to play.

He turned the corner with a dramatic flourish, the stick high above his shoulder, only to be confronted with the image of Nanna Doris scrubbing down his kitchen bench.

'You can throw that but I'm not gonna fetch it,' she said.

He slowly lowered the stick. The ball rolled away from the handle. Pup wandered into the room and followed the slow rolling ball, picking it up in his mouth and holding it up to Norm, asking for another roll.

'Some guard dog you are,' Norm spat.

'Don't get wild at him. Us old folk never know when to butt out.'

'Can I make you a cup of tea?'

'I don't know, can you?'

Her smile gleamed with mischief. He took his cue and turned towards the kettle, only to find a teapot already filled.

'Oh, you've made one already.'

'That's right. Now, bring it over to the table and pass me that stick so I can flog ya.'

Norm gulped. He brought the plastic stick and the teapot to the kitchen table, carefully setting down the teapot in front of Nanna Doris as she took her seat, then anxiously held out the stick.

'You don't hand someone a stick when they say they're gonna flog you with it. What's wrong with you?'

She took the stick and hit him over the shoulder with it. She began pouring herself a cup of tea. 'Now, this is none of my business, so if I am overstepping the mark you go ahead and say and I'll leave you to sort it out yourselves. God knows I've got enough problems of my own without dealing with all of your issues. Milk.'

Norm jumped to his feet and brought a bottle of milk back to the table, where it was sniffed suspiciously. Nanna Doris then reached into her purse and pulled out three scotch finger biscuits from a ziplocked bag. Norm took his seat and immediately began to shuffle his hands nervously. His movements were as quick and darting as those of a hopping mouse. He looked at Nanna Doris and looked away. He put his hands on the table then back in his lap. His foot tapped on the floor to its own rhythm, seemingly independent of any input from Norm and unresponsive to any command to stop.

'Your eyes are red,' Nanna Doris said as a dry fact.

Norm squirmed. 'Oh, yes, sorry, allergies.'

'You think I was born yesterday?'

'No, sorry.'

'No what?'

'No, I don't think you were born yesterday.'

'So you think I'm old then? You're saying I look old?'

Norm was taken aback. 'No, not at all. You ... you weren't born yesterday but you weren't born that long ago. A while ago but not heaps long ago.'

'Don't be stupid. I'm old. Are you too thick to notice that I'm old?' A small smile appeared on the corner of her lips, the first crack in her facade. She was enjoying torturing the boy. 'I don't care if you're smoking that ganja. What else are you going to do around here?'

Norm was taken aback, both by the older woman's casual attitude and her use of the word 'ganja', which he hadn't heard outside of '70s cop movies.

'You understand the position I'm in here, don't ya?' she asked, dipping a biscuit into her tea. 'Ella is my granddaughter. My only granddaughter. Without her mother here, it's up to me to look after her.'

Norm nodded and sipped his tea to avoid having to make eye contact. His shoulders hunched. He braced himself for another lashing. Nanna Doris brushed the crumbs off her hand and dipped her biscuit again. 'You never knew your Nanna, but I have known you since you were a little thing, so, I think it's only right that I yarn to you on her behalf. But first, I need to do this.'

With a sharp move of her hand, Nanna Doris pulled on Norm's ear, ripping it down towards the table. He cried out in pain, shocked at the strength of the old woman. His ear burned and for a second he feared it would be torn clean off his body. Then, as sharply as it began, the pain stopped.

'There we go. Now, use the ear you've got left and listen to me. Someone should have told you this a long time ago. You're being a sooky la-la.'

Norm sighed. 'Actually, I have been told that quite a bit lately.'

'For years I've seen you walk in and out of this house following my granddaughter like a lost dog on the street. You're more of a dog than your dog.'

She hit the word 'dog' hard.

'Then, when things don't work out, or they don't go the way you've dreamed them up, you come back here and you have your little sook. Well, what are you doing?'

'I don't think she wants me to do anything,' Norm answered. 'She should go. It's right for her to go. I can't stand in the way of that. I thought you, of all people, would understand that.'

Nanna Doris broke another biscuit in half. 'I did not ask you about Ella. Listen. I am talking about you. Your life. The kind of person you want to be. That's not about her and it can't be about her. You've got two scenarios here. One, she walks out of your life forever. Too bad, so sad. But what then?'

She was emotive in a way that Norm had never heard before. Each word shot like a bullet, pinning him to his chair. 'You're just going to pack it in? You're done? Life over? Don't be stupid! If she's going off to live her life, you need to live your own. You can't live or die for Ella. She doesn't want that and you shouldn't want it!'

She smacked her hand against the table to emphasise her point then paused for breath. In a moment, the anger in her expression turned to kindness once again. 'Here's the thing, Norman. If she does want to be with you, the same questions still apply. What man is she coming home to?'

Norm stared back at Nanna Doris, lost for words.

'You know why it kills me to see you sooking about like this?' she continued. 'It's because you've made this whole thing a foregone conclusion. This is who you are and she either loves you or she doesn't. You haven't worked on yourself. You're so busy looking behind you, you've taken your eyes off the road ahead. Ella is a smart girl, Norman.'

'I know that,' he blurted out. Norm hadn't realised it but the hairs on the back of his neck had risen. A defensiveness had grown inside of him, the kind that only bubbles when you know you're dead to rights. Nanna Doris didn't react, she just poured herself another cup of tea.

'I know you do. You're a smart boy. Smart enough that you should know she wants to be appreciated, not worshipped. Smart enough to know that your life has to be worth more than that, too. You need to know what you want and find someone who wants to go on that journey with you. If that's my Ella, then I will be very happy for you both. If it isn't, it's best that you find that out now. If you try and find your happiness in another person, it will turn to resentment. I have seen it before, in this very house.'

Norm felt the breath leave his body. He tried to speak but couldn't. He swore he could see the beginnings of tears in the old woman's eyes.

'You listen to me, this is your grandmother speaking. Find your own happiness. Find your purpose. Live for yourself and see who shows up for the journey.'

6

The sounds of 1228 AM Radio Norman played from inside the store. INXS's 'Original Sin' had just been followed by Bizet's 'Habanera'. Jasper had introduced both tracks as 'one for the lovers', which is something he liked to say when he wasn't sure which track was about to play.

Ella could smell the blueberry muffins. She made a note to mention it to Mr Baylis when he brought over the tea. That way he could be reminded to take them out of the oven while still saving face. And anyway, they smelled much too good to allow them to burn.

There were facts that she still couldn't piece together. Norm's mother was alive, somewhere. Where was she? Why didn't she come back for him? Did she know he was left all alone? And then the bigger question, the one that really hurt: why hadn't he told her?

Ella wanted to confront him. To show up unannounced and bang on his front door demanding an explanation. But how much of that feeling was wanting to see him? How much of it was wanting something to be mad about, instead of this unshifting sadness.

She was stuck in an endless week. One life over, the next refusing to begin. She knew she would miss the town, that she should savour every minute she still had in Norman, but it wasn't the same. Not without him.

Ella's eyes drifted to the next table, where the newly unemployed former council secretary Daisy Peach was engrossed in conversation with Mrs Langham. Ella didn't want to eavesdrop but if she couldn't help it, then it wasn't her fault. At least that was the justification she gave herself that allowed her to blame the laws of physics and not her own desperate desire to disappear into someone else's drama for a few minutes.

'He thinks we should take it. He said it's nearly twice the value of the land. Says we'd be mad to sit on it,' Mrs Langham said, leaning over her scone, the purple frames of her glasses sparkling in the light. She nervously clutched the turquoise pendant on her necklace. 'I don't know what to tell him.'

'What would that mean for—' Ms Peach's voice shook. She couldn't bear to even ask the question. She thumbed the turquoise stone on her pinkie ring.

Ella leaned closer so she wouldn't miss a beat. Ms Peach's voice had dropped to a low whisper.

'It's the Marshall Group, isn't it?'

Mrs Langham didn't answer. Ella's mind was racing. What was this group and why were they interested in buying up property in a dying town? Then, something clicked. Rona had mentioned signing a non-disclosure agreement. Ella had dismissed it as a short-lived lie to quiet Norm, but what if she had been telling the truth? It would explain a lot. She had to talk about it with Norm. Then, she remembered, of course she couldn't. The same old sadness came strolling back.

Ms Peach slammed her fist on the table and Ella jumped involuntarily. At the worst possible time, Mr Baylis approached Ella's table.

'And how are you doing, little miss?' he asked.

She gave a strained smile. 'All good, thank you.'

Mr Baylis walked around the table and leaned on the empty seat. 'Where is your little friend today?'

Another thump rang out from the other table. Cutlery clattered. Ella was in a tight spot. She couldn't ask Mr Baylis to leave so that she may eavesdrop on his other customers better. The strain on her face must have shown because all of a sudden he was pulling back a chair, fluffing out his apron and sitting down with a groan and a loud crack from his knees.

'I know that look,' he said kindly. 'Do not worry about him. You are too sweet a young woman to worry about that boy.'

'Oh, uh, no, I—' Ella began.

'It's okay.' He leaned forward on one elbow, raising his hand to his grey moustache to whisper, 'I never really liked him anyway.'

178

Despite herself, Ella giggled.

'Forget him. Tell me about you. What is it that you wish to do?'

'No, it's silly.'

'Everything worth a damn is silly,' he said.

Ella took a sip of her peppermint tea, forgetting about the drama unfolding between Daisy Peach and Bettsy Langham.

'I want to study the stars.'

Mr Baylis furrowed his brow. 'You and I have different senses of humour, I think.'

'It's a little silly. Stargazing makes you feel so small but so important because there's this big grand thing going on out there, further away than we can imagine, more complicated than we could ever understand, but we get to witness it. We've been witnessing it for a long, long time, too. The same constellations I see at night lit the way for my great-great-great-grandmother.'

Mr Baylis smiled more broadly than ever and pointed a thick finger right at Ella. 'You are a lot like your mother.'

This took the oxygen right out of her lungs.

'You knew her?' she asked.

'Knew her!' Mr Baylis waved a hand dismissively. 'She sat right where you are, every day. She and Mrs Baylis loved talking about how the plants were growing, and every little thing going on in the town. They're probably still doing it right now.' He looked up to the sky and just for a moment, his expression turned impossibly sad, the weight of the years hanging on his forehead. Then, as quickly as it had appeared, it was gone again, replaced by the big, broad smile Ella knew so well. 'Of course, she was a painter, your mother.'

Ella was stunned. 'Really? No. Really!?'

Mr Baylis pointed over Ella's shoulder towards the old weather-beaten shed. 'That is you, no?'

Ella turned her body and stared at the mural of the young girl dancing by the riverbed. The world seemed to hold still around her, her heartbeat slowing to a crawl. She had never paid it much mind. It had blended into the background of her world, never remarked upon. Yet, there it was, there she was, painted by her mother's hand.

It made her sad to think she hadn't recognised herself. There were so few photos in the home. No baby pictures. It must have been because her mother was in them all. This woman Ella hardly knew yet missed so dearly. Ella so rarely felt seen. But there it was, hiding in plain sight. Proof that she was real and loved and once filled with joy.

There was only one other person in her whole life who had ever made her feel like she was truly special, and he had walked out of her life.

'You wait here,' Mr Baylis said, leaping from his chair with a sudden vigour. 'You wait.'

He hopped back inside, bouncing from foot to foot with youthful energy. Ella sat transfixed by the mural and her mind slowly turned back to Norm. Norm, whose mother was out there somewhere. Every little morsel of her mother's life was like gold for Ella. How could Norm know there was not just a story but a real person out there somewhere, and sit still?

Ella heard a clatter behind her. Ms Peach stood suddenly and raced past her table. Ella couldn't be sure, but she thought that she'd seen tears in her eyes. Before she could dwell on it, Mr Baylis had returned, holding in his arms a painting of him and his wife, some thirty years younger, standing arm-in-arm surrounded by white roses. It was by no means a masterpiece of the form, but what it lacked in technical prowess it more than made up for in heart. Ella studied the painting carefully. Warmth radiated from it. She couldn't help but smile. And there, in the bottom right, scrawled ever so delicately in white paint, was her mother's signature.

'This was a gift she gave us,' Mr Baylis said. 'We had a photo, a beautiful photo from our wedding day. It used to sit by the register in a little silver frame. But when the flood hit, and the banks overflowed, it was ruined. The whole store was, of course, but it was the photo that broke Maria's heart. Then, a few weeks later when we reopened the store, your dear mother brought us this. She had painted it from memory. We cried. We all cried.'

Even now, as he recounted the memory, Mr Baylis pulled out a large white handkerchief and blew into it. 'She was a wonderful, wonderful woman, your mother.'

Ella sniffed. And then sniffed again. What was that smell?

'Oh, god. The muffins!'

7

Well, I love utes. How good are utes? And how good would a Big Ute be? That's what I'd say.

Prime Minister Scott Morrison, 9 December 2021

One of the candles promised tranquillity, another promised wisdom, a third promoted positive vibes, a fourth would instil self-love, the fifth captured the smell of the Amalfi coast, and the sixth just said 'Sandalwood' in Arial font. They combined to give the distinctly not calming sensation of being trapped in a fire hazard. There were no smoke detectors, either. A code violation, Billy supposed, but it would be out of keeping for a psychic to need one.

Michelle laid out another card in front of Billy. It showed an oddly peaceful blond boy, suspended upside down, his legs crossed and his arms seemingly lashed to a post.

'The hanged man,' she said.

'Is that good?' Billy asked.

Michelle's brow furrowed in a way that concerned Billy. He had never put too much stock in the occult, but he'd still rather good news to bad.

'It's not necessarily bad. It could just mean you need a new perspective on things, or there will be a greater sacrifice required.'

'Oh, terrific,' Billy said, loosening his tie and wiping the sweat off his brow. His shirt was already sticking to his body and the thick, incense-filled air was doing little to help his claustrophobia. He tapped his fingers on the table twice in quick succession. 'Hit me.'

Michelle pursed her lips and drew another card.

'The Devil,' she announced, causing Billy to throw his hands up in dismay. Michelle quickly drew another card. 'Alright, alright, here.'

With a flourish she placed the card on the table. Billy caught a glimpse of a cartoon drawing of the grim reaper before Michelle swept the cards aways with one hand and placed them all into a small wooden box.

'Let's forget the cards, shall we?' she said. 'We still have a lot of work to do. I've heard that the Batchen girl is moving away. Word is she got a spot at the university.'

Billy made no effort to hide his disinterest. 'I'll be sure to send a letter of congratulations,' he said, dipping his finger in the candle wax and watching it congeal over his finger. He slowly picked away at it, leaving shreds of wax on the table. The process fascinated him, like acquiring and shedding a second skin. He reached back into the candle and coated his finger again. Michelle grabbed his wrist and the wax dripped down, freezing in mid-air like a purple stalactite. 'Listen. The Batchen girl is leaving.'

8

Ella sat cross-legged in front of her mother's mural and tried to place herself within it. She was too young to form an actual memory. Even if she could, it would be of the things that delight a child, the blur of the riverbank as she twirled and twirled, a butterfly she chased, the sounds of the rushing stream. She would not have known then to linger on what was important, the flash of a smile, the smell of her mother's hugs. Maybe this particular day never existed, or maybe it was a hundred days melded into one. She imagined her mother, in the shade of the river red gum, not much older than Ella now, wearing paint-flecked overalls, washing her brushes in a bucket.

Ella had spent the last hour on top of Vodafone Hill. With a flick of the wrist, she would twirl her phone into the sky, twisting in the wind, slowly rising, then crashing back to Earth, each time carrying with it a new piece of devastating news. She had learned the Marshall Group was a predatory arm of a major energy conglomerate, famous for sucking the last drops of mineral wealth from country towns and moving on to their next victim.

From the top of Vodafone Hill, she could see the borders of Norman, surrounded in all directions by dead land. She found no beauty in the view. It was all too fragile.

Then there was the house at the very edge of town. Norm hadn't been seen for days. He had shut himself off from the world. He would want to know about the Marshall Group, surely. He needed to know the town was under threat. Maybe they could put everything else aside and focus on saving Norman for one more day. And then ... and then what?

A slow rumbling interrupted Ella's train of thought. Was it a car? She put a palm to the ground, wondering if she could feel some far-off vibration. She felt the brush of wind on her cheeks and tried to remember the last time she'd felt a breeze on the main street of Norman. The small stones by her side rolled down the riverbank and into the dry bed underneath.

She turned and rose to her feet, her brain refusing to process the spectre on the horizon. At first, Ella thought of fire, and felt her heart jump into her throat, but this was something different. It did not have the smell of fire, nor the darkness of the smoke. Rather, the colours of the cloud evoked inappropriately delightful words in her mind like 'tangerine' and 'persimmon'. What it did have was the same impossible scale, as if the whole world had been engulfed. It looked like a crashing wave, threatening to swallow the world before it. As if to make good on the threat, within a few seconds, Vodafone Hill was completely enveloped. The sky took on an unnatural orange-tinted darkness. The wind began to pick up the small stones in the streets, whipping them at her ankles.

She turned towards the riverbed, and for a moment considered crawling under the upturned troopy.

She was about to take off down the riverbank when she heard a crash. The door of Maffezzoni's Metals warehouse had been flung open, and in the gulf stood Ella's salvation. Rocko stood in the doorway, his calloused hand cupped against his yellowed beard as he called out to Ella.

'Girly, get in, quick!'

She didn't need to be told twice. She put her head down and ran for the open door.

Ella couldn't remember a time when the old metalworks warehouse had looked open and inviting. The plyboard reinforcing the broken glass shopfront and the occasional dull orange light inside had been a perfect starting point for primary school ghost stories.

From inside, the building was remarkably unremarkable. Perhaps this had once been the foyer to greet customers, but it had been a long, long time since anyone had stepped through that door. A single bulb hung from the ceiling, its shade caked in dust, the light low enough that everything appeared in black and white. She could see the words *Maffezzoni's Metals* painted in delicate cursive on the window, long since hidden from the street by chipboard.

'You're Mr Maffezzoni?' Ella asked.

'Aye, what's it to you?' Rocko said. 'You're not that little prick from the council that's been hassling me, are you? I told you, I'm not paying the rates because you lot don't empty my bins. I burn everything in a barrel at the back of the shop. That's legal. You don't own the sky.'

The boards rattled and the light flickered. The dust cloud had arrived. 'Might as well settle in,' Rocko said. She followed him along a cramped, dank hallway which opened out to a spacious workshop. Decommissioned workstations with cobweb-covered machinery hinted at a productive past that Ella could not remember.

In a flash, Rocko disappeared deep into the bowels of the building. With anyone else, Ella might feel nervous, but Rocko was a weirdo, not a creep. An important distinction. Also, if needed, she could snap him like a twig.

A halogen light hummed and Ella tried to imagine Rocko working diligently at one of these stations. An impossible thought. Something caught her eye, a sharp spike poking out from underneath a dusty tarp near her feet. Ella slowly pulled it back, revealing a large metal sculpture, a razorback pig, five feet long at least and three feet wide. Its skeletal structure made it seem oddly delicate, yet the thick-legged stance and bent head projected pure strength. Ella swore she could practically see the steam snorted out of its nostrils. It was powerful, beautiful and above all, absolutely and undoubtedly a pig.

Echoes of footsteps suddenly reverberated around the room. Rocko had returned with two cans of Melbourne Bitter.

'I see you've spotted Sarah,' he said. 'Don't get any ideas. She's not for sale. Come round, I'll show you the rest.'

They walked together, weaving through equipment in the warehouse. Rocko lifted a heavy door and they walked through an enclosed greenhouse set-up, along a short gravel path towards a large corrugated-iron shed, the door wrapped in a thick chain and secured by padlock.

Rocko dropped the lock to the ground, unwrapped the chain and opened the hanging door with great exertion, the hinge unleashing a godawful cry as the bottom corner dragged into the gravel. They stepped inside and Rocko pulled on a cord above his head. Dull lights blinked on in three stages, reaching deeper and deeper into the recesses of the shed. Ella stood in awe with a dash of fear.

Before her stood an unfathomable menagerie of metallic creatures, like a zoo where the exhibitions had been forged from the bars themselves. They were skeletal frames, yet somehow felt delicate and tender. The tapir dug at the ground with its snout, the meerkat's ever-so-small paws rubbed its ears, the kangaroo standing proud, chest out, weight on its iron tail, ready to leap into the unknown. These creatures were at once impossible, harsh and unearthly while still being vibrant and alive.

Ella turned to look Rocko up and down, trying to comprehend how this man, who seemed as if he had been unfrozen from a slab of Antarctic ice, could be capable of such intricate work. Suddenly, she was struck by a brilliant idea.

'Rocko, I reckon I have a job for you. A big one.'

9

I have been a neighbour of the prawn for eight months. It certainly draws a lot of people to the area, especially around my fence outside ... It does throw out a lot of light, as well. Those eyes, as you see, the eyes on the prawn, they're a beady-looking thing. It can be a real horror story if you tend to think of it that way. I'm actually frantically growing trees out there now.

Kevin Santin, interviewed by ABC News, 9 September 1991

Botany Street was dressed up like a carnival. Trestle tables out the front of storefronts were overflowing with fresh fruit, honeycomb, homemade candles, pottery, garden sculptures and for some reason an ice sculpture, a protest fist, melting in the sunshine. The water ran from the base of the sculpture off the table and formed a puddle at Sandy's feet.

Shelby laughed, and the sound rang on and on. She was riding on Tony's shoulders, and young, so very young. It was not real. It couldn't be real. But was Sandy caught in a dream or a nightmare?

It was the town as it used to be, her friends as they used to be. Jen and Mick, hand in hand, skipping through the streets. Shelby guiding Tony from above, like he was a racehorse. Together, they retrieved a frangipani, and passed it down to Sandy.

She watched on with dread. She was torn over whether to warn them or let them live on in this perfect bliss. Mick turned to smile at Sandy. It was a smile she hadn't seen before. He didn't look at her like that. Not back then. His hand loosened and Jen's slipped away.

Then, in a second, she was on the roof of the Elephant, alone with Mick. She had to warn him. She grabbed him by the shoulders. He leaned down and kissed her. This wasn't right. This didn't happen. She kissed him back. They would have never done this. His hands were on her back. They were strong but gentle. She leaned into his chest. Jen was out there somewhere. What if she walked in? This was wrong. She shouldn't be doing it. She had to warn him. His hands moved to her jeans. She had to warn him.

And in a moment, it was gone. Replaced by the repeating pattern in the plaster on the ceiling. Sandy was short of breath. She resisted the urge to look at the bedside clock. Better not to know. Her eyes traced the fan pattern. They'd been right there, the other side of that ceiling, on the roof of the Elephant.

It had been so long since she'd seen their faces. They replayed in her mind as she slowly lifted herself out of bed. Sandy told herself she would make something of the morning. She pretended that she wasn't afraid to sleep again.

She took a cardboard box and moved through the pantry, selecting tins of food, grateful for the prepper instincts that her father had passed on. She worked quickly, talking to herself, trying to distract from the memories, now disturbed, that would not go quietly.

Tony had come to her, as everyone did. Such is the life of the bartender. You are the community's shoulder. This time was different. The strong man bereft, looking Sandy in the eyes and asking where it had all gone wrong, asking when his wife was coming back, asking if Sandy had known, asking how he was going to take care of this baby alone. All questions that she couldn't answer.

It had been raining that night. Back then, an unremarkable fact. It was raining because it rained sometimes. She took the box to the fridge and packed in a bottle of milk and half a dozen eggs.

Apparently there were seven stages of grief but she never really made her way beyond anger. She was the extra friend, the disposable one. When they were around, she was a utility, there to carry burdens, to listen to the things they couldn't say to anyone who mattered. Then, one way or another, she could be tossed aside. Her existence became a bad memory of a time they'd rather forget.

It had also rained the night Tony died. What did that mean? Probably nothing. It rained sometimes. It used to rain sometimes.

The stars had retreated and a pink hue crept over the horizon. The phrase 'rosy-fingered dawn' came to mind. She started the car, its rumble disproportionally loud against the backdrop of the sleeping town.

Sandy had tried to contact Shelby. Her last known address, at least. A postcard years before had said she was moving on with her life, that she couldn't look back anymore. It didn't say where she was going or how to find her. Sandy had thought that she might now reconsider, for the good of the boy. It hadn't happened.

The only person who did seem to step up was Mick. From what Sandy had heard, the kid was already at his house most nights. He was given the option to make the move permanent but the kid refused. He'd turned down Sandy too. He wanted to stay in his home. He wanted to wait for his mother to return, even if he waited forever. So, the town had stepped in where Shelby wouldn't. Norm became their responsibility.

She stopped the car, choosing to walk up the driveway. No need to wake him. She left the box of supplies by the old redback boots on the front porch. Maybe now Tony would let her rest.

10

The memory sounded like gunfire and smelled like pig. It was the second-happiest moment of Rocko's life. A one-in-a-million shot. His father's excited laughter sounding closer to gibbon than man. Sharp exhales of breath with a *ha-ha-ha!*

Rocko could still hear it as he walked around the empty warehouse, preparing for the night's work. The first thing Rocko had taken down were the meat hooks. He would have no use for them. Nothing would hang in his home. He melted down the composite parts and forged a cross, which he placed atop of his old man, to rest with him for eternity.

Ha-ha-ha! It was a happy memory. His father's sweaty hands taking the rifle with one hand and lifting the boy with his other. It was the first time Rocko could remember thinking that he might just be worth a damn after all.

'We've got a prodigy on our hands, I reckon,' his father said, lifting little Rocko's hands up like a prize fighter. Rocko wasn't too sure what a 'prodigy' was but he assumed it was a kind of pig.

Pig hunting was somewhere between service and sport. Rocko's father told him they had to be culled to protect the local wildlife and vegetation, but that it didn't mean they weren't allowed to have fun while doing it.

Then, the memory turned sour. Collecting their trophy, Rocko and his father discovered that the shot was not perfect. The pig had not been slain. She had collapsed on the ground, releasing a low guttural groan between pained breaths. She looked Rocko in the eyes. He saw only pain and fear.

His father had considered this a teaching moment and handed his son a bowie knife. He might as well have been handing over the Olympic torch the way his father revered that blade. He tended to it with enough care and attention to evoke feelings of jealousy in Rocko. Now, it was in his hands.

Rocko lowered his mask and fired up the angle grinder. The sparks lit up the room like New Year's fireworks. A fountain of flame, bursting into the air yet never seeming to touch the ground. It was that impossibly beautiful yet dangerous spectacle that first drew Rocko to the craft. To take something so powerful and curl it to your will was one thing. But to use it to build something truly delicate was something else entirely.

Again, it was his father who had fostered the fascination. Rocko remembered playing in the street and hearing an ungodly noise rip through the air from the warehouse. There was nothing the young boy craved more than chaos, so it drew him like a moth to the flame.

He had teased the door open and was greeted with a vision of hell. Fire in the sky, the screech of metal, and orchestrating it all a terrifying figure in a metal mask, thick gloves and a dark apron, the master of the flame. Here, before Rocko, the Devil himself worked on a terrible machine that would bring about the end of the Earth. It was the coolest thing he'd ever seen.

The Devil looked his way and Rocko screamed. The Devil matched his scream, their voices booming over the screech, as if a thousand souls screamed along with them. Then, it all went quiet. The flame was extinguished, silence prevailed once more. The Devil removed his mask to reveal Rocko's father, still out of breath, but now with a curious smile on his face as he noted his son's interest. Soon, Rocko had his own mask, heavy enough to pull his whole head towards the ground as sparks filled the air around him. That was the happiest moment of Rocko's life.

It had been far, far too long. It wasn't so much that art was meditative for Rocko. Really, the opposite. It gave him a brief escape from his head. His entire being became about bringing these sculptures to life. Even if it was as simple as a sculpture of a little frog wearing a top hat, that could keep the darkness at bay for hours. Plus, when do you ever get to see a little frog wearing a top hat?

He had thought his machines had turned off for good. There were no more customers, no materials, and worst of all for Rocko, no more wildlife to capture his imagination. He was uninspired. That was, until Mick's daughter walked through his door.

The girl's idea resonated with him immediately. A Big Thing in Norman. It tickled something in the back of his head as if he had heard it before somewhere but he couldn't place it. Then, the kid explained the shape of the sculpture to him and Rocko laughed until a hacking coughed threatened to shut his lights off for good. They were going to piss people off, no two ways about it. It felt good.

He was happy to work for a case of beer and a pouch of tobacco a week, but the metal wouldn't come for free.

He ran a hand over the razorback that had served him so well over these years. 'I'm sorry, girl,' he said to her, his voice cracking more than a little. She would understand, he told himself. She would know that this was the right thing to do. The angle grinder whirred. He felt the bowie knife in his hand.

To Rocko, these statues were proof that there was something beautiful inside of him. If his father was right and someday we would all face judgement, then surely these statues would show he had a soul worthy of saving. Had he found himself in purgatory one day, he could point to these creatures as proof that he had brought joy to the world. Now, he'd have to hope that St Peter had made a note of it. Anyway, what was the point of holding onto a relic of your goodness? The time had come to pay the piper. The town had a lot of heart but this project was, as Rocko's father would put it, running on a fart and a prayer.

It was the right thing to do. There was no other choice. There could be no redemption without sacrifice.

Maybe it was only right that Sarah would be up there, atop the hill, looking over him for however long he lasted.

11

Kimba is home to Australia's biggest galah – the famous 'big galah'. The galah is 8 metres tall and 2.5 metres wide and weighs 2.3 tonnes. Every year the bird, which is made of fibreglass, is painted to keep its pink and white coat in good condition. It was built in 1993 by hand by the owner of the gem shop ... Kimba Gem Shop employee Doris Griffiths said many tourists were interested in stopping to see the Big Galah and also check out the shop's local gemstones.

Port Lincoln Times, 30 September 1999

It was a lie to save face. Mick and Sandy both knew it. Unspoken, as so many things were between them, but understood nevertheless.

'I needed somewhere to hide,' he said, eyes to the ground like a child. 'There was nowhere else to go.'

Who would believe that? As if his truck would not protect him. As if there was some reason he should have been idling in front of the Stumbling Elephant in the first place.

Why couldn't he say that he wanted to see her? Perhaps it was that other unspoken truth sitting deep inside of him, that he knew he had no right to be forgiven. He had slammed the door shut, as if grief belonged to him alone. Cruel though that was, this was worse. To walk back into her life at a time of his choosing and reopen the wound.

They stood at either end of the empty bar like two kids at a school disco. When was the last time they'd been alone together?

Sandy looked at him for a long while.

'I suppose you feel like garbage,' she said.

'I do,' he replied.

'Good,' she said. 'I'm glad.'

'You have every right to be,' he said. 'I am sorry.'

'You have every right to be,' she said.

'Is this pointless?' he asked.

'Depends what you mean by *this,*' she answered.

'You know, the strangest thing happened the other day,' Mick said, as he took a seat at the bar stool closest to Sandy. Only the taps stood between them now. 'I was on my way here, actually, and I was listening to Radio Norman.'

'By my count, that's two strange things,' Sandy said.

Mick smiled as he continued, 'This song comes on. Jasper must have introduced it but we both know that's not worth a damn. So, the first thing I hear are the drums. And I recognise them, you know, but

I haven't heard this thing for about twenty years. Then the thing kicks in properly and it's "Wide Open Road".'

Sandy took a sharp intake of breath. 'That was Jen's and your song.'

'You remember that? Of course you do. You remember everything.'

Sandy placed a pint in front of Mick. He took a long sip and wiped the foam from his lips.

'I loved that song,' he said. 'When the kids were little, we used to move the kitchen table, play that song, and dance the night away.'

Mick disappeared into the memory as Sandy studied his face. He wasn't the young man she knew anymore. His features had softened, the sun had taken its toll. The same could be said of her. How was she supposed to compete with a memory? Still, in the red light of the dust storm, sitting at her bar, flashing that old smile she thought she might never see again, he was beautiful.

'I loved that song,' Mick said again, treating himself to another long sip. 'It made me dream of the future, you know? All the places we were going to go.'

His heavy eyes rested upon Sandy and she felt as if she might dive into them forever.

'Twenty years and I just didn't listen to it. I don't know why. Maybe I was worried that by trying to relive something I'd corrupt it. Or that I couldn't listen to it without Jenny, like I was betraying those old times. So, I let it get quiet. All too quiet.'

He let his voice trail off. When he spoke again, it was as if the words were scraped from his throat. 'It sounds different to me now. But I still love that song.'

Sandy placed a hand over his and felt his warmth radiate up her arm. 'I have lost a lot of people in my life, Mick,' she said. 'Only one of them has ever come back.'

12

With great effort, Ella dragged herself off the bed and started lazily placing books into the bottom of a cardboard box. She came across one of Norm's old yellowed science fiction things and for a moment considered reading it but decided that would be ultimately sadistic and, worse, boring. Next was a copy of *Wuthering Heights,* a bookmark stuck halfway through, around the point of Cathy's death. The bookmark was a card featuring a cartoon of a dog in a party hat. It was from Norm, of course. Inside, he'd written about how he got a feeling this was the right present when Ella had elbowed him in the ribs and demanded he buy it for her. He ended the note saying that he'd write something sappy but 'it would only earn me another shot to the ribs and they're still tender'. She closed the book, card still inside, and placed it into the box.

There was something existentially depressing about the thought that her entire life was supposed to fit inside a hatchback. She found shoving clothes into a suitcase was a therapeutic way to relieve her frustration. They'd look terrible on the other side but that was a concern for future-Ella. After only a few minutes of work, she lay down on top of her blankets and willed the rest of the room to pack itself.

Minutes passed, maybe an hour, she stared at the ceiling and let the time drift. Jasper's voice broke through the haze and announced that the next song would be 'Wide Open Road'. Ella groaned. She wasn't sure whether she could emotionally handle it at this moment. Though, part of her enjoyed the thought of leaning into her misery. Sushi life. Fortunately, she was granted a stay of execution when Jasper accidentally played 'Thunder Road' in its place.

'It must be fate,' she muttered.

There was no point avoiding it, anymore. She was thinking about him again. As if he'd ever left. Those last words still echoed. He had held her gaze. Norm never did that. He was always looking down at his hands, or around the room.

'I thought I saw something,' he had said.

And again Ella wondered – had he?

Ella rolled over, reached under the bed and extracted a yellow shoebox. She paused for a moment and considered throwing the contents all in the garbage bag. She was starting a new life, after all. Why be encumbered by the past? But curiosity is hard to resist at the best of times, and painful curiosity is near impossible.

She opened the box and was greeted first with a flurry of notes, presumably most, if not all, from Norm. She pushed them aside and looked deeper. Something near the bottom felt strange. She pulled and revealed a blue-and-purple string bracelet weaved for her by Murray Tate when she was in Year 7 and he was in Year 8. It was, at the time, the most romantic moment of her life until she found out a week later that he had also made one for Tandy Blake. That could go in the bin. She plunged her hand once more into the nostalgic lucky dip and retrieved a photo.

Christmas morning, a lifetime ago. Zeke was barely visible, buried under a pile of wrapping paper. Ella had a wild expression on her face, furious at the person taking the photo, which must have been her dad. But of course, it was her mum who caught her attention. She looked impossibly beautiful even first thing in the morning, kids clambering all over her, dressed in Dad's white polo that fit her like a dress. Ella felt sick at the thought of how close she'd come to throwing the photo away.

She walked out and found her father in his natural habitat, the recliner, staring at a telly that was stuck on the History Channel. He laughed when he saw the photo, a deep laugh that Ella hadn't heard in a long time. She wanted to hear it more.

'You're allowed to be happy, Dad,' she said.

He scoffed and looked away.

'I want you to be happy,' she said, taking his hand. 'We both lost Mum. We all lost her. You did, Zeke did, I did. Gary never even knew her. It wasn't fair.

It still isn't fair. She didn't want to go and we didn't want her to go. But she did.'

He gripped her hand tighter. 'But she left us with a great gift. She gave us a dad who loved us so dearly that he would sacrifice the rest of his life for us. He did that for us and for her, but we did not ask for that. Look, I'm not saying you were perfect.'

'You've been pretty clear about that,' he said.

'And you've deserved it,' Ella replied. 'You're real annoying, and boring, and annoying. But you're annoying because you care about us so very much and sometimes you show that in weird ways because you're properly boring. We don't need you to be miserable to know that you care.'

Ella could feel him shrink again but she wasn't finished. So, she changed tactics.

'Do you know what makes Roman concrete so special?' she asked. In an instant, the expression on his face changed from uncomfortable sadness to open-mouthed fascination. Ella might as well have announced that she was leaving that afternoon to live on Mars.

'It survives,' she continued. 'Much, much longer than modern concrete. Our structures need constant repairs. Highways are closed. Infrastructure crumbles. But Roman bridges are still standing. And sure, time wears them down. Roman concrete has lime in it, though. There are pockets of lime in little clusters and when it cracks, they come into contact with water and the cracks heal over. It's tough because it knows when to break, and how to break. You try and be rigid, and you crumble. There's no repairing that. It's tougher to not be tough. You get what I'm saying?'

He smiled, his eyes again watering. He pulled her in for a long hug and kissed the top of her head. 'I must have done an alright job if I raised a kid like you,' he said.

'Don't flatter yourself. I was born this way,' she replied, playfully pushing him back.

'Too true that is,' he said. Then, because he couldn't help himself, he added, 'By the way, you know that the reason the lime was in there was 'cause they used to mix it hot instead of cold? Ancient mixing method, hey.'

Ella's expression turned to outrage. 'You already knew! Why didn't you tell me?'

He shrugged. 'I liked hearing you say it. Who taught you that, anyway?'

Good question, Ella thought. Then she remembered – the other most boring man in her life. Norm spent days looking up obscure concrete facts that he could nonchalantly slip into conversation. The memory warmed her. That dork. All of that work just to impress her dad.

She paused.

All of that work just because he cared about her family.

Ella said something about having picked it up watching the telly and raced back to her room. She started pawing through the box again.

She'd always been waiting for the big thing. The theatrical gesture, the bold declaration, something grand and cinematic that told her love had finally come to town. Yet, here in her hands were a thousand tiny declarations. That was Norm, of course. He would never appear on her front lawn holding a boombox over his head. But every single day, he would prove that he loved her again and again.

A rush of electricity filled Ella's senses. A new vision of the world had opened before her. It was as if she could suddenly see ultraviolet light. Something pervasive and beautiful that had surrounded her for years was now right in front of her face and in a single moment everything about her life had changed.

Then, with a crushing realisation, she remembered that it had not. Before she realised what was in front of her, it had already been ruined. She remembered his words again. 'I thought I saw something.'

The radio played a familiar tune – 'Forever Now' by Cold Chisel, a certified banger, could not be dampened by Jasper's mistaken claim that he was about to play 'the song that inspired Charles Manson'.

She ran her hands again through the pile of notes. She had saved them for a reason. She had known they were precious to her, somewhere deep inside. She thought of her father, the way he let happiness walk out his door time and time again. She had two days left in Norman. Saturday morning she would hit the road. There was still a chance.

Norm might not have been the kind of person to make a grand gesture, but Ella was. Go big or go home, she always said. He thought he had seen something in her eyes that day. He did see something. As always, he had seen her, even when she couldn't see it herself.

He wanted to see something. She would give him a sign he couldn't miss.

Ella raced back into the living room. She swung around the doorway with great force, holding onto the frame to stay upright.

'Dad, I need a favour. A big one.'

'I knew there had to be a reason you were being so nice,' he sighed. Then, without a second thought, he lifted himself from the chair and took his keys from the coffee table. 'What do you need?'

13

He sat on the back porch, Rayburn Fink book in his hand, and pretended he didn't know that it was Friday night. He pretended his interest was in the words he'd read a hundred times before and that he was not listening for the sound of a car rumbling down his street. He pretended that he would have the strength to stay in this spot, had he heard it, and not raced to the window just to watch her go. He pretended that he had made the right choice walking away.

Norm thought that he'd been protecting them both. It would be too painful to sit together knowing that Ella was leaving town. He couldn't trust himself not to beg her to stay. He wouldn't allow that. She had to go. It hurt, but it was right. He couldn't stand in the way of her future.

How had his dad felt the night his mother had left? He felt pained by the thought, then embarrassed to have even considered it. How could Norm's pain possibly compare? They were married. They had a baby.

He tried, as he had tried on so many nights, to remember what their family life had been like when they were all together. Were they ever happy? One of the downsides of parents who grew up in the digital age was the lack of physical evidence of their love. In one sense, *he* was the physical evidence of their love. In another sense, that was gross. What he wanted were photographs, printed and framed, of a family on a picnic or at the beach. He didn't know whether he wanted proof of a time when everything was good, as if he could fall inside and live there forever – or a sign that things were doomed to fail. A hidden expression in a photograph, a moment of tension revealed in a video, that would explain why she'd left.

Maybe he *was* having a sook. But why shouldn't he? Isn't one of life's great pleasures to indulge in a sook when you have been wronged by the world? Exactly what kind of hell did they live in where a human being wasn't allowed to pity themselves?

Ella would be taking off at first light. The sun was coming down. Maybe she left early. Either way, Ella was gone. That's all that mattered. Whether he liked it or not, he had entered a new phase of his life without ever realising it. This was After-Ella. A desolate time, to be sure. Worse than any future that he or Fink could imagine.

Norm decided to take his dad's old bike and ride into town, as if he did not believe such a time could exist until he had seen it for himself.

Pup climbed into the wheelbarrow and looked expectantly at Norm, who shook his head in reply. He opened the door trying to coax the old dog back inside, but Pup wouldn't budge. Norm gave him a scratch behind the ears and pushed the wheelbarrow into the entranceway. The old dog let out a sad little moan in response.

Norm wrapped the old dog in his arms and gently dropped him on the couch. He flicked through his DVD pile and put on *Amélie.* Something suitable for a discerning dog, he reasoned. The film began and Norm slipped out the front door.

He had planned to ride as far as his legs would take him. There were no towns beyond Norman anymore, he knew that, but maybe he'd ride until the trees died out, the grass turned to red dirt, and all signs of human life dissolved away. That plan would last for about three minutes. Norm had only just reached the top of his street when something caught his eye.

He dug his bike into the dirt and leaned it against his leg as he stood, mouth agape, trying to process what was in front of him. It had to be a hallucination or a trick of the light. What he was looking at was a dream. Not just a dream. His dream, come true, before his very eyes.

There was a scaffold atop Vodafone Hill, a tower of Babel reaching into the blue sky. A metal frame, impossibly high, imposing itself over the town below. A large hessian tarpaulin wrapped around the structure giving it the look of a precariously stacked column of hay, backlit by the setting sun, glowing beautifully over all below.

And on the façade facing him, there was a message, painted in a navy-blue paint, each letter at least as large as Norm. His throat closed, his eyes widened. It said:

NORMAN,

BELIEVE

WHAT

YOU

SEE

But how could he believe it? An impossible dream was suddenly made real. It had been cast into metal and thrust into the sky. Ella, brilliant Ella, had kept his dream alive when he was certain it had died.

Believe what you see.

To the town, this would be a defiant statement of purpose. It would be a sign that the Big Thing was not a flight of fancy but a real object that would soon be built in this very spot. But to Norm, it was so much more than that. A message in the sky, from Ella, just for him.

Colour returned to his world. He felt an energy pulse through his veins that had been lost for days. She loves him. Ella *loves* him. Ella loves *him*.

A cold chill swept over Norm. How long had that message been there? What if he was too late? Perhaps she had waited for days then, having not heard from him, had driven away from Norman once and for all. Happiness may have passed by his door and kept going.

He had to find out for sure. Norm stepped back onto his bike and pedalled desperately. His thighs burned as he pushed down the road with all the force he could muster, sliding down the bank and into the dry river. The handlebars bounced violently as Norm struggled to stay balanced. The dying trees by the riverbank blocked the fading light and Norm pushed on in near darkness, his mind filled with visions of Ella, the chance that he might see her before she left, images of her loading the last boxes into her car and reversing down the drive.

His tyres sprayed the red dirt across the husk of the old troopy as Norm leaned hard into the turn, pushing to propel the bike as fast as he could into the embankment. Hitting it with force, he took off into the air, sailing into Botany Street.

The next thing Norm heard was a sickening crunch that he prayed was his bike. The whole world seemed to slow and he felt that eerie calm that tells you that you're definitely, truly, indelibly stuffed. The screech of the brakes from Reggie Piper's beaten-up Yaris sounded like the pull of a bow on an untuned violin. He could see the large pepperoni in Reggie's front seat drift in slow motion, the box opening as it gracefully hovered in the air, only tethered by strands of melted cheese that one by one were giving way.

Deep in his subconscious Norm understood that it must be 7pm. That pizza was meant for him. Reggie was delivering the standard order for Norm's Friday nights with Ella, Pup and three choices of DVD. And as Norm floated up into the air, his eyes turned to the patrons of the Sunshine Deli on the other side of the road, their mouths slowly opening in horror watching him. He had always hoped when his time came to leave this Earth he would have one last profound thing to say, the kind of thing that a character would say in a Rayburn Fink novel that paid due to the beauty and fragility of life. But at this moment, all that came to his mind was the thought, *Oh, Mr Baylis could use a haircut.*

And then the world went dark.

PART THREE

Believe What You See

BIG, BRASH AND FINALLY TREASURED

Long dismissed as tourist kitsch, Australia's 'Big Things' – giant models of everything from koalas to pineapples – are now being heritage-listed and recognised as works of folk art.

The gaudy structures, commissioned since the 1960s by rural towns keen to put themselves on the map, have gathered such a following they are even being compared to Egypt's pyramids.

'They're like our pyramids, our temples,' respected artist Reg Mombassa said.

'Because European settlement was so recent, Australia doesn't have historic old buildings like in other countries and the Big Things are a way of saying "we're here, this is our place".'

The Sydney Morning Herald, **14 July 2009**

1

Sandy tossed away the dregs from a plate of chips and wiped down the thick oak table that her father had built a lifetime ago. The dust had painted the town red. The result was altogether less fun than the idiom suggested. It made Sandy think of the first snow of winter, something she only knew about from movies. She imagined Mick's boot prints heading out the door and away from the Elephant. Maybe she could follow them and see if he ever turned back, if he'd even considered it for a moment.

It was raining hard in her memory. Was that right? It felt wrong now. It had been so long since she'd seen rain fall in Norman. Jen was dead, the baby was alive. Mick, poor Mick, with no time to grieve. Three kids now. The oldest one starting primary school in the New Year. He was a shell. Only operating because he had no other choice but to continue on.

A black cloak hung over the town. The tragedy belonged to everyone. They all carried the burden, slogging slowly through the streets, tears conjured without warning, falling to the dirt and being absorbed. There were care packages left on the porch, of course. Maria Baylis had cooked a lasagne. A 40-degree day and she left a lasagne. Sandy understood. You wonder what to do, though you know in your heart there's nothing you can do, really. There's nothing anyone can do to heal this pain. So, you cook a lasagne.

The bar of the Stumbling Elephant had turned into a pulpit. Each night the parishioners would enter, happy to see away another day, looking for some relief, hoping there could be some meaning or moral to be found among the ruins. Sandy became the town's official supplier of depressants and hope. She preached the message of Norman – endure, believe that better days would come.

Shelby had been lost, too, on that day. They just didn't know it yet. Everyone grieves differently, they said. Some reach for community, some disappear inside themselves. There is no correct answer.

Sandy took a broom and began work on the front porch. A useless task. She could not sweep the whole town. Soon dust would be tracked in on the bottom of boots and coat the floor of the bar. Nothing to be done about that. Her time would be better spent lying out in the street and making a blood-red dust angel. Still, she swept. Fish gotta swim, birds gotta fly. Roll the boulder up the hill. Keep your mind busy. Don't let the past take hold of you.

Tony was on the road, the rest of the town asleep. The rain had come. Sandy had sent the final stragglers on their way when she saw the headlights. The hatchback stopped in front of the Elephant. Sandy braced for terrible news.

She could remember thinking, *What more? What else do we have to lose?*

Was she crying already or was it just the rain? All she remembered was Shelby's offer. They would run away. They would escape this life and build a new one. They would go where grief couldn't find them.

Endure, Sandy begged. That was always her answer. Endure. Survive the unthinkable. Survive.

Shelby said she wanted proof of life. Those were the words she had used, proof of life. It wasn't about Jen. Or, at least, it didn't begin with Jen. It had always been there. There was an unshakeable feeling of a deal that had been violated. A promise that if she took the right steps, found the bloke, built the family, lived the life, then happiness would follow. Jen had found that happiness. Whatever else happened, she got to taste it. Shelby was scared she would never know it. She said she refused to die without ever having lived.

Sandy had nothing but hollow pleas to answer. What about Tony? What about Norm? Shelby spoke as if outside of her own body. 'Not all parents are capable of sacrifice.'

They were chilling words. Sandy knew in an instant her friend had already leapt from the cliff face. She was lost. There was no way to bring her back. Shelby stepped back into her car and Sandy knew she would never see her friend again. She had become another tether to a life Shelby needed to escape. Her tail-lights disappeared in the rain.

Sandy had been there when the boy awoke, unaware his life would never be the same. She had stayed with him until Tony returned.

Shelby was gone. Jen was gone. Mick had cut himself off. So, Tony drank. He would sit alone by mutual agreement. The rest of the town considered him cursed, or thought his story was too sad to fathom. It was best not to think about him. Leave him to it, they'd say. Sandy kept him close when she could. Better he drank there, where she could monitor him, water down the drinks, drop him home safely. But there was only so much she could do. More than once he had called Sandy from some far-off pub, slurring his words as he told her he wouldn't make it back that night.

Sandy would keep watch, take care of the boy, stay the night, leave before he woke. She never spoke of it. She refused to taint the image of his father. It was all he had left.

Tony would be too full of pride to ever take money from her. Even as his decline began in earnest and the work dried up. Sandy began pocketing the Keno money. She'd fill the house with food. Leave any extra in an envelope in the letterbox. Let him save face. Another half-measure. An attempt to endure. Then, when Simon Glassner lucked out (or so he thought) on the Keno draw one night, it all came to a head.

Of course, Sandy couldn't tell them the truth. It would humiliate Tony.

She didn't know if he ever worked it out. He was a smart man. He must have known but he wouldn't say a word. He'd finish his drink, walk his glass over to the bar, say goodnight and take the troopy home.

Then they lost him, too, and a great silence had taken hold of the town as each member of Norman grappled with a question they dared not ask, for fear of the answer.

Sandy knew the truth. There was no way to avoid it. He knew those roads. He drove for a living. He wouldn't try to cross the river in a downpour.

But as soon as she opened that door, the other questions stormed in. *Why that night?* What answer could possibly satisfy that? Then there was the even more painful one, *What more could I have done?*

In the aftermath, denial had become a necessity. For practical reasons as much as emotional. She was the last person to see Tony alive. The insurance would only pay out if it were an accident. His state of mind was important to know. The future of his kid required her to lie. It was the least she could do for him – for them both. She lied to keep him fed. She lied to keep him close. She lied for Tony, one last time.

In cruel hindsight, Sandy could feel the inevitability of that night, yet at the time it felt impossible. The

sun would shine tomorrow, she'd been so sure of it.
Hold on. Just hold on.

2

Reggie Piper was in shock. At least, that was one explanation for his slow reaction time and dilated pupils. Though, if Occam were here, he might disagree. There were a few cheese-inflicted burns on his arms but ultimately nothing life threatening. He would keep. Arthur Baylis handed him a paper bag to breathe into and took the keys out of the ignition.

The Perkins boy needed more serious attention, certainly beyond anything Arthur was able to provide. He scratched at his moustache as he considered the scene.

'We've gotten ourselves into a real pickle here, Mrs,' he said, tucking his apron under the boy's neck. He was breathing, that was a start.

By the time Arthur reached the top of Vodafone Hill he wasn't sure whether to order the ambulance for the boy or for himself. His face was red, his brow thick with sweat. The sun had disappeared and a full moon rose over the town, bathing the scene in an eerie glow. The call made, Arthur sat on the concrete slab, his back against the metal structure. How long either of those had been there, he wasn't too sure. Perhaps his head was also swimming, either from the adrenaline or a contact high from Reggie Piper. Gently, ever so slowly, he eased himself off the top of the hill, remembering the days when he and Maria would fly down full of reckless abandon. A lifetime ago and yet only minutes.

He wet a tea towel and applied it to the boy's head and sent Reggie to the Elephant in search of help. Alone with the unconscious boy, Arthur said a little prayer. He wasn't sure why it embarrassed him to do so. Perhaps because he had never been a particularly religious man. He was a fair-weathered friend of God. More than that, he felt he was owed one for all that he had endured. This boy, too, had been through more than enough.

Call him an old fool but that helicopter sure looked like an angel to him, a spectacular sight flying in, spotlight on, landing right on the main street of Norman. They asked if he would like to accompany the boy but that did not seem right. Bless Sandy for arriving at that very moment. She did not need to be asked twice. Frankly, Arthur thought, good luck to anyone trying to keep her off it.

The helicopter flew away and Arthur looked up to the moon.

'He's in your hands now, Mrs,' he said.

***

Arthur woke slowly the next morning, his bones aching from the climb, a painful reminder that he hadn't dreamed it all. Whatever may happen with the boy, he considered his role in the matter closed.

Imagine the old man's surprise when, as morning broke, an old dog walked into the Sunshine Deli. The poor thing didn't move too well anymore, either. Lord knows how he made it all the way into town.

'Alright, Mrs,' Arthur muttered to himself. He was responding to the voice of his wife, heard only in his own head. Over many, many years of marriage her voice had become the sound of his conscience. It was her voice that told him he should bake that apple strudel that poor Ms Peach loved so dearly, and it was her voice that told him if no one climbed that hill, the poor boy might die. Now, her voice was telling him to get that poor dog out of the heat and give him something to drink.

There had been no word from Sandy. No way of receiving it even if she tried to call. Arthur had about as much chance of ascending that hill a second time as the old dog did of performing a backflip on his chequered floor. So, the old man sat, nursed his sore muscles and sipped his coffee.

He thought of the incredible adventure the boy must be on now, whether he knew it or not. The boy had probably never flown before. Yet through the night he had glided over half the state. A curious sight it must be these days. So few lights still on in these parts, what with entire towns going dark. But when that city shimmered on the horizon, it must have looked like the gates of heaven itself.

3

McDonald's is building a Big Big Mac in Tamworth for Australia Day. The Big Big Mac is around 36,000 times bigger than a regular Big Mac.

AdNews, 25 January 2017

At last, Billy was being taken seriously. This was the kind of respect he deserved. If he was going to move into the higher echelons of society he would have to get used to rooms like this, only bigger, higher up, and with views of the whole city, not just the parking lot opposite.

He was destined for big things. Michelle had told him that the first night they had spent together. He corrected the thought. They hadn't spent the night together, so to speak, but in the most literal sense he had visited her home at night and they'd drunk a bottle of wine together. Or, he had drunk the wine. She didn't drink. Or she didn't drink wine or something like that. It was hard to remember. He'd had a whole bottle of wine that night. But he did know they'd be toasting with champagne when he finally pulled off this deal.

She always said to look for the signs. He'd seen one on the highway. It was a picture of a businessman with maracas dancing up a storm. The copy said that real movers and shakers had their superannuation with SuperOz. *That's me,* he thought. He would close this deal, sign up to SuperOz, buy himself a pair of maracas, and take a bottle of champagne home to Michelle. She would know what had happened, of course, being psychic and all. That's probably why she'd told him to wait. She knew this would be the perfect moment. She really was brilliant.

A small cough brought Billy back to the room. One of the younger suits in thick black frames was asking if his legal representation would be arriving soon. Billy projected confidence, leaning back in his chair the way Brando did in *The Godfather.* He pursed his lips as if considering the question. The truth was, he didn't have any legal representation but he had seen enough movies to get the gist of what happened in meetings like this.

'I assume one will be provided for me,' he said, tapping both hands on the table in feigned impatience.

'That is not a service we provide,' Glasses replied. He shared a smirk with his colleague that he thought Billy would be too slow or half-witted to notice, but Billy had seen it clearly.

'I am perfectly capable of representing myself.'

Billy eyed them sternly, the way he would his mechanic when he asked for the bill. A look that said, 'I might not know what I'm talking about, but I know funny business and I want no funny business.'

Glasses hid a laugh with a cough. 'It is not so much a matter of representing yourself. This isn't a court case. It's just with a property matter such as this there is a lot of paperwork—'

'Which I am extremely capable of handling, thank you,' Billy interrupted. Glasses shrugged and shook his head, clearly bested.

Allison had been gone a long time. Her phone had flashed minutes into the meeting, a name Billy didn't recognise, but she did catch him looking. Did that seem suspicious or just nosey? It could be any number of things, Billy assured himself. Maybe it was her dog sitter and her dog had died. God, he hoped her dog had died.

It was understandable he would be a little thrown. He had called this meeting in haste, he had driven through the night. That was not his fault. Time was suddenly a factor.

Michelle, wonderful, vivacious Michelle, had been ever so slightly wrong about Mick Batchen. Perhaps her abilities had been clouded by a full moon or something that Venus was doing. Billy rocked up on Mick's front porch expecting an easy sell. He was prepared to make an offer right then and there and purchase his run-down property as a personal favour before the town was decommissioned. One would expect that, being met with such an offer, Mick Batchen would shake Billy's hand and thank him for his tireless generosity.

But that is not at all what happened. Mick had all sorts of questions he wanted answered. He had questions about why the mayor would want to buy up property in a town that was about to cease to exist. He wanted to know exactly when this defaulting of Norman was due to happen and why he, as a citizen of said town, had not been informed yet, as if Billy was a secret-keeper and not merely reading the tea leaves the way anyone else could. Then, more impertinent, he wanted to know the particulars of Billy's financials, specifically how he was able, on a mayor's salary, to afford to purchase his property. Strictly speaking, that was none of his business. Seeing that there would be no business done on that day, Billy thought it best for both parties for their discussion to be concluded.

He would have been happy to cut his losses and bide his time for the next opportunity were it not for the sight in his rear-view mirror. How he hadn't noticed it before was anybody's guess. Too focused on the needs of the citizens of Norman, most likely. But there it was, openly defying him, a tower on Vodafone Hill.

A memory flooded back into his mind. Those two kids, one of them a Batchen, as he recalled. They had plans for just this kind of thing. What they didn't have was any kind of approval. That would be a big problem for the two of them. Vodafone Hill was property of the council. Erecting an illegal and potentially dangerous structure on top of that hill would be a very serious offence. Anyone who assisted them might even be forced to forfeit their concreting licence.

Allison re-entered the meeting, her eyes disappointingly dry for someone who may or may not have discovered tragic news about a beloved pet. She took a moment to confer with her legal team. Billy wished he had brought someone along to confer with, but lacking that, he conferred with himself.

'What do you know about the Big Thing?' Allison asked.

Billy raised his eyebrows as if he had not heard the question. He glanced around the room, wondering if someone else might answer it. With no one to defer to, he took a deep breath in, let out a small cough, and said it was a non-issue.

'What do you mean a non-issue?'

'It's Latin.'

'It isn't,' Allison pressed.

'Well, who can say. What I mean is that you don't need to worry about it.'

This comment, while perfectly rational, seemed nonetheless to bristle Allison. 'We will decide what we consider necessary to worry about, Mr Fitz. Our firm is interested in completing this purchase without any unfavourable media attention. Were there to be, say, a large statue being erected specifically to attract media attention, that would be a problem for us.'

She had Billy banged to rights, but he wasn't willing to let on. Instead, he stroked his chin thoughtfully and only said one word. 'Quite.'

'Quite what?'

'Mm,' Billy answered.

Allison was somehow unmoved. 'Either you kill this project, or we kill the deal,' she said.

4

Launched at Ballina ... The Big Poo was created in an attempt to win the title of beach sewage capital of the North Coast ... After the launching, the poo will travel to Manly's sewage festival in time for the Australia Day weekend.

***The Canberra Times,* 14 January 1992**

At least Ella wasn't the only one crying on the tram. Behind her, a twenty-something wearing a tight t-shirt that read 'No Date to Celebrate' sat with headphones on and tears in his eyes had a hand on the window and a withered gaze that said a very meaningful six-week relationship had just come to an end. At the front of the tram was a much sadder scene. A businessman, tie loosened, head down, absolutely bawling. This wasn't a performance for anyone. This was plain old misery. A group of high schoolers with Australian flags painted on their cheeks were taking turns guessing what had happened to him. One guessed that his wife had found out about an affair. Another believed he'd run over his own cat. A third speculated that the cat was probably in the driveway when he pulled in. He would have discovered the affair when he walked in, cat in his arms. Then, when he tried to reverse away, he would have crashed his car into a post, which is why he was on the tram.

God forbid the teens would notice her, the sad girl standing in the vestibule. Something about their vicious eyes convinced her that with one quick glance they would know that she was a lost girl far away from home, who had publicly humiliated herself, been rejected, and driven down the highway crying ugly, snotty tears for hours over some weird boy.

She imagined their cackles when they heard that Ella spent all afternoon taking her dead mother's paints to her sad, lonely father's wet weather covers for a cricket oval in a town where it never rained. They would know she dragged that heavy hessian up the hill like Christ with his cross, a public execution. She'd sat there all Thursday night and into the next morning. She had fallen asleep on the hill and awoken to find she was still alone. She had wondered if he had somehow missed the sign or worse, he hadn't missed it at all. And in those final hours in Norman, as the sun began to wane, she thought of her dad and her nan, and slid down the hill to spend one more night with them.

They would know how small she felt sitting alone on the edge of her bed in her sad, empty room in her sad little town waiting for a boy who would never follow her anyway. A boy who she could have had at any time but only realised she wanted the moment it became impossible.

She had taken off early the next morning and even then, she believed. She'd expected to see Norm racing out into the front yard as she left, ready to throw himself under her tyres just to slow her down.

By the time the sun had risen, she was breathing normally again, even smiling as she drove past the turnoff to Glenrowan. 'Sushi life,' she whispered to herself. The car moved slowly, weighed down by all her earthly possessions. The rearview mirror was completely blocked, which she found half romantically symbolic and half a massive safety hazard.

She sniffed then froze, worried the noise might be a drop of blood to a shark. She didn't dare look in the direction of the high schoolers. Instead, she focused on the roof of the tram as if she found the whole thing innately fascinating. *Dumb country hick,* they must have thought, *can't believe this carriage is travelling without a horse.*

But she did see something. A small sticker, black on yellow, among a collection of government warnings about paying for your fare and undercover cops patrolling the carriage. She knew she wasn't being logical. This was more pathetic than the declaration, really. To have her heart touched by generic safety advice issued by the Victorian state government was perhaps the second-lowest point of her life. Still, there it was, worming its way directly into her heart. The sticker said:

Hold on. Sometimes sudden stops are necessary.

236

It was going to be alright, she told herself. Everything worth doing is scary. No one rides a flat rollercoaster. That's a ... well, a tram.

At that moment, the tram pulled to a sudden stop. Ella, having been mesmerised by the poetic implications of the sign, had forgotten to heed its literal instructions. As the tram lurched to a stop, she was thrown forward. And as time slows at all moments of crisis, she found herself suddenly, gracefully floating, her arms flung back behind her as if she were performing a beautiful swan dive.

Ohh, she thought. And with that, her head slammed into the wall of the vestibule. The world slowly faded away and somewhere a million kilometres away, one teenager laughed while another said, 'Oh my god, no.'

***

I could be a doctor, she thought, watching the important, busy people race from room to room around her. It all felt so dramatic, like living in a movie. Deep down she'd always wanted to have a go on those paddles that shock people back to life. The sight of blood made her want to throw up and pass out, but maybe there was a type of doctor that didn't have to deal with blood. Or people, she definitely didn't want to deal with people.

This flight of fancy was the concussion talking, but Ella was happy to take any distraction from the stitches being sewn into her forehead and, even worse, the shit-eating grin of Zeke watching her from the end of the hospital bed.

'Oh, that's nothing. You're being a sooky la-la,' he said, exactly the response she'd expected from him the moment she'd texted.

She considered calling Norm. But the thought of him rushing to her bedside was immediately doused by the prospect of once again waiting for him to never arrive. Perhaps the rest of her life could be a series of calling on Norm from increasingly pathetic situations only for him to never show, until one day she was buried alone in twin side-by-side plots.

At least Zeke was enjoying himself. He saw a med student he knew passing through the foyer. An attractive med student, Ella couldn't help but notice. Zeke must have noticed too, as he immediately disappeared down the hall.

Stitched up and with no sign of Zeke, Ella went looking for the gift shop, hoping to eat a feeling or two. What she found was perhaps the saddest room she could fathom, which is impressive in a hospital. The shelves were almost bare, save for some stationery and a greeting card display where the Sympathy section had been picked clean. There were a few cards left in the 'Sorry to hear about your uncle's hernia' section, while the congratulations cards were still thoroughly well-stocked. Next to them were three small, white plush bears each with their own love-heart nose and semi-deflated balloons reading in

238238238

order 'Get well soon', 'Love you' and 'Sorry to hear about your uncle's hernia'.

Ella treated herself to a Golden Rough. She also bought herself a legal pad, a pen and a card. In the uncomfortably rigid plastic chairs in the corner of the waiting room, Ella tucked her feet underneath her body, leaned the legal pad against her thigh and wrote a note she had no intention of sending.

Dear Norm,
I was so sorry to hear about your uncle's hernia...

5

He thought he saw her. A flash of her hair passing by his door. But there was no chance it was actually Ella. Norm turned to the plastic chair where Sandy sat slumped, green trucker cap over her eyes and denim jacket laid across her body like a blanket.

'Did you tell Mr Batchen?' Norm asked as nonchalantly as possible, a feint wasted on Sandy, who knew the real question: *Does Ella know I'm here?*

'I'll do it now,' she said, rising out of the chair, only to be waved down by Norm.

'No, no. I would rather keep this quiet.'

It was an absurd suggestion. As if the gossip-starved town of Norman would ignore a helicopter landing on Botany Street.

'You can head back if you need,' Norm added. 'I'm going to be here a while.'

Sandy didn't respond save for a small pursing of her lips.

Norm spoke not because he had anything of importance to say but rather to break the monotonous hospital sounds.

'Should have known this was coming. It's all pretty obvious in retrospect. There I was thinking something nice would happen in my life for once, but what I forgot is that nothing nice ever happens and it's stupid to think otherwise.'

He let out an ungodly huff. Still, this didn't rouse Sandy. Resigned, Norm was reduced to mumbling to himself.

'Awful things happen suddenly.'

'Finish the quote,' Sandy answered, unmoving beneath her jacket, the cap back over her eyes.

Norm was confused. He didn't answer. Sandy eyed him seriously from under the bridge of her cap. 'Finish the quote.'

Norm tried to remember but it was a struggle. The line had become a personal mantra for so long he had disconnected it from its origins. It was Rayburn Fink, obviously, one of his earlier stories, following a naturalist at the end of the world. The plot was a strange kind of inversion of Noah's Ark. The world was no longer inhabitable due to a nuclear holocaust, and all life was slowly extinguishing. The naturalist was writing a book called *The Book of the Dead.* This is also what Rayburn Fink named the novel. *The Book of the Dead* was to be the final record of the plants and animals on Earth. Most of the creatures were dead or dying by the time the naturalist reached them. The naturalist was also dying, slowly and painfully, of course. It was a comedy after all. But the context of the quote escaped his memory.

'It's the seeds,' Sandy said, as if reading his mind. 'The bloke has a pocket full of seeds and is searching for uncontaminated soil to grow them in. Why spend your last days growing seeds on a dead planet? Well, because, as he says, awful things happen suddenly but hope grows slow.'

Sandy stood and pulled her jacket over her shoulders.

'Hope is a choice. I'd have thought you of all people would have understood that, seeing as you stole all of my books from the cricket sheds. Don't give me that look. You should have known they were mine. I'd read them when Mick and Tony were playing. I hate cricket.

'Now, I am going to get us some actual food and bring it back. If you feel the need to sook, press the blue button and you can annoy one of the nurses, alright?'

6

He had to quit the drink. Rocko knew that. It was going to kill him. It had probably already done a number. He just hadn't really cared up until now. 'Something's gotta kill you,' he'd say. 'May as well be tasty.'

Anyway, that was a problem for another time. No point quitting when you're tipsy. He took one of his roadies out of the pocket of his cargo shorts and cracked it open. The sun beat down on his weathered face and he felt as if he was sweating out the beer faster than he could drink it.

He had managed to give it up for a while. A little over a week, by his count. Not intentionally, or unintentionally, just a side-effect of getting lost in his work. In fact, he had wandered up to the Stumbling Elephant in search of food having realised he hadn't eaten in a day and a half. As the town's only declared vegetarian, Rocko had struggled to find a menu that would cater to his needs, until Sandy caught on and taught herself to make a risotto, a vegetarian curry and even the odd quiche. They tasted truly awful. She was no cook. But it was the best feed Rocko would get when he tired of two-minute noodles for breakfast, lunch and dinner.

Now, Rocko had the distinct impression he was getting screwed. The pub was closed, a remarkable event, one that he couldn't remember ever happening before. It didn't matter if Sandy was trapped in bed with the shivers, she'd still manage to unlock the door and let Rocko serve himself. Or maybe she'd just forget to lock the door. Whichever was the case, they had a system.

The Melbourne Bitter was foamy and warm, the aftereffect of a long journey in the pocket of his shorts. He took a sip and nearly spat it out, but for once it was not for reasons of Rocko's refined palette. A truck had slowly turned the corner and rumbled onto the road ahead of him and it had given him an idea. He took the beer in his hand and, with what was quickly becoming a practised arm, he flung the can like he was returning a shot from third man. The can spun in a long arc and crashed into the side of the truck, spraying beer all over the logo that read 'Norman's Concreting: Where else are ya gonna go?'

Mick Batchen slammed on the brakes and the wheels ground into the dirt, spraying dust through the air. He stuck his head out the window and bellowed, 'What's wrong with you, you dumb dog?'

Rocko was quite pleased with himself, really. That had worked exactly as he had planned. Maybe he hadn't completely fried the old noggin after all. 'Mick, I've gotta talk to you.'

'Then wave, mate. Don't chuck beer at my truck.'

Rocko shuffled his feet like a school kid getting detention. 'Yeah, I suppose you're right. Anyway, got a minute?'

Mick hung out of the cab of his truck as he considered the question. Rocko put on his best puppy-dog eyes and with a groan Mick turned off his engine.

'Yeah, go on, mate,' he said. 'Pub?'

'Elephant's closed,' Rocko said, pulling another can out of his cargo shorts and handing it to Mick.

Mick looked at the beer for a long time, weighing it up in his hands. He pulled back the tab and foam shot in all directions. With a shrug of his shoulder, he gestured for Rocko to sit down on an empty milk crate. Mick leaned uncomfortably on a rounded concrete pillar, knowing that if he sat down, his knees would not let him back up.

The two men stayed there for a long time, neither in any hurry to move on. They spoke about the good old days, though it wasn't clear if they were referring to the same ones. They cracked more cans. Rocko let the foam roll down his wrist. They spoke about the final days of Norman. They spoke about Mayor Billy Fitz and his indecent proposal. They allowed a great anger to pulse through their veins.

'The man's a bully. He's a prick, and a dog and a rotten dog prick bully prick,' Rocko said, spitting every word, shifting from foot to foot, waving his arms about. He never gave up a fight. He was the proud owner of a nose that bent at three impossible angles. 'There's nothing I hate more than a bully,' he said.

'Weren't you the one that falconed Norm with the can?'

'That was just a bit of fun. Not my fault if the kid can't take a joke. This bloke's a dog.'

'He's a proper dog,' Mick confirmed. 'But that's the way it goes, I guess. Nothing to be done about it.'

'Bullshit,' Rocko shot back, letting the word ring with a low drawl. 'You ain't seen nothing yet.'

***

Rocko led him through the workshop and backwards in time. Back to those good old days, when the Norman market was still thriving, Rocko would have an entire menagerie of metal animals. Mick remembered the Saturday mornings spent with Jen, heavy with Ella, still determined to spend hours on her feet, stopping at every stall for a chat. Tony and Shelby arguing over something unimportant. Was that true? Had his memory been clouded by time? It was so hard to differentiate what he saw back then and what he imagined later. Had Shelby known she was pregnant yet? They were happy, right? They had to be happy at some point. It wasn't always bad. Sandy would have been there, too, lost somewhere in the haze of his memory. How strange to think that she hardly attracted his attention back then. She was just

Sandy. It had taken him too long to realise how special it was to be just Sandy.

Rocko directed him to a large blue tarp in the back of the room. He shuffled over and, with a gruff little 'voila', ripped the tarp away.

Mick was dumbfounded. He squinted to try and work out if he was missing some grand abstract meaning in the sculpture.

'What is it, mate?' he asked.

'That's a torso, that's one arm, and that's a hat,' Rocko said.

Mick scratched at his beard and feigned interest. 'Oh yeah, a hat, is it?'

'It's an old hat,' Rocko clarified.

Mick could see it now. It reminded him of the tricorn worn by pirates in books. That was something, at least. He didn't understand how it was supposed to save Norman, but it was undoubtedly a hat.

'That's great, Rocko. Alright, mate. You have a good one.'

'Wait, wait, wait,' Rocko said, grabbing Mick's arm so he couldn't leave. 'Don't you see? This is gonna be the Big Thing. And I reckon it'll work, too.'

Mick nodded, starting to understand. Then shook his head. Nope. Still didn't get it. 'The Big Hat?' he asked, trying to imagine pulling off a highway to see that.

'No, no, no, it's a whole thing. Some assembly required. I ran out of metal, but your girl told me all about it. The hat is just the start.'

'This was Ella's idea?'

Rocko nodded. With a start, Mick realised he still hadn't called Ella. He pulled out his phone but of course there was no reception. It would have to wait. As soon as he was done with Rocko he'd climb the hill again. Maybe he'd call Sandy, too, just to check in. His heart did a little *rum-pum-pum-pum* at the thought. He swallowed the feeling.

'What's the plan?' he asked.

Rocko looked around the empty workshop conspiratorially. The next moment, the space was echoing with Mick's laughter. He ran his hand over his stubble once more. 'Those cheeky little pricks. I should have known.'

There had to be some way of making this wild dream a reality, but how? Ella was gone, Sandy had gone AWOL, Fitz was on their backs and Rocko was out of materials.

'What do we do about Fitzy, then?' Mick asked.

Rocko picked up a hammer and banged into the metal hat. An oddly beautiful note rang out across the warehouse. 'We build this bastard,' he said. 'Then, he can either admit he has no idea what's going on in his own town or pretend it was his idea all along.'

Rocko was off again, hopping around the warehouse banging his hammer on anything he could reach, laughing like a mad thing. 'Think about it, Mick. Whatever he's up to, he's trying to get it done quietly. So, I reckon we make as much noise as we can. Who knows what happens next but at least it'll stuff him around.'

'Give me another beer, Rocko,' Mick said with a laugh.

Outside, poor Reggie Piper sat in his crumpled car, leaning on his horn, trapped behind an abandoned concrete truck with two pizzas rapidly cooling in his passenger seat. But Mick and Rocko didn't know that. They were busy nursing a tiny flame of hope.

'Okay, what do we need?' Mick said, circling the pieces on the workshop floor. 'I've got some paints still in the shed. We need something we can paint on though ... more flexible than the frame.'

'I had a thought about that, too,' Rocko nodded. He pulled back another tarp to reveal a pile of empty beer cans.

'Are you sure, mate? You've got at least thirty bucks worth of recycling here.'

'Anything to help the cause,' Rocko said, throwing another can on the pile. 'But we're going to need more. Whatever metal we can find. If it isn't bolted down, grab it. If it is, take the bolt, too.'

***

Had you arrived in Norman that evening, you might not believe what you saw. On its face, it seemed like a town asleep. Lights were off. Doors were shut. The streets were empty, bar one snoring delivery boy. But if you looked carefully enough, creatures were stirring. At the edge of town, on Vodafone Hill, two men were struggling up a steep incline.

For anyone else, it would be frustrating work, but they were filled with glee at the mischief they were undertaking. Twice they lost grip of a metal leg, sending it rolling back down the hill, but rather than grumble or curse their luck, these grown men would squeal with delight as they slid on pizza boxes back down the hill, chasing after it.

Their efforts were rewarded with an astonishingly beautiful sunrise. Rocko and Mick sat side by side at the edge of the hill, watching the town awaken in a golden glow as the concrete dried behind them. Rocko slid down the hill to relieve himself at the bottom of a tree and Mick was left alone with his thoughts. It took less than a minute to decide to call Sandy.

7

In 2009 Australia was given a brand-new attraction – The Big Slurpee – a 50ft Slurpee erected in the country town of Coffs Harbour...

Unfortunately, it was not to last long, being dismantled later that year. The Big Slurpee – for those that were crazy enough to go, it was one big memorable summer.

Team Slurpee blog post, 10 August 2010

White canvas stalls stretched deep into the university. Each had a colourful roof, standalone signage and a group of overeager students promising you friends, social events and, best of all, a free t-shirt if you signed up to their society.

'It must be fate,' Ella whispered to herself. Zeke had dragged her out of his apartment with the promise of distraction. Yet, the ghost of Norman was right there waiting for her.

Two young men in matching mesh singlets and high-and-tight haircuts raced to see who could be the first to drink an entire jug of beer through a straw then complete a backflip. As far as she could tell, this seemed to be a promotion for the Table Tennis Society. In the end, the display was a better promotion for St John Ambulance as neither were able to fully complete their backflips, instead performing a balletic movement best described as 'crumpling like a sack of crap'.

As always, Ella made a note to tell Norm about it. She had a thousand of these notes written on her legal pad or on her phone. She'd even walk through the streets talking to herself as if he was right there. Saying things like 'get a load of that' at the sight of a protest out the front of the State Library calling for a reduction of late fees, or 'oh, you would hate that' at a fully grown man in a rabbit suit standing out the front of a cosmetic surgeon's office shredding on an electric guitar.

The frantic city scenes that she had hoped would fill her with excitement instead made her feel profoundly lonely. She tried to call Norm once, knowing that he wouldn't have reception. That was probably a good thing. She didn't know what she would have said if he had picked up.

Zeke grabbed her by the arm and escorted her through the crowd. He glided confidently through the campus as if he owned it. With a wave of his hand he told Ella to never drink coffee from one portable coffee cart, directing her to an identical cart two hundred metres away which he claimed had 'the good stuff'. Ella was suspicious. Her brother was never this nice without facing the direct threat of a wooden spoon.

'Eugh, Zeke,' she cried, her face scrunched in disgust. 'This tastes as bad as the Sunshine Deli.'

Zeke took a long swig from his cup and smiled. 'Right!?'

Ella wondered if she'd ever feel so confident in the city. Zeke hadn't transformed. He was born assured that he, and he alone, was made in God's image. He was handsome enough that the girls of Norman agreed. Coming to the city was just a chance to show off to more people. Gary was another creature altogether. Zeke had organised a video call that morning, making it late evening London time. Gary had appeared in a black singlet, one long earring dangling from his left ear. He looked toned and tired but assured them he was only at the beginning of what was going to be an incredible bender. It warmed Ella's heart to hear his voice, to see his face again. There was no way they could talk like this in Norman.

She watched the other first-years wander through the grounds in wide-eyed wonder. They were a few years younger than her, enough for Ella to feel the difference. It was as if those lost years in Norman had lasted a decade. She was worried she had a stench of sadness hanging over her.

She turned back to her brother, who was entertaining himself by swiping wildly through his phone.

'Zee, what if this is a mistake?'

Zeke drummed his fingers across the plastic lid of his coffee cup, considering her question. Then, he shrugged his shoulders and let out his brilliant smile.

'Yeah, what if it is? Isn't this the perfect time to make a mistake? You're young. You're supposed to be making mistakes. You can't get everything right. Only one of us is perfect.'

'Shut up,' she laughed, shoving him in the arm.

'Come on,' Zeke said, placing an arm around Ella as they walked.

'You wanna know what I reckon?' Zeke asked. Before Ella could snipe at him, he'd already continued. He knew her too well to leave space for that. 'Don't bother, I'm gonna tell you anyway. I could tell you that you're smart and curious and hard-working. I could say that you're the equal or better of just about anyone who walks through those gates.'

Ella shot him a sceptical look.

'Oh, don't get me wrong, it'd make me physically sick to admit,' he said. 'I paid sixteen dollars for a sandwich today and I'd rather not have to throw the whole thing up.'

Zeke put a hand on Ella's back, guiding her around the corner. They were at the top of an arterial road looking down into the city. There were hundreds of people going about their days. Thousands, maybe. School students mulling about the shopping centre, people in suits with dour looks on their faces rushing from one place to the next. Cyclists attempting to fistfight any pedestrians who stepped into their lane to board the tram.

'By coming here, you're either going to find out exactly what you want or exactly what you don't want. Either way, it's good to know.'

'I don't even know where to start,' Ella protested.

Zeke smiled. 'That's great. What's the point of coming all this way if you already had all the answers? You know who you are, that's more than most people can say. For better or worse, by which I mean strictly worse, you are you. But what can you do? That's worth finding out.'

After a while, Zeke had to head into the office and left Ella to wander around the grounds alone with strict instructions to wear a helmet while riding the tram. She weaved through the maze of buildings, getting lost in the heart of the campus. This didn't feel like home. She liked that. She sat on an uncomfortable wooden bench and picked at the flecks of dark green paint as the clouds slowly cleared above. And for one moment of quiet repose, she let her guard down and let herself think about Norm again.

Ella tried to imagine a world where she'd walk out of a high-energy particles lecture and find Norm having skipped his film studies tutorial to watch *RoboCop* for the four-thousandth time, telling her that it was a real education. They'd get coffees and walk arm in arm all the way home.

The dream was so simple and the reality so cruel. Ella was entirely happy to force her will on Norm when it came to where they ate or what they watched, but she couldn't control his life. Ella hadn't wanted to leave Norman because she was scared of all that was out there. Norm didn't want to leave because he didn't want to leave.

She felt her pocket vibrate. For a moment, her heart leapt. She retrieved her phone and saw her dad's face on the screen, all scrunched and grumpy from when she'd forced the phone in his face demanding a photo for his contacts page. Ella made a pact with herself that no matter what cocktail of emotions she'd been feeling, on the phone she was going to sound cheerful and excited about her new life, otherwise her dad would worry himself sick and she'd be fielding calls all night.

'Hi Dad,' she said, her voice sugary sweet. Immediately, she knew something had to be wrong. He'd only said hello but his tone was so serious and his breath so laboured that she couldn't stop her mind from racing through all the worst-case scenarios.

'Dad!? Is everything okay? Is Nanna alright?'

'Oh, she's fine,' he said, a small touch of light returning to his voice. 'Your nan's an ox.'

Ella felt her heart beat again, but it wouldn't last.

'I'm not supposed to tell you this. I promised I wouldn't. Ella, it's about Norm.'

***

Ella couldn't wipe the thought from her mind. Norm bleeding on the road. Norm alone in a hospital room. Norm scared. Norm needing her. Norm abandoned.

She felt selfish and sick. All this time she held the resentment of having been scorned. She thought she was being punished for daring to leave. She thought that his love for her had died. Now she knew better. He had come running after her, the way he always did. She had cried hot tears in anger wondering how she could have been so easily discarded. She had sat with her phone in her hand waiting for him to call.

But then, why hadn't he called?

She knew him better than he knew himself. She could piece together his exact thought process. He would have considered himself a bother. He would have known that by the time he had awoken in hospital, she would have crossed the border and left Norman for good. He'd have relegated himself to a relic of her past. He would have decided not to interrupt her new life with his problems. He'd have told himself she didn't care anymore. He couldn't have been more wrong.

There had been a slow realisation growing within Ella that had caught alight and burned like a falling star.

She wanted everything the city had to offer, she wanted the life that lay at her feet, but she wanted all that *and* she wanted Norm.

She broke an impressive raft of laws driving to the hospital, assured in the knowledge that if she had caused a car crash she'd probably end up there anyway. She pulled into a parking spot on the street, spraying black exhaust fumes all over two patients smoking in front of the hospital.

She impatiently waited at the back of the triage line wanting to scream, 'Out of my way, it's an emergency!' Instead, she folded her arms and resented the clod in front of her, wasting the nurse's precious time with his little dislocated finger. *That's God's punishment for playing indoor soccer, idiot. Jog on.*

As she walked through the halls, she wished she had something in her hands, some kind of gift that would say, 'I am sorry to hear about your accident but perhaps a lifetime of sex would make up for it?' She thought about the gift shop. Maybe a balloon lamenting his uncle's hernia would be the perfect way to say that she wanted to be together forever.

What would that look like, anyway? She'd trundle her little hatchback up the highway every Friday night to steal a day and a half with him in Norman only to say a teary goodbye and return in time for her Monday morning lectures?

The line moved. What should she say? How would he react?

At last, she raced through the hallways, dodging patients slowly pushing their IV drips. She took a deep breath and opened the door to Norm's room. Only, Norm wasn't in Norm's room. In fact, the only person inside was a middle-aged man with thin hair and thinner lips. She was too late. Norm had gone.

'Can I help you?' the orderly asked, tucking in the corners of fresh white sheets. Disappointment was engulfing Ella, so thick she could hardly breathe.

'I was looking for Norm,' was all she managed to say.

'Yes? I'm Norm,' the man replied.

Ella was already emotionally exhausted, and it took all of her remaining processor power to understand what he'd just said. All the while, the orderly was looking increasingly worried, as if Ella might have escaped from some dark corner of the hospital.

'Not you. A different Norm. A patient. He was hit by a car.'

'Well, sounds like he couldn't have gotten far. I could check the morgue?'

Ella gasped in horror. The orderly, too, looked distraught.

'Sorry,' he said. 'Just a joke. A bit of gallows humour. Please don't mention it to my supervisor. He says I'm not supposed to talk to anyone anymore.'

8

Sandy couldn't sleep. She'd been haunted by the sight of Norm unconscious, strapped to the gurney as the paramedics worked on him, the blood on his face lit by the landing lights, his expression oddly peaceful.

She didn't know what made this boy special. She'd never noticed this dogged determination in him before. Even these days, when Sandy watched his leg be manipulated by the physiotherapist, a daily routine as embarrassing for Norm as it was painful, she could see the fire behind his eyes. *No wonder Ella loves him,* Sandy thought. That kind of thing was rare. The kid was a dreamer and a worker. He was mature beyond his years, but not at the sacrifice of his playfulness. To see the young man he had become filled Sandy with a strange kind of pride and doubled her resolve to not let him down.

She should have known that the second she announced she had to return to Norman he'd be begging to be discharged. Maybe she had known. Just as he knew that she'd never leave him behind.

***

The painkillers worked their magic. Norm opened the sunroof and bathed in the light of the uniform blue sky. He felt a peace sweep over him, the likes of which he hadn't felt in weeks. They were on the road to Norman.

The radio died on the outskirts of the city and they drove on in silence for a long while. Norm wasn't sure if he truly drifted off to sleep or if he lost himself in the hypnotic rhythms of the road and allowed the hours to wash over him.

Then, from what felt like a long way away, he heard Sandy's voice.

'Must feel good to be going home,' she said.

It wasn't really a question, yet it still gave Norm pause. Was he happy to be going home?

'Yeah, I guess,' he offered.

'Well, I'm convinced,' Sandy replied. 'It's a shame you weren't able to see some of the city. You might have really liked it.'

Norm didn't answer.

'I wonder how Ella is going out there. It's always hard starting again at some place new all on your own.'

'She's got her brother,' he said, trying to keep his voice neutral.

'I suppose you're right. And I suppose whenever you feel like chatting you can just climb the hill and give her a call, when your hip is a bit better of course.'

Again, he didn't answer. He considered feigning sleep, but the drugs were starting to wear off and the pain was too great. His performance would be interrupted by constant writhing and seething as he tried to find any relief. That must have been why Sandy started this line of inquiry, an attempted distraction, though he'd prefer to feel every searing second than to discuss Ella.

'I don't really have a choice, do I? I've got to stay.'

'Oh really, why's that?'

'I'm Norm from Norman, you know? Without Norman what am I? Just Norm? Yuck.'

He could hear Sandy shift in her seat. 'You do know that you're not named after the town, right?'

'What?'

Sandy's laughter filled the car. 'Are you playing with me right now? Did you think your name was one of those things like when a couple conceives their kids in Paris or Brooklyn or whatever then name the kid that? We don't really do that with Australian towns. Here's my boy, Dubbo, and my twin girls Wagga and Wagga.'

Norm was rocked by waves of laughter meshed with waves of pain.

'Here's my beautiful daughter Albury, and my awful son Wodonga.'

'Don't make me laugh, don't make me laugh,' Norm pleaded.

Sandy relented and gave him an opportunity to catch his breath.

'Wait, if it's not the town then why did he name me Norman?'

'You sure you're ready for this?' Sandy asked. 'Greg Norman.'

'Oh, yuck,' Norm replied. 'We almost built a Big Greg Norman.'

'What? His big nude arse looking over the town. No thanks.'

'You knew my dad pretty well, didn't you?'

'Yeah, yeah I did,' Sandy answered. 'Though all he ever wanted to talk about was his kid. You know those people? You're trying to have a night at the pub and they want you to look at a bunch of pictures of some annoying little squirt. Really boring chat.'

She spent the rest of the drive telling Norm stories of his father's exploits, embarrassments and long history of bold boasts that would be immediately undone, such as his claim that he could 'easily' do one thousand sit-ups, only to quit before he reached forty. According to Sandy, he couldn't lift himself up and instead requested beer be poured directly into his mouth as he lay on the floor. It was nice to hear stories of his father as a man, not as a tragic symbol, not as a saint, but as a kind of knockabout loser. Someone like Norm.

Yet as she spoke, Norm's thoughts didn't dwell on his father but rather on Sandy, the woman who had sat by his side day and night. She had immediately put her life on hold without question or complaint, for the sake of his recovery. Norm had always thought of himself as the boy left behind, the debris of his parents' mistakes, unwanted and forsaken. Slowly, quietly, he realised that he had never really been alone. All this time he'd had a guardian angel looking out for him.

9

'Have you ever in your days seen anything like this?' Arthur remarked, his arms shaking under the weight of his serving tray, clay mugs rattling as the teapot threatened to drop, cascading tea over Patty Lu.

'Watch what you're doing!' Doris barked.

Her sudden eruption was enough to panic him further, and he placed the tray on the table with an indelicate thud. Patty took a napkin and wiped up the drops of tea.

'Grab a seat, dear,' she said.

Arthur slowly shuffled inside and returned with another wrought-iron chair. 'I've had to hide these. Some nasty beggar stole a couple of them the other night, and a table, too!'

His buttocks had almost touched the seat when Doris spoke again. 'What, no biscuits?'

With great strength and resolve, Arthur managed to reverse his momentum and rise once more. He returned with a small glass jar of Florentines he had baked the night before.

Doris scrunched her face like she'd just smelled a rotten egg. 'You got anything else?'

He raised himself once again, sending a quiet curse up to the heavens as he returned with a jar of shortbread.

'Lovely,' Doris announced, unscrewing the jar and allowing Arthur to take a seat. His knees cracked as he flattened out his apron with both hands. He'd forgotten to get himself a mug but would rather dehydrate than need to rise a third time.

He stretched his neck, feeling the heaviness in his shoulders. Yet, Arthur was not tired. He felt oddly invigorated. 'This town has something.'

'Well, I'm sure they'll get rid of it,' Doris said. Patty snorted into her tea.

'No, no, there's an energy again. You can feel it.'

'I think that might be your medication kicking in, dear,' Patty said, giving him a tap on the arm.

Arthur waved them away. He could tell there was something in the air. This Big Thing had the town buzzing. He had wiped down the specials board inside for the first time in fifteen years to keep a tally of everyone's guesses as to what it might be. Cheating was discouraged by the town's inherent code of honour, which was reinforced by persistent rumours that Rocko was camping atop the hill, firing buckshot at anyone who dared approach. According to Gavin Walsh, his call to his aunt for her birthday was done at gunpoint.

Rocko's misplaced exuberance aside, there seemed to be a growing sense of solidarity among the townsfolk. Arthur had thought the town was dead but as it turned out, it was only locked in stasis, waiting for the perfect moment to return, like the frog that hid in the sand on the animal documentary he wished he'd watched more closely. One by one, the people of Norman had offered whatever they could to help the cause.

Mick needed gravel and sand, which meant Angela had to unlock the chain on the landscape suppliers. They needed muscle for the heavy lifting, which gave Stephen and the crew from Shifting Bricks something to do other than waste away playing pool at the Elephant. The heavy work had Eka doing double shifts at Lucky Duck while Pete's Chinese had brought on extra staff for the first time in years. Reggie Piper was playing both sides of the street, rumbling his crumpled car down Botany Street, giving Arthur chills every time he passed.

All this activity spawned more. Mrs Langham donated a storefront of flowers to fill garden beds around the concrete slab on top of Vodafone Hill that had been dug out by Trevor G. Arden's frustratingly named business, Trev's Landscaping. Arthur, too, had been kneading dough until the arthritis necessitated a break, all under the watchful supervision of a sleepy old dog. Boards were coming down from shopfronts. The streets were filled again. Life was returning to Norman.

The whole system ran on I-O-Us, in a sense. It wasn't a future prospect. It was more an acknowledgement that at some point along the way, everyone in the town in one way or another owed everyone else something. It was the collective mentality that it would all come out in the wash.

Try as they might to act above it, Arthur knew that the only thing bringing Patty and Doris out this afternoon was a desire to witness the commotion for themselves. Though, it was not their only focus. Doris had salacious snippets of gossip to share. 'Did you hear Sidney packed up yesterday, ready to go, and Bettsy tells him that she isn't going with him? She's staying right here, she says. Her heart is in Norman, she says.'

'Good on her,' Patty answered over her tea. 'Life is for the living, after all.'

'Yes,' said Doris. 'And we all know she'll be pushing up daisies in no time.'

Both women snorted and cackled, leaving poor Arthur, who had not the faintest idea what they were talking about, to stare down the street and wonder what was to become of this little town.

10

The giant Big Mac at Waler Park has been voluntarily removed by McDonald's after causing outrage in the community, leaving behind only a dead patch of grass to mark where it was.

The Northern Leader, **31 January 2017**

Billy leaned on his horn. When that didn't achieve the desired result, he revved the engine. Fear, after all, was the great motivator. As if to prove his thesis, Bettsy Langham immediately snapped to, redoubling her efforts to cross the street in a timely fashion. He rolled on, satisfied. In this town, William L. Fitz was God, and these little ants could choose to feel his warmth or his wrath.

There certainly was an odd concentration of activity today. Billy slowed as he perused the streets. He watched the voters filling the tables of the Sunshine Deli. They stared back at him with a look he read as somewhere between admiration at his achievements and jealousy of his success.

The sound of a truck horn brought Billy back to reality and he swerved sharply to avoid the flatbed coming the other way. His front tyre struck a pothole and the car bounced uncomfortably, knocking Billy's head against the leather upholstered roof. Through the rear-view mirror he watched the truck rock down the street, the rusted chassis on its back threatening to escape its bonds and fly free. He made note of the number plate, which he diligently added to his enemies list.

This was all the result of those kids and their irresponsible flight of fancy. They had no idea what they were risking for some little vanity project. It was borderline criminal to get these people's hopes up. It was sickening to think what such a promise would do to this community's already battered psyche, not to mention his profit line.

Taking a handkerchief from his pocket, Billy wiped the thick sweat from his forehead. He turned back to the road and followed the hive of activity towards the Stumbling Elephant.

The applause when he walked in sounded like a gunshot. Indeed, Billy, already on his guard against the more unscrupulous elements of the town, performed a dramatic and surprisingly flexible evasive manoeuvre. Specifically, he ducked low and spun his frame behind an old woman sitting near the doorway.

His shock turned to delight when the true nature of the sound registered. At last, Billy's work was being fully appreciated. He had assumed the backwards folk of Norman were too obsessed with the minor issues of bin collection and street maintenance to truly comprehend Billy's dedication and vision. The applause swelled as he bowed and waved to the adoring public.

Through the appreciative crowd he saw Sandy polishing glasses, a nasty expression on her face. How it must kill her to see Norman so enamoured with their mayor. He sauntered over, in part to force Sandy to bathe in his reflected glory, and in part to ask the question that was gnawing at the back of his mind.

'What the hell is going on?'

Sandy didn't respond. Instead, she chose to flick her tea towel over her shoulder and retire to the back room. Billy snorted. Then, he felt a clap on his shoulder, strong enough to make the whole area fall entirely numb.

'Three cheers for the man who saved Norman!'

The crowd erupted, as Billy felt a pint forced into his hand. He took a sip and gave a nervous thumbs-up, leaning over to whisper under the din, 'I did what?'

'Feels good doesn't it, Mr Mayor?' Mick said. 'They love you.'

He was right. It felt great. Billy kept his eyes on the crowd, waving and nodding to each table, but allowed a smirk to grow between his round cheeks. He decided to gift the crowd a taste of his trademark humility to let them know that he was still one of them, only slightly superior.

'Yes, well, you must not forget that politics is really about people. Everyday, salt-of-the-earth types with blue collars and red necks and green ... uh, envy directed at those who are doing better in their black cars and yellow ... houses. You know, it's a rainbow.'

Mick nodded along. 'Oh, I think these people deserve a bigger speech than that.'

Billy watched as Mick strode through the crowd of revellers and walked onto the corner stage, leaning down from his great height to speak directly into the microphone.

'Norman,' he bellowed. 'We are all here today thanks to one man. The saviour of the town. The architect of Norman's very own Big Thing!'

A roar of approval washed over him, but his heart sank. That damned statue? And what did they just call him – the architect?

Mick bellowed over the crowd noise. 'Welcome to the stage our mayor, Billy Fitz!'

Had he an extra second, Billy would have made a quick exit, but it was too late now. Every eye was on him. The crowd were chanting his name. 'Fitz! Fitz! Fitz!'

Gingerly, Billy approached the stage, his back sore from pats.

'Thank you, you're too kind. You're ... you're far too kind.'

For so long he had wanted the town to love him the way he had deserved, and now, in an instant, that dream had become a reality. He decided to bask in it. Celebrate it. This was the second-best moment of Billy Fitz's life. There, in the crowd, he saw Michelle, wonderful Michelle, her eyes looking upon him like he glowed. Maybe he did. Maybe he really was exactly as brilliant as he thought. No wonder she loved him.

'They said Norman was dead,' Billy cried, 'and we said you ain't seen nothing yet!'

The crowd roared. He had them in the palm of his hands.

'We will rise from the ashes! We will save our town! And when the cover comes off and this monolith is revealed, remember that this is a gift to you from your Mayor, William L. Fitz.'

Billy was drunk on the approval of the crowd.

'What's it gonna be then?' asked a young, mousy-haired woman.

'Sorry?' Billy asked, wheeling around the stage to address her.

'The Big Thing. What is it? The Big What?'

Billy took out his handkerchief, already a little moist, and patted his upper lip. He crossed his arms, feeling the sweat patches in his pits, hoping they weren't visible through his shirt.

'Any guesses?' he asked.

All at once, members of the town shouted their suggestions. The list included a Big Greg Norman (no thank you), a Big Norman Gunston (better, but no), a Big Dirt Mound (that's just a hill), a Big Pineapple (been done), a Big Banana (come on, think harder) and a Big Norman (no clarification about what this meant).

Once the crowd exhausted itself, Billy concluded his speech with a chuckle. 'Maybe you're right,' he said. 'I couldn't possibly spoil the surprise before the Grand Unveiling. This Saturday, at Vodafone Hill, where you and the whole world will see the unveiling of the next Big Thing!'

11

Perhaps he hadn't survived the crash at all. Perhaps this was all a hallucination, conjured as he lay bleeding out. Surely that was more believable than the scene before him – Norman alive and operating as one. Some carried sheet metal, others arranged plastic garden chairs, while the rhythmic sound of beating hammers rang down the main street as for the first time in years the market stalls were reassembled.

Norm slowly approached Vodafone Hill, carefully manoeuvring a walking frame he was already growing to resent. He looked as if he'd been suddenly cast into old age. He had been away for too long. The town around him had changed so much. He was drifting through a dream.

But there was something missing. The hessian tarp obscuring the Big Thing still displayed Ella's message, the call he'd failed to answer. *Norman, believe what you see.*

But how could he?

What part of this was believable?

Their impossible dream was coming true, and she wasn't here to see it.

Norm thought back. Back when the world was simpler, when they had been sitting side by side in the shadow of the Big Ned, when Norm had felt the electricity between them only for Ella to jump up, animated by her own spark of inspiration.

'I've got it,' she'd cried. 'What was it about the Big Ned that drew people in? What made it so interesting? We travelled halfway across the state to see it. Why this one and not the Big Orange or whatever?'

Norm, lost in her smile, had taken time to properly rouse himself. 'You mean the one in South Australia or the one in Western Australia or one of the two in Queensland? There are a lot of them, come to think of it. You know what town should have a Big Orange? Orange. That's a missed opportunity.'

'Focus,' she'd said, with a stamp of her foot. 'What makes the Big Ned compelling? It's because it's a little dark, right? It's his last stand. We're looking at the bloke right at the end. The time he doesn't get away. The only thing people like more than a hero is seeing him fall, yeah? It's grotesque.'

'So, you want a fallen hero?' Norm answered, jumping to his feet. 'What should we have then? What's controversial? A Big Pineapple but we put it on a Big Pizza?'

'Yawn. Think harder.'

'The Big Cricketer sandpapering the Big Ball?'

'Too emotional,' Ella answered. 'That made my dad cry.'

'Okay, what do you suggest?'

Ella flashed a brilliant smile. 'Who do white people love the most?'

'Jimmy Barnes?'

'Captain James Cook,' Ella announced with a flourish.

Norm choked. 'You ... you want us to make a Captain Cook statue?'

Ella nodded.

'Ella, are you sure? Considering you're uh ... that you are ... uh...'

'That I'm what?' she said, before making a grand display of checking the colour of her arms. 'Oh my god! Oh no, what's happened!?'

Norm rolled his eyes. 'Anyway, there are like fifty of them. That's not even unique. One of them is even doing a Hitler salute like this.' He raised his arm to demonstrate. Ella pulled his arm down.

'Best not. Anyway, I've got something even better.'

She pointed to the Big Ned.

'His last stand,' she said.

'You mean—'

'Hawaii.'

Norm was struggling to process this image. 'You want the Big Thing to be Captain Cook getting speared to death by Hawaiians?'

Ella held his gaze. She was serious, and more than a little frightening.

'Yup. The Captain gets cooked.'

It was a horrifying suggestion. It'd outrage the Australian public. It would be like spitting on Gallipoli. There'd be endless reams of thinkpieces, angry comments, complaints that they'd taken the joyful kitsch of the Big Things and made them sickeningly political. In other words, it'd get a lot of attention. The fear and excitement had wrapped around him like a cloak as the idea was spoken into existence. 'It'll certainly get people talking,' he said with a nervous laugh.

'There's no such thing as bad publicity,' Ella answered.

Norm nodded. He wasn't sure about the idea, but he trusted Ella the way you trusted the sun would rise the next day. So, he took a deep breath and nodded. 'Let's do it.'

Now, as he took the undignified gentle slope up the back of Vodafone Hill, Norm shook his head in wild wonder at how his harmless little idea had grown to this. The rhythmic noise of his walking frame scraping into the dirt matched the beat of his heart. Reaching the top, he peeked under the hessian covers to spy Rocko, hanging by one arm off the scaffolding frame, spot-welding the epaulettes onto a jacket constituted entirely out of recycled cans of Melbourne Bitter. There was no walking away. It was a reality. It was a monolith.

She should have been here to feel this rush.

Perhaps there was enough romance in this moment already. The perfect blue sky over Norman, the sounds of a town back at work and, even better, the sounds from the Stumbling Elephant of a town at play. Norm considered it all, the life in flux around him, Ella lost to the city, and a town and country primed to be stunned. Standing on the precipice of his new life, Norm felt a terrible retching in his stomach and before he could control himself, he was vomiting onto Vodafone Hill.

If reincarnation was real, maybe the smart thing to do next would have been to climb to the top of the Big Thing and jump right off, then maybe he would have the good fortune to return to Norman as a snail with no anxiety issues, relationship dramas or weak constitution that cannot handle one life-changing revelation and a bit of microwaved egg. Norm wondered for a moment what would happen if he just turned and ran. What if he blew through the city limits of Norman and ran until his legs gave out then crawled until he couldn't crawl anymore? It was a family tradition, wasn't it? To abandon ship when things got tough was what the Perkins did. A sharp pain shot down from his hip, up his spine and down his leg as a little reminder that escape was impossible. If reincarnation were true, Norm thought that he must have committed some horrible acts in his past life. He was probably the worst sea cucumber to ever slime its way across the ocean floor. What else could possibly justify the torture he had been forced to endure in this life?

'You alright, mate?' Mick asked, giving him a reassuring if far too aggressive clap on the back. 'We didn't get your design wrong, did we?'

'Is he dead?' Rocko shouted, now dangling by his legs from the scaffolding like a chimpanzee.

'Keep working, stuff ya,' Mick called back. He turned and smiled expectantly at Norm. 'So, what do you reckon?'

Norm stood silently as he took it all in. 'It's unbelievable,' he said, and meant it in every sense of the word.

'Ah, I was worried this whole thing was just some fever dream that Rocko had burped up.' He took Norm under his arm. 'You know, they say we're living in the digital age or the microchip age or whatever but they're wrong. This is the age of concrete. That's what they're gonna call us when they dig all of this up one day. We are in the concrete age. When all these digital things have disappeared into the ether, this statue of yours will still be standing. How about that? None of this whole "look upon my works, ye mighty, and despair" bizzo. It's more like, "look upon my works, ye mighty, and say – you know, not effing bad mate."'

To think that this statue would live longer than Norman itself was anything but reassuring to Norm. This statue was a quick fix. A scam, really. Now, it would literally cast a shadow over Norman for all time. Mick was lost in his own thoughts now, gazing up at the structure. 'To think, we are creating our own Colossus of Rhodes. A wonder of the world, right before our eyes.'

Norm wasn't too sure that the Big Thing would be considered a wonder of the world, but he appreciated the sentiment.

'Do you know how the Colossus of Rhodes was built?' Mick asked, and Norm suddenly realised asking this question was the only reason he'd mentioned it in the first place. It would be rude to not play along. Norm let his mind wander as Mick told him the story of Ptolomey's liberating of a Rhodes under siege by someone and a statue erected in the honour of whatshisname, the god of whatever. He was thinking about more important things. Like, how would the town react when the scaffolding came down, the tarp dropped and the Big Thing was revealed?

'Sorry, sir,' Norm said, interrupting what was surely a riveting monologue about how you made rivets in the ancient world. 'I just need a moment. I think I might take myself home.'

'Oh, of course,' Mick said, with a nod.

They paused uncomfortably for a moment.

'I need you to carry me down.'

'Ah, well, I'll finish my story on the way,' he said, putting two strong arms under Norm and beginning the slow and now exceptionally painful journey down the hill.

From his vantage point, held aloft by the large, sweaty father of the girl he'd loved for as long as he could remember, Norm took a long, mournful look at the town. Some dark part of him understood that while a vivacious and active Norman had been what he always wanted, it wasn't the Norman that he knew.

'Oh, let me show you something I spotted,' Mick said, dropping Norm and his walking frame onto the grass. Moving slowly and wobbling unsteadily, he took three slow steps to where Mick was kneeling, on the edge of the path that marked the entry to the Stumbling Elephant. There he saw the marks where, half a lifetime ago, he and Ella had carved their names into the fresh concrete. He could still remember the anger on her father's face, as if he'd caught them taking a sharpie to the Mona Lisa. The memory, impossibly frightening at the time when he was certain he was about to catch a flogging, now filled him with an incredible warmth, as if reminding him that in some way he would always be a part of Norman. He had already made his imprint on the town and, for better or worse, the story of Norman would always have to run through him and Ella. In that way, they would always exist together. And in spite of everything, he smiled a little. Mick grabbed his shoulder.

'Now, if you ever do anything like this again, I will flog you.'

Norm declined a lift, preferring to take his time to walk down the old streets of Norman once more. Painful though it would be, he could tell himself it was good mobility training, and he would thoroughly self-medicate when he finally made it home in an hour or two. He wouldn't walk alone, either. As Norm shuffled down the street, the door of the Sunshine Deli pushed open and from the darkness emerged Pup the Old Dog. He was limping painfully but then so was Norm. Slowly, delicately, Norm eased himself onto the ground just in time for Pup to give him an affectionate lick around his ears. He had the thought that someday, he would awaken to a world where he would no longer know the feeling of this comforting, hideously noxious breath on his face. He would wake not having to force a 30-kilogram weight off his legs. He would not be followed from room to room, toilet included, lest he have a single moment of peace. He hugged the old dog close to him. He remembered the day his father emerged from the cab of his truck holding a perfect little puppy, carried by the scruff of his neck.

There, in the street, he had a sudden moment of clarity. His father had known. Norm had always assumed it had been some kind of cosmic coincidence, the puppy arriving full of love and joy only a few weeks before his father departed. The mornings he spent, his face down on the mattress, sick and rigid, unwilling to face the world, only to feel the back of his neck tickled and his ears bitten by a puppy who knew nothing of tragedy, and wanted to play. It had been his father's attempt at a salve, to give him something to cling to, to remind him that his heart contained the potential for happiness, to keep him a child.

His dad had known. Maybe not when. Maybe he hoped he wouldn't go. Maybe he tried to stay. But he had known all along that he would also be leaving Norm behind.

Something remarkable triggered inside Norm. Tears began to fall from his eyes. A guttural cry erupted from his throat and he howled into the sky. There was sadness, yes, but this was deeper than just sadness. It was release. He was saying goodbye to a tension that had been inside for so long he had confused it for being a part of him. Pup, loyal to the last, sat on his hind legs and howled along with Norm.

When he arose, he was reborn. Not healed, never healed, but no longer waiting to be healed. It was as if he understood that his power came from resilience. Awful things happen suddenly, but hope grows slow.

12

Zeke had found her lying facedown on his couch, perfectly happy wallowing in her own misery, and attempted to cheer her up in the way all brothers do. First, he'd sat on her legs and turned on the footy, pretending he hadn't noticed her sitting there, then stolen the pillow she'd been lying on, causing her head to bounce against the cushion. Oddly enough, neither of these techniques had worked.

'Some deal you've got going here,' Zeke said, kicking off his shoes and swinging his legs up on the couch so they were perilously close to Ella's face. 'You get to lie about here while I get the groceries, cook the dinner, run all your little errands for you.'

Ella mumbled something into the cushion.

'What was that? I don't speak couch.'

She shifted her head a few centimetres to the side. 'What errands?'

'What errands, she asks! Just acting as your personal postie.'

'I don't know what you're talking about,' Ella answered, shifting her head back.

'Don't worry, one of my perks as personal postal employee of this facility is I get to read all of the outgoing mail, so I know all about that poor little fella that you *love oh so much* and *miss every day* and whose uncle has a hernia apparently, which is way too much information for a love letter in my opinion. Who even writes letters anymore?'

Ella felt her blood run cold. She turned around, propping up on her elbows to face her smugly smiling brother. 'What did you do?'

'I think the words you're looking for are *thank you, brother.*'

Ella's jaw hung low. 'Zeke, you didn't.'

'I know, right? What a bloke. This wasn't just a pop-it-in-the-box job, either. I had to go inside and buy a stamp, too. A stamp! I didn't know you could still buy stamps! You know, some say the term hero is thrown about too much these days. I like to think that I just show up and let the Lord work through me.'

Ella screamed and screamed and screamed.

Zeke looked confused and more than a little scared. 'What?'

***

Ella had her arms draped over the dashboard, head against the steering wheel. They said you could never go back home. She didn't know this was what they meant.

She had left the city in a mad rush. No clothes, no supplies and only a quarter tank of petrol. The further she drove from the city, the more the panic had set in. The road back was no longer marked. Street signs had been stolen or vandalised beyond the point of usefulness. The abandoned towns were too uniform to act as markers. Dead farmland sprawled for hectares in between. Crumbling roads gave no indication of what was an important arterial route and what was a dry country track.

She pulled over and considered turning back. At least she'd be able to refuel, pack, and kill Zeke.

There were no cars coming from either direction. The sun was disappearing behind the hills and with it the heat was dropping rapidly. There was still a blanket in the back that Norm had used on their road trip, a million years ago. It smelled like him. Ella pushed her chair back and hugged into it, getting a little bit of rest before she had to push on.

By the time she awoke the stars were out, and she stepped out of the car to bask in their glory. This was something she didn't get in the city. The world felt so restrictive when you couldn't see the stars. Here, she was once again a part of the universe. Venus, the sister of the Sun, burned bright in the sky.

She took a breath and thought about how long people had stood in this spot and sought guidance from the stars. The heavens gifted knowledge, and those who paid attention could find all they needed to know. That's why she had travelled all this way, to learn what she could from the stars. That thought played on Ella's mind as she remembered all those nights in the old tree, looking at the blanket of starlight above her, trying to spot the exact centre of the galaxy with the supermassive black holes. She remembered how hard Gary had laughed when she told him about supermassive black holes, and how he'd called her a supermassive black hole for a month afterwards.

Something clicked for Ella in that moment. She knew how she'd make her way back to Norman. There was a constellation that could be seen all year round. She had always kind of resented it because of the way it had become the tattoo of choice for the Australian racist, but it was one of the brightest constellations in the night's sky by apparent magnitude. It would guide her home.

She laughed at the thought of having to decolonise the Southern Cross to make it back home. The constellation didn't belong to them, anyway. It was on about forty flags, the stars were around three hundred light years away on average and her people had been navigating by it for millennia.

The hills were west, reversing the direction of the cross would show her north, and by their powers combined she could approximate the direction of Norman. She turned the radio on. When 1228 AM Radio Norman clicked in, she'd know she was close.

She was coming home again.

13

Goulburn has the Big Merino, Ballina has the Big Prawn and Augathella has ... the Big Meat Ant.

_AM,_ ABC Radio, 27 October 2015

Jasper had been sitting in his chair for so long he couldn't remember a time when he could stand up out of it without making a series of loud and embarrassing noises. Every day he would sit in his studio, a window looking out to Norman, and he'd talk to the town, even when he wasn't sure there was anyone listening. He'd long considered himself the morale officer of the town. The way he saw it, it was his duty to keep the town dancing even through the darkest days. A while ago he had resigned himself to the fact that dark days were all the town had left. How wrong he had been.

Not only were there people out in the streets, but he had also received calls from out of town. Journalists from the city were calling to ask him if the rumours were true about a rogue mayor who had taken it upon himself to build Australia's Next Big Thing and save his town. It was an inspirational story, for sure, and Billy Fitz had been out in front of it. Jasper had always been sceptical of Billy. He'd never liked politicians of any stripe. Billy's father was a politician and told him firsthand that they couldn't be trusted, a point he proved by cheating on Billy's mother and leaving town. Besides, to his memory, this story began with a boy dragging pipes up Botany Street in the middle of the night. But of course, Jasper was sworn to secrecy on that detail. Instead, he told them that there was a bigger story here than local politics. This was the story of Norman, the little town that could.

A television producer asked Jasper if he would be interested in being part of a news story about the Big Thing. They said the mayor himself would appear on Jasper's program for an interview Friday morning, a day out from the unveiling, the whole event captured by television cameras. 1228 AM Radio Norman would be broadcast across the continent. Together, they'd make Norman famous.

'You might have noticed some exciting times in the town of Norman,' he said into his microphone. 'Well, I am here to tell you we have the mayor himself, Billy Fitz, visiting us tomorrow morning on Radio Norman, to preview the grand unveiling of the superstructure that has our little town the talk of the country. And that means it's time for one thing.'

Jasper pressed play on the console and was very surprised when the first notes of David Bowie and Mick Jagger singing 'Dancing in the Streets' didn't kick in. That surprise turned to terror when, instead, an organ playing Chopin's 'Funeral March' blasted from the Radio Norman speakers.

Still, nothing could quell Jasper's excitement. That evening he took a rare wander through the streets of Norman, which had woken up from their long, long slumber. The tables were back out the front of Pete's Chinese as Mrs Langham shared what seemed to be a friendly dinner with Ms Peach from the council. And there at the next table was Sandy on a rare break from the Stumbling Elephant. She was sharing a meal with that Batchen fellow.

Jasper took up a table outside Pete's Chinese, ordered the butter chicken tacos, and watched as five different cars over the course of an hour drove down the main street. He'd hardly seen so many cars enter in the last three years. *Probably the media,* he thought.

He absentmindedly wondered if the discount motel was still open. It might shock old Ben half to death to see someone actually pulling into his driveway after all this time. The mints that Ben used to leave on the pillows weren't too fresh back in the day. They might be purely lethal to ingest now.

***

Jasper was back on the microphone at first light.

The circus was in town. You could always tell when city people came to a country town. It wasn't the clothing or the accent but the way that they looked at locals. Not with disdain, as one might expect, but rather with a smiling curiosity. Gawking at them as if they were charming wildlife, a mob of wallabies that might be frightened off by any loud noises.

On this particular morning, the observers were themselves being observed, though they would not know it. Only Jasper could recognise, idling at the top of Botany Street, the refurbished 1978 Holden Torana that belonged to Mayor Billy Fitz. He loved the car so dearly. Jasper often thought that, were he to try and create heaven itself for Billy L. Fitz, all he'd need to do was stick him in the Torana and point the mirrors to reflect his own face back at him. Whenever the 'results' came through from these uncontested sham elections, Billy would celebrate by revving up and down the streets of Norman. There were rumours that he used to do doughnuts in the cemetery, but Jasper had never witnessed that himself and wasn't one for idle gossip.

The engine revved as Billy tore down the street for a dramatic forty-metre journey, swerving just metres ahead of the assembled pack of journalists, who had a table at the front of the Sunshine Deli where they were sharing a laugh about their 'deeply authentic' muggaccinos. Jasper watched, fascinated, as Billy emerged from his car, dipping his head to accommodate the absurdly large akubra hat he had cracked out for the first time. His forehead was already awash with sweat. It seemed the tuxedo he'd decided to wear on this 43-degree day wasn't breathing quite as well as he would have hoped.

Jasper sighed to himself as he watched Billy pretend to nonchalantly bump into the journalists as he picked up his morning coffee.

Jasper tried to keep his focus on the bigger picture. This little experiment was good for the town. There was a distinct feeling that, against all odds, the town had been offered a future. A miracle drug had been produced.

Coffee in hand, Billy arrived for his interview. As Jasper sat down, a pedestal fan placed only inches from the mayor's face, on the agreement that it would be switched off before the recording began, he decided to play his part in this dance, however absurd he might personally consider it.

'That was chapter thirty-two from the audiobook of *The War of the Worlds*,' Jasper said. 'And now, we have a very special treat indeed. We've been teasing it for a while. At last, the moment is upon us. Without further ado, which, for those of you who might be unaware, is an expression that means without any further dilly-dallying. That's an odd term in itself, isn't it? Dilly-dallying. Where did that come from, I wonder? It certainly is evocative – and fun to say, I must admit. Quit your dilly-dallying, I say. Do you think perhaps there was once a man, or perhaps a pair of brothers, Dilly and Dally, who were notorious procrastinators, so much so that their names became synonymous with the entire practice?'

The mayor paused for a long time, turning to glance back at the reporters before answering. 'Is that really your first question?' he asked.

Jasper gathered himself. 'No, sorry, of course not, no. Though, if you are listening and you know the answer, make your way to the top of the hill and text it in or come and knock on my window. But of course, today is no day to dillydally since I was just in the process of introducing a man who needs no introduction, except, I suppose, on radio, since you cannot see him, unless you are at the window outside Radio Norman, where there are a great number of people gathered right now. Hello, everyone! What a treat this is for us all. For sure, the biggest day in Radio Norman's history, I would say. Wouldn't you?'

Again, Billy paused, a flash of anger reaching his eyes and dissipating as he smiled for the cameras. 'That's right, I'm Mayor William L. Fitz and it is a pleasure to be here on Radio Norman.'

'First thing is first,' Jasper said.

'Oh, is it?'

'Yes, now, Mr Mayor, it's the question the whole town is asking. When that scaffolding comes down and the tarp drops tomorrow, what are we going to be looking at?'

Billy turned to the window and flicked a smile, making sure to hold it long enough for a good shot from the cameras. 'Now, Jasper, you'll have to wait and see like everyone else.'

That soundbite would be carried on every station, and he knew it. Jasper had to begrudgingly admit the mayor was in fine form. He took a few minutes to pontificate about the long history of ingenuity in Norman. He even claimed that this was the first town in Australia to ever have a stop sign. Particularly as he coupled it with a pointed line about how things in Norman weren't stopping anymore, they were just getting going.

Yet, somehow, the never humble Mayor Fitz would not be drawn into questions about whether, once all this noise died down, he'd be interested in running for another term as mayor.

'We will have to see what the future holds,' Billy said, with a glint in his eye. 'We never know what opportunities might arise for any of us.'

With horror, Jasper realised that the man before him saw a window to actual power. This wasn't merely a press conference for his own ego. For Billy, this was a job interview. The media were here and he was prepared to put on a show.

It must have worked, too. By that evening, Norman's discount accommodation Motel Can-Afford-Ya and premium lodgings The Norman Continental, both of which sat side by side opposite the old tip, were both entirely booked. There were no rooms left above the

Stumbling Elephant. There were reports that some of the more enterprising members of Norman had taken a blow-up mattress and a few curtains to convert their garages into what they called an exclusive bed and breakfast. One national network broadcast van had already been spotted parked behind the Elephant, and there were whispers that the unveiling might be covered on breakfast television the next morning.

Before Jasper's very eyes, Norman as he knew it was changing forever.

14

'Who goes there!?' Rocko bellowed, pointing the rifle menacingly into the darkness. His handheld spotlight was blinding, and Mick's picnic basket rattled as he lifted it to cover his eyes.

'Watch where you're pointing that thing, Rocko,' Sandy shouted, the light sliding across to blind her.

Rocko squinted into the dark. 'What's the password?'

'You didn't give us a password, ya nong,' Mick bellowed, causing Rocko to spin rapidly on his heels, his finger inches from the trigger.

Rocko's lips pursed as he scratched his chin with the rifle barrel. 'Didn't I? I could have sworn I came up with a password. It was a good one, too. What was it? Oh, yeah, Norman. The password's Norman.'

Shaking his head, Mick continued to climb the hill, only to come face to face with the end of Rocko's rifle.

'I asked you for the password.'

'It's ... Norman,' Mick said.

'Hang on a minute,' Rocko said, tensing up. 'I hadn't told nobody that was the password. Just how exactly do you know it?'

'Rocko, put the gun down,' Sandy said with enough authority that Rocko, dejected, dropped it at his feet, firing a round off into the darkness. They all froze. Sandy picked up the rifle. Rocko reached forward and she pulled it away, leaving him to hang his head in a disappointed but unsurprised way.

Mick placed the basket down and pulled out three shot glasses and a bottle of whiskey. 'Sit down, you silly prick,' he said, lying on the grass overlooking the town. Sandy settled in beside Mick, offering the whiskey bottle to Rocko who politely waved it away. Sandy looked at him, making no effort to hide her surprise.

'I'm not drinking,' he explained. 'Three days now.' He paused to consider. 'Wait, breakfast yesterday. Day and a half.'

'That's still good, mate,' Mick said. 'I didn't bring anything else, though.'

Rocko lifted himself off the ground. 'It's alright, I'll duck down to the Elephant and grab a bottle of Passiona.'

'It's already locked up,' Sandy said.

'I know how to get in. Back soon,' Rocko replied, already lining up his Lucky Duck pizza box. He slid away, leaving the night to Mick and Sandy.

Sandy picked up the whiskey bottle but Mick snatched it from her hands. 'Hey, you're off duty,' he said, pouring them both a shot.

'Rocko not drinking, hey?' she said with surprise, taking her glass.

'I knew that, actually,' Mick said. 'Thought it might buy us a little bit of time to talk.'

'I might need more whiskey for that,' Sandy replied, making quick work of her shot and exhaling steam into the air. 'Look, we're grown-ups, I've done this dance before. We don't need to sugar-coat this. You've been through an awful lot. If this is all too much for you, just rip the bandaid off and tell me.'

There was the sound of a crash somewhere below, but Mick and Sandy gave it no attention. She was watching him as he looked out to the city below and sipped his drink.

'You know, I haven't actually tasted whiskey in years. Not for health reasons or anything like that. I had a damn stupid reason. I lived in a town with one pub and I was scared to go there because of the bartender.'

'Damn, she sounds beautiful and interesting,' Sandy said, topping up both of their glasses.

'That's the funny thing. I thought I'd be scared that I could never love again, but really I was scared because I knew that I could. I didn't know how to explain that to the kids, so I tried to hide it away. Did a pretty good job of it, too, I reckon.'

He turned to face her and felt his heart flutter. 'But that was a mistake,' Mick continued. 'A better dad would have tried to teach them that there's all different kinds of relationships, and ways to love, and experiences you'll have in your life and all that. Pretty sad that Ella had to teach it to me.'

He smiled and hoped it would hide the fear in his eyes and the sadness for all the time already lost.

'She's very wise, that girl. Must have had a good dad. The kind of bloke who would put his whole life on hold for her and her brothers.'

Mick leaned in closer, his words barely above a whisper. 'Sandy, I did you wrong. You deserved better. But if you give me the chance, I will spend every day—effing Rocko!'

Sandy was taken aback. That was not the offer she had been expecting. Most likely because Mick was not expecting Rocko to appear inches from his face, proudly holding aloft a 1.25-litre bottle of Passiona.

Rocko's grinning face fell as his eyes darted between them. 'What did I do?'

Sandy took the bottle from Rocko and patted him on the shoulder. 'Nothing, Rock. Mick was just telling me something I already knew.'

She twisted the bottle cap and passionfruit-scented foam sprayed all over the three of them.

'Aw, Rocko, you shook it up!' Sandy cried.

'Not my fault. I had to jump through the broken window.'

'You what!? Rocko, what have you done to my pub?'

Mick took the bottle and stepped between them. 'Hey now, let's just ... Rock, how about you just drink straight from the bottle?'

'Nah, I want it in the glass for a proper toast and everything.'

Mick shrugged and filled Rocko's glass.

'To making good trouble,' Mick said. They clinked their glasses and emptied them.

'How do you think they'll react?' Mick asked. 'It's pretty out there.'

Surprisingly, it was Rocko that provided the incisive answer. 'Stuff 'em. Look at this place,' he said. 'The kid's plan has worked already.'

He was right, too. The town was lit up in a way they hadn't seen for years. There was action and excitement. If this was the death rattle of Norman, at least she was going out with a bang.

'You know the best part?' Sandy said with a satisfied grin. 'Either way, Billy Fitz ends up humiliated.'

'I'll drink to that,' Mick said, topping up the glasses again.

They sat together for a long while, savouring the cool air. Night and day they'd worked on this statue. The project had quickly turned from rebel graffiti to industrial operation. Now, the paint had dried, the scaffolding had been brought down, and all that was left to do was remove the covers and let the town do the rest.

'Oh, I almost forgot. I've gotta show you something,' Rocko said, leading the others behind the statue and disappearing over the back of the hill.

'Where'd you go, Rocko?' Mick said, stumbling around in the dark.

'Hang on, it was around here somewhere,' Rocko answered.

'You took the torch, dickhead,' Sandy called.

'Oh yeah,' Rocko said, a half-second before a loud thud rang out, followed by a yelp. 'Never mind. Got it.'

They listened as Rocko rustled around in the dark until, in a flash, they were blinded by a floodlight that revealed itself only inches from their face with all the subtlety of a freight train.

'Christ,' Sandy yelped, shielding her eyes. Then, blinking as her eyes adjusted, her cry of pain turned into a cackle of laughter. 'Rocko, you mad bastard,' she said with delight.

'The kid said he'd promised the mayor something here would be named after him. I couldn't think of anything more appropriate.'

'A fine job, mate. A fine job,' Mick added. 'That deserves a toast.'

And the three of them poured a drink to christen the newly unveiled Mayor William L. Fitz Commemorative Outhouse.

15

Back in 1964, I felt that it was a most interesting challenge to be asked to produce a 40-foot-long banana ... Then the problem was, how do you actually design a Big Banana? Not being a great artist, I had to seek the best banana I could to copy.

Alan Chapman, Consulting Engineer, ABC News, 21 August 1991

The pain in Billy's throbbing head could not detract from the stars in his eyes. He sauntered through town receiving applause breaks along the way, feeling like a champion gladiator triumphantly marching through the streets.

The rattle of his key in the lock was a little too loud for his liking but he endured, as heroes do, and pushed open the door, ready for another day of serving the Norman community to the utmost of his ability between the hours of 11am and 2pm.

But he was not alone. As he opened the blinds he realised Allison was already sitting at his desk, waiting for him.

'How did you get in here?' Billy asked, startled. Allison tilted her head towards the large chunk missing out of the opposite wall. Billy cursed himself. He had really meant to get around to telling someone to fix that.

'Take a seat,' Allison said.

'Why thank you, they're mine,' Billy answered with a touch of snark. Uneasy, Billy settled in. He'd been so caught up in the energy of the town he hadn't thought about the Marshall Group. By the time they came to mind later in the night, he'd drunk enough to melt a breathalyser. The thought of having to deal with them caused him to down a couple more drinks to help forget. Then, he had become suddenly preoccupied with seeing Michelle, who had claimed to not be ready to see him that night and sent him to stumble on home.

Now, he was paying the price. He'd stupidly thought he'd have at least a day or two to gather himself before they found out. News travels fast, it seems.

'Can I start by saying I'm sorry,' Billy said.

'No, no, we're sorry,' Allison said. 'We were under the impression we had an understanding. You help us and in return, you would be generously compensated.'

'Well, it's a funny story,' Billy said.

'Is it?' Allison asked, raising an eyebrow.

'Depends on your sense of humour, I guess. Anyway, I think this can still work out for us. You might have to pay a bit more but whatever. Just pitch it as jobs for the community.'

'Actually, I have my own funny story,' Allison said, taking a sheet of paper out of her folio. 'It goes like this – a minerals company was ready to handsomely reward the Mayor of the Arse-End of Nowhere for his work in securing land that could be useful for a mining operation. Then, against all logic and sense, the Mayor of the Arse-End of Nowhere decided to draw a lot of attention to his town with some insane publicity stunt. This made the executives of the minerals company wonder if it would be worth all the hassle. So, they conducted their own independent analysis of the soil and found that the cobalt in your soil is of a very low purity and would produce a low net yield.'

She pushed the paper towards him. Billy's blood ran cold. 'You're not laughing, Mr Fitz? I guess you had to be there.'

Allison's expression turned somehow colder. She stood and walked to the door. 'Oh, and good luck with the unveiling. I hope it's worth it.'

***

Billy slunk into Michelle's store, his entrance announced by the door chimes. She had been expecting him, of course. She knew something was wrong. His aura must have been exuding negativity or his chakra had cracked or whatever. She'd lit candles for the occasion, but no amount of sandalwood could still his beating heart. His world was collapsing. Overleveraged financially, the proud owner of worthless property, the

308

whole nation waiting for him to unveil a statue he'd never seen, dreams of a beachside villa crumbling in his hands.

She took his head in her hands, her long red nails playing with his ear as she clutched him to her bosom, comforting him as he hyperventilated.

'I've seen what fate has in store for us,' she said. 'It is my curse that I cannot warn you what will happen, or it might not. But I can tell you this: when our stories were written in the stars, they were written together.'

Did he really believe she could see the future? He didn't know. But she believed in him. Maybe she was the only one.

'What is it going to be?' he asked. 'Tomorrow, the Big Thing, what is it?'

Her dark eyes studied him. 'It will be the start of our new lives.'

16

Pup heard the noise first; his old ears were still sharp at times. Norm could tell him to get off the couch a hundred times and he wouldn't hear a word. He could say that he wasn't sharing his dinner and Pup would look at him with those confused big eyes. But he could clearly make out the sound of wheels hitting gravel from a kilometre away. Nothing motivated that dog like the promise of pizza.

Norm had turned down an invitation of a night at the Big Thing, preferring to spend the last day of Norman as they knew it in his favourite way, at home on the couch with pizza, the dog and a selection from the DVD tower. The bit that made those nights magical was missing, but there was nothing to be done about that.

Pup scooted towards the door, a spryness in his legs that had not been there the night before. Norm took a little more effort to get off the couch lately.

There was a gentle knock at the door. Then another, less gentle, knock and finally a persistent banging on the door.

'Just leave it there, Reggie,' Norm said, not bothering to hide the frustration in his voice. First you hit a guy with your car, then you get mad at him for not coming to the door fast enough. That takes some nerve.

Another knock. 'Reggie, I swear to God,' Norm began, gripping his walker ready to strike as he opened the door.

Right at that moment, a day earlier than he'd expected, and in a way he'd never predicted, Norm Perkins felt his world change forever. It was the single best moment of his entire life, yet he only managed to say one word.

'Ella.'

***

He looked at her as if seeing her for the first time, as he always did. This moment was all she could think about as she drove through the night. This was the dawning of her new life and she wasn't going to wait another second for it to begin.

Ella stepped through the door and grabbed him by the collar. She pulled him close and kissed him long and hard, his shock seemingly overtaken by instinct as his hands found their way to her back and held her tightly.

After what felt like a lifetime, she pulled back and they stood, looking at one another. Norm blinked as if trying to check he was truly awake, wrapped his arms around her and pulled her back in. She felt entirely absorbed by him. She fell into his chest and gripped her hands onto his shoulders, straining her neck up to kiss him again.

Their eyes betrayed what they weren't able to say. Their words could never do it justice. This was more primal. It was abstract, ethereal and yet perfectly clear. Unspoken not out of fear but unspoken because it was already understood. They refused to break apart. Ella closed her eyes and kissed Norm again, slowly and passionately, desperate to live in this moment as long as she possibly could. She opened her eyes and saw him looking at her so lovingly, holding her so tenderly, that all she could do was smile and think how nice it felt to be whole again.

He smiled and so did she. Then, Ella, always the mature one, scrunched her face and stuck her tongue out. She ran her hands down his arms, took hold of Norm's hands and stepped back. 'Sorry, I interrupted you. What were you saying?'

'Well, actually I ... you know I had this whole thing I was going to ... actually,' Norm said, pulling her back. He bent down and kissed her neck softly, over and over.

'No, you're right. Let's just keep doing this,' Ella said, wrapping her arms around Norm.

She felt a little wet nose press into her leg. Norm waved his hand frantically, clicking his fingers in the old dog's face.

'Pup, go away. Go away.'

Ella smiled, extracted herself and bent down to scratch the old dog. 'I missed you, too, buddy. Yeah, I missed you, too. Now, I am going to take Norm into the bedroom so you go somewhere and block your ears, okay?'

She gave Pup a smack on the backside and sent him off towards the lounge room. She curled her way back up to Norm and put her arms around his neck.

'What was that?' he said.

She smiled. 'You heard me.'

Ella took his hand and guided him through the hallway. Norm moved slowly, his hip staggering. She paused. 'Are you going to be okay?'

'I don't care if I die in there.'

'Suit yourself.'

Their movements were nervous yet tender. She undressed him slowly, running her hand lightly over his scar, tracing it down his side. Naked, lit only by moonlight, Ella thought about how strange it was that they could know each other so well yet not at all.

Norm's hands took her feverishly, holding her tight, the warmth of their bodies causing her skin to tingle as he kissed her hard, lowering her onto the bed gently yet with a strength that she did not know he possessed. He climbed on top of her and slowly their breath became one.

The moments after seemed so delicate, embarrassing really. She stared at the ceiling in silence, then she turned to face Norm, only to notice he was already staring at her. They both smiled, then laughed at how dorky that felt.

'So, we should have been doing that for ages,' Ella said.

'We can always make up for lost time,' Norm replied.

She intertwined her fingers with Norm's, holding them above their heads and turning them in the moonlight.

'I shouldn't have left.'

'Yes, you should have,' Norm said. 'There's a whole world out there. You deserve the chance to go and make everyone fall in love with you.'

He didn't say 'fall in love with you, too' but Ella heard it all the same.

'I should have told you,' Ella replied.

'Okay, maybe that's true.'

Ella let out a small laugh then buried her head in his chest. She knew what she wanted to say. She wanted to tell him she wasn't ready to say goodbye to him. She wanted to tell him that she loved him and hear him tell her that he loved her, too. Really say it. But that was too much to face. Not right now. Instead, she asked something much simpler. 'So, should we watch a movie?'

They made their way out of the room, still wrapped in each other, kissing as if they'd waited their whole life to do it, which, she supposed, they probably had. She wore a green t-shirt she'd taken out of Norm's drawers, while he wandered out of his room in his boxers. They found Pup scratching at the front door.

Ella left Norm to investigate and found a fresh box of pizza at the door.

'Oh my god,' she laughed. 'Do you think Reggie heard us?'

Norm shrugged. 'Sushi life.'

17

'It has stood for over half a century but at the weekend the iconic ten-metre statue of Captain Cook was removed after being deemed a controversial symbol of colonialism. Local Martin Anton bought the landmark for just one dollar ... bargain of the century.'

Karl Stefanovic, *The Today Show,* **30 May 2022**

Nothing about this day felt real. It was cloaked in the soft haze of a dream, from the very first moments as Norm awoke to find Ella in his bed, wrapped in his sheets and nothing else. She had already been watching him, for who knows how long. They locked eyes and smiled. Ella's face immediately scrunched up.

'That felt too schmaltzy,' she said.

Norm comically rubbed his eyes and poked her cheek. 'Oh my god, you're actually real.' He poked her again. 'You're really, really real and you're actually here.'

'Keep poking me and I won't be here for long,' Ella laughed. 'Here, I'll prove it to you.'

They kissed and she rolled on top of him. Norm screamed in pain and Ella shuffled off. 'Sorry! Sorry, sorry, sorry!'

His screams turned to laughter. 'No, you proved your point. I believe you're real now.'

They took their time getting out of bed that morning. It was as if they had a silent understanding that while they were in these sheets, they were safe. Time would stand still for them. Outside those doors, the future beckoned. Where would they be when it finally arrived?

***

Everyone wanted a piece of Billy Fitz. He danced from interview to interview appearing on three major breakfast television programs as well as the one put to air by the national broadcaster that was shown to hospital patients and members of the Qantas Club. Having long resigned himself to being a big fish in a small pond, it looked like Billy was beginning to aspire to becoming a regular-sized fish in a polluted estuary. He was built for the camera, energetic, folksy, just ridiculous enough that it made good television.

Norm kept his distance. If the mayor was happy to take the credit for this, then all the better. Michelle the town psychic followed the mayor from appointment to appointment, beaming with pride for reasons that Norm didn't understand but he put down to a true inability to know a single thing that the future might hold. Norm, at least, understood what was about to happen. He felt sick with excitement and dread. There must have been hundreds of people spilling out onto the road and the fields surrounding Vodafone Hill. The dirt was covered with picnic rugs, plastic chairs, milk crates, and stools stolen from the Stumbling Elephant. The crowd competed for the best space, which was any spot where your view wouldn't be blocked by the towering figure of Big Gavin Walsh.

Reggie Piper, in a surprising display of ingenuity, had set up his own merchandise stand at the base of the hill. The business seemed an instant success even though the shirts for sale were clearly from Reggie's own wardrobe, with crude slogans written on with sharpie. He'd already sold out of 'I whipped my Big Thing out in Norman' shirts and he was running low on the accompanying 'I Saw Norman's Big Thing' designs.

The Big Thing stood proudly, draped in the cover that still had Ella's message of love emblazoned on it. Above the statue, there was an even more remarkable sight: dark clouds over Norman.

Sandy, Mick and Rocko had set up a kind of viewing platform on the roof of the pub, a prime location that also promised a safe distance from everyone when the cover came down. They'd even created a little pulley-and-winch system to lift a basket containing Pup all the way to the roof.

Mick had been stunned to see his daughter back in town and wrapped her in a powerful hug, his eyes immediately watering. It was as if they had been apart for a year. Ella had to fight to extract herself.

Norm checked his phone and realised, miracle of miracles, he had reception. Mick saw him looking and leaned down. 'Noticed that, hey?' he said with a satisfied smile. 'We put a repeater in Cook's hat. As long as the Big Thing is up, the whole town gets reception. Now, we need a new name for the hill.'

Norman may not have joined the twenty-first century, but it was at least finally entering the late twentieth.

Moments later, Mick approached again, this time shuffling his feet nervously like a schoolboy. 'Ella, there's someone I need you to meet.'

He took her by the hand and escorted her to the other side of the roof. Ella shot Norm a confused look as she was dragged along by the now eager steps of her father.

'Sandy, this is my daughter.'

'The daughter I've known her whole life? That daughter?' Sandy asked.

Mick blushed. 'Oh, yeah. Sorry. I—'

'Dad, are you blushing?' Ella laughed, dumbfounded at what she was seeing.

'Shut up, nah I'm not, I was just...' Mick stammered.

Sandy grabbed him by his paint-flecked shirt. 'Oh, you big softie,' she said, planting a kiss on his lips. She turned back to Ella. 'He's a good bloke, your dad.'

'That he is,' Ella smiled.

Sandy popped a bottle of sparkling and poured everyone a glass, except for Rocko, who had lemonade in his, complete with strawberry on the rim.

'Look at all you've built here,' Ella said, turning to Norm.

'We built,' he said, giving her a nudge.

'Oh, you're not pinning this on me,' Ella replied, giving him a poke in the ribs. 'The Big Thing was your idea.'

'The design was your idea!' Norm was worked up now. He turned from the crowd to look down to Ella's grinning face. 'Why are you messing with me today of all days?'

'Because it's fun,' she answered, hopping onto her toes to give him a kiss. Over her shoulder, Norm saw Sandy give him a private smile and tilt her glass.

When he looked back, Ella had wrapped her arms around his stomach. 'You never told me why,' she said.

'Why what?'

'Why a Big Thing? What inspired that?'

Norm shook his head. 'It's stupid.'

'That has never stopped you before,' Ella said.

He took a deep breath in. He shrugged. 'You know, I always knew you would go one day. Don't look at me like that. I really did. You had to – a town this small couldn't hold someone like you. It wouldn't be fair. So, when I was standing at the bottom of the hill that day I was thinking about how I couldn't stop you from leaving Norman, and all I could ever hope is that every so often you would find your way back. So, I came up with a way to make that a little bit easier.'

Ella looked up at him in silence. She pulled him close, digging her fingers into his back with the kind of grip that made it clear to him that she would never, ever let him go again.

'Look,' Rocko called from his vantage point, his legs dangling off the edge of the Stumbling Elephant rooftop, binoculars in hand, gesticulating wildly towards the base of the hill. 'They're about to start.'

It had taken Billy Fitz four attempts to get to the top of Vodafone Hill. He had made the unwise decision to wear Italian leather wingtips this morning, the height of fashion but a choice that made it impossible for his feet to get a purchase on the steep hill. Instead, he had to crawl up on all fours – an undignified look, particularly when a clump of grass came off in his hand, showering the mayor in soil.

But at last, a reverent hush fell over the crowd as the mayor, his tuxedo now sweat-logged and dirt-stained, approached the makeshift podium on top of Vodafone Hill.

'Now, I don't know about you, but I have no interest in listening to anything that man has to say,' Mick said, putting his arms around Ella, Norm and Rocko. 'So, we thought we might have our own little ceremony.'

'Hear, hear,' Sandy added, popping a fresh bottle of sparkling. 'I think it's only appropriate that someone says a few words.'

Mick looked to Ella, who looked to Norm, who looked back to Mick, each waiting for the other to take the mantle. In the end, it was Rocko who stood atop the esky and addressed the group.

'It was Pericles who said that what you leave behind is not engraved into stone but woven into the lives of others.'

They listened enraptured. Two days off the booze and the man was a savant.

'I don't care what happens with the statue or Fitz or any of that crap. You mongrels have already saved Norman. That's what makes a community. If this plan doesn't work and a month from now we're all back downstairs hearing those sad pricks talk about how the town is dying, we will know that's crap. We are Norman.'

With that, the gang raised their glasses and let out a cheer that drew the attention of a few of those gathered at the base of the hill, who then quickly turned back to the scheduled festivities.

Rocko paused, overcome by the moment. He wiped his face with the dirtiest handkerchief Norm had ever seen and spluttered, 'To think, if I hadn't hit you with that can of beer none of this would have ever happened.'

Norm hardly had the heart to tell him that, if anything, it had made the whole thing a lot harder. Instead, he patted the old man on the back and was brought in for the most pungent hug of his life.

The booming voice of Mayor Fitz echoed around the town. Surprisingly, the mayor had chosen to open the morning's ceremony with the national anthem, performed by himself. There was an initial buzz of excitement from the spiteful observers on the roof of the Elephant, knowing that nothing spelled disaster like an a cappella anthem. It was much to their disappointment to discover that all this time, Billy Fitz had been hiding a beautiful, operatic voice. In his hands, the dull, old, uninspiring song was impossibly compelling. His thick vibrato resonated across the ground, shaking the windows of the Stumbling Elephant. For a moment, Norm worried about the structural integrity of the old building. He took a deep breath, scared he might hyperventilate. It was really happening. For better or worse, their lives would all change from the next moment. Ella took his hand and squeezed it tight.

'It will be okay,' she said, as if she could read his mind.

The noise in the crowd began to rise and they realised the unveiling was getting close. Billy Fitz's voice boomed over the crowd.

'People of Norman, as your mayor, I promised to put this town on the map. Today, that promise is fulfilled. In the future, as you look upon this structure, know that this is the work of William L. Fitz.'

'Ella,' Norm said, leaning down to whisper into her ear. 'Promise me something?'

Her usually joyful face suddenly became very, very serious. 'What is it?'

'Next time you leave, take me with you.'

The crowd had started a countdown, chanting as one. 'Ten! Nine! Eight!'

Ella looked up at Norm, a look of utter shock on her face. 'But it's Norman,' she said.

'I've always wanted to say this,' he told her. 'This town ain't big enough for the both of us.'

Mayor Billy Fitz took the thick rope into his hand, preparing to pull down the covers. 'Six! Five!'

'You helped build my dream. I want to help build yours. That is, if you'll have me.'

Ella scrunched her face up. 'I'll think about it,' she said. Then before Norm could react, she gave him a long, deep kiss, her arms wrapping around his neck as she pressed against him.

'Oi, lovebirds,' Sandy shouted, snapping them both back to reality. 'Here it comes!'

'Two! One!'

With a cacophony of cheers, claps and whistles calling him on, Billy Fitz pulled at his rope, the cover fell and for the first time the people of Norman saw the Big Thing. The hundreds of people gathered were stunned into silence as they tried to process what they saw before them.

The all-too-familiar figure of Captain James Cook, bent over as if bowing to the crowd. But there was something very unnatural about his pose. Then, with horror, they realised he wasn't bowing, he was doubled over in pain, a large serrated chunk of metal entering the figure's stomach and bursting through the other end, blood shining off the edge of the blade and soaking the shirt of Cook. His hands, also soaked in blood, held his stomach, as if trying to keep it together. Then there were the eyes, which captured the perfect mix of shock and fear of a man who has just become acutely aware that he is about to die.

The gigantic figure was gruesome and grotesque, the wound truly sickening to behold.

The shock rippled through the crowd. Parents covered their children's eyes. Groans of disgust began to cry out. Even Ella, who had conceived of this figure, felt a deep sickness in her stomach. Norm bent down and whispered in her ear, 'As I was saying, I think it's time for us to leave.'

The sounds of displeasure turned to anger, a fury that was directed at Mayor Billy Fitz, still holding the rope that revealed the monstrosity. Slowly, triggered by the crowd's reaction, he turned and looked up at the figure. All the colour drained from his face as he saw his political career end before him. Cameras flashed and a can of Melbourne Bitter flew through the air, narrowly missing Billy's still-gaping mouth.

'We've been had!' one man shouted.

'This is sick,' cried another.

Some members of the crowd began to rush the hill, while others threw projectiles at the mayor, who had to seek refuge behind the shin of the colossus.

Then, all at once, the clouds erupted.

Rain!

Rain over Norman!

Not a small drop but a deluge, unleashed all at once. A monsoon, striking with force, heavy enough to make the Big Thing impossible to see. It felt as if they had received a message from heaven, but such was the ferocity of the rain it was impossible to discern as either damnation or salvation.

Norm looked for Ella and found her on the other side of the roof, her back to the Big Thing, facing the town. Her beauty shone as she stood proud, her chin held high, watching the rain wash away the red dust from the facade of the old shed to reveal the portrait of the young girl dancing by the river's edge.

'Time to go,' Mick said, opening the hatch that led back into the safety of the Elephant. Rocko stayed sitting on the ledge, soaked from head to toe, sipping his lemonade and watching the chaos unfold underneath him.

'You go on, mate,' he said, toasting Mick. 'I'm happy right where I am.'

18

...a disgraceful revisionist attack on an icon that speaks to the depravity of left-wing culture. We encourage all Australians to visit Norman and be sickened in person...

The Australian, 15 February 2039

...Big Thing that shows the Cooked Cap'n himself copping it right in the gussy. I know I'm endeavouring to take a road trip to Norman immediately!

Pedestrian. TV, 15 February 2039

...after all, we are a nation of larrikins, and if we wish to preserve this carefree attitude it's essential that we immediately convict Mayor Billy Fitz...

The Full Chudd, Sky News Australia, 15 February 2039

...an artistic controversy reminiscent of the furore that followed Picasso's *Les Demoiselles d'Avignon*, which has personally filled me with such ennui I could hardly finish my madeleine...

The Guardian, 15 February 2039

19

'Bon appetit,' Norm said, placing a plate of scrambled eggs down in front of Ella. Pup sat on the floor by the end of the table, waiting expectantly. Norm placed a metal bowl in front of him and gave his ears a scratch.

'Wow,' she said, picking through them with a fork. 'Didn't use the microwave today, Chef?' She tried a mouthful. 'Edible! You are learning.'

Norm smiled. 'Oh, you know, I'm a fancy city boy now.'

He shuffled to the kitchen bench. In his hand, he held the cane that Rocko had gifted him, complete with a metal topper that looked just like the head of a razorback. It was a little cool and a lot frightening, just like Rocko. Norm retrieved his plate and took a seat opposite Ella, who watched him intently.

'Do you hate it here?' she asked. 'You can tell me.'

Norm looked through the window of his small apartment, knowing that somewhere in the distance, beyond the hills, Norman was out there. The thought comforted him even if, by all reports, it had changed, too. Not only was Norman famous, it had become infamous. The Big Thing had made the front page of the national broadsheet, which declared it a disgrace. The breakfast shows had kept a week of rolling coverage and late-night commentators threatened to tear it down themselves. They had their knives out for Billy Fitz in particular, who according to them had 'offended the sensibilities of every fair dinkum Australian'.

His claims that he'd been set up had been dismissed by one writer as the complaints of 'Australia's absolute worst sooky-la-la'.

Elsewhere, the Big Thing was a cult hit. The story had run on youth media websites with headlines like 'Cook Fkn Cooked As Norman Whips Out Its Big Thing', while social media influencers were taking day trips out to get photos posing bent over with the statue.

With a disgraced mayor on the run and no one else interested in taking charge, Sandy had assumed the position of Interim Mayor. She made her second act as Interim Mayor the paying of all invoices related to the construction of the Big Thing, which she happily reported had indeed revitalised the economy of Norman as people travelled far and wide for the opportunity to be horrified in person.

Of particular note was Reggie Piper's merchandise store, which he operated out of the old mayor's office, now that the official office of the mayor had been relocated to the Stumbling Elephant, since Sandy had to be there anyway. By all accounts his 'Nothing's Normal in Norman' shirts were the second-best seller, a fact that Norm absorbed with glee. Though, he was a little miffed to lose out to 'Norman: Home of the Massive Cook Up'.

Newly flushed with cash, Sandy's first act was to fund a reticulated water system that would use recycled water to irrigate and revive Norman's historic agricultural industry. Of course, this new irrigation system needed a name, and she was more than happy to declare it the Mayor Billy Fitz's Memorial Irrigation System, with a little plaque that explained that, while the mayor himself lives, this system only exists thanks to his political career literally going to the shitter and dying.

Norm's own payments, for innovation, development and planning of the Big Thing, netted him enough money to afford the rent for his small apartment and gave him enough time to settle in and decide what it was he wanted to do next.

'Nah,' Norm finally answered. 'I'm really starting to like it.'

Ella checked her watch. 'Ah crap, my first lecture starts in twenty minutes. I'd better get a move on. What are you up to today?'

'Well, there's the German Film Festival that Pup wanted to see today but first I've got to catch up on my mail,' Norm answered, reaching into his satchel and removing an envelope which he placed on the desk, removing a single piece of paper torn from a legal pad. Ella's eyes threatened to bulge out of her head. She had forgotten all about the letter. The drama of the day had overtaken the thought, and then everything was going so well she hadn't even thought to ask.

'You are absolutely not reading that,' she said in a panic, trying to snatch the paper off him. But Norm was too quick, pulling it away.

'Hey, hey, hey, this is my mail.'

Ella shrank in her chair. 'Look, I was in a bad place when I was writing that. I didn't know if I'd ever see you again. I thought I'd messed everything up for good.'

'Oh no, it says here my uncle has a hernia. Poor guy. I didn't even know I had an uncle.'

Ella tried to swipe the letter out of Norm's hands, but he held it at arm's length.

'Fine,' Ella said, grabbing her bag and heading for the door.

'Wait, can you post something for me?'

Norm handed her a card. The picture showed a sad cartoon dog with a speech bubble saying 'Sorry to hear about your doggone haemorrhoids'. Ella scrunched her face involuntarily. She flashed Norm a suspicious look and opened the card.

> *To Ella,*
> *Thank you for believing in me, even when I didn't.*

Thank you for loving me, especially when I couldn't.
You made my dreams come true.
I can't wait to do the same for you.
Together, we will fix your uncle's hernia.

'Yuck,' she said.
'Keep reading,' Norm urged.

I love you, Ella.
That was the real Big Thing all along.

'What? That doesn't even make sense.'

'I'm glad you liked it.'

'I like you.'

'I like you.'

With that, she left.

While Norm stayed, and dreamed about their future.

Big dreams.

Acknowledgements

The first reader of this book was supposed to be my dear friend Steph Doohan. But I was too slow. All the same, her spirit is felt throughout this book. It's filled with her humour, her attitude, and I am certain every grammatical error I've allowed is being met with her scorn somewhere.

This book would not exist without the tireless work of Tom Langshaw, who took a chance on this book, and from the very first moments understood it better than me. Thank you to Kirsty, Léa, Kajal, Lauren, and all of the incredible team at Pantera have all been impossibly kind through this whole process, answering a series of annoying questions from the world's most nervous nerd. And of course, thank you to Hazel Lam for making a gorgeous cover.

To all the people who gave me early advice, read incomplete extracts, offered advice and put up with me throughout the process, I would like to offer my endless gratitude. Namely, Bridie Connell, Kara Schlegl, Bridie Jabour, The Penrith Lot, Bec Shaw, Wil Anderson, Tony Armstrong, Alice Nolan, Maria Lewis, Shirley Evans and the World's Least Encouraging Group Chat.

To all the lovely people who risked their reputation to endorse this, thank you. Virginia Gay (who transported a photocopied version of the book across the world), Annabel Crabb, Andrew Denton, Nakkiah Lui, Jan Fran, Susie Youssef, Benjamin Law, Rachael Johns, Clare Fletcher and Brydie Lee-Kennedy.

Finally, my wonderful family. You give me purpose and make it possible to fulfil. Everything from reading early copies of the book to family members who could no longer read it to themselves, to making illegal merch that you will be prosecuted for, I appreciate all your support.

To Grace, thank you for putting up with a father trying to play peek-a-boo from an office chair and for throwing all the books in my office onto the floor to show me that all art is fleeting.

To Miranda, oh how to even start? This book is filled with your wit, your kindness, your rudeness and your beauty. You provided endless support on the page and in our home. Without you, I would not be able to write, I would have no one to write for, and I would not know the love that I write about.

To Brando, you were no help. If anything, you are a hindrance. Get out from under the desk. I know you've been fed. I was the one that fed you. It was fifteen minutes ago. You are fooling no one.

Text credits

Chapter 14: 'Ned is a money spinner in Kelly Country', *The Canberra Times,* 18 March 1990 © *Canberra Times*/ACM

Part 2: YouTube video uploaded by MrAgm65, 23 November 2012

Chapter 2: *The Today Show* via YouTube, 8 July 2022

Chapter 4: *The Canberra Times,* 27 January 1989 © *Canberra Times*/ACM

Chapter 7: Prime Minister Scott Morrison, 9 December 2021

Chapter 9: ABC News via YouTube, 9 September 1991

Chapter 11: 'Halfway mark of continent', *Port Lincoln Times,* 30 September 1999 © *Port Lincoln Times*

.

Part 3: 'Big, brash and finally treasured', *The Sydney Morning Herald,* 14 July 2009 © *The Sydney Morning Herald* The use of this work has been licensed by Copyright Agency except as permitted by the Copyright Act, you must not re-use this work without the permission of the copyright owner or Copyright Agency

Chapter 3: 'Maccas build giant Big Mac for Australia Day', *AdNews,* 25 January 2017

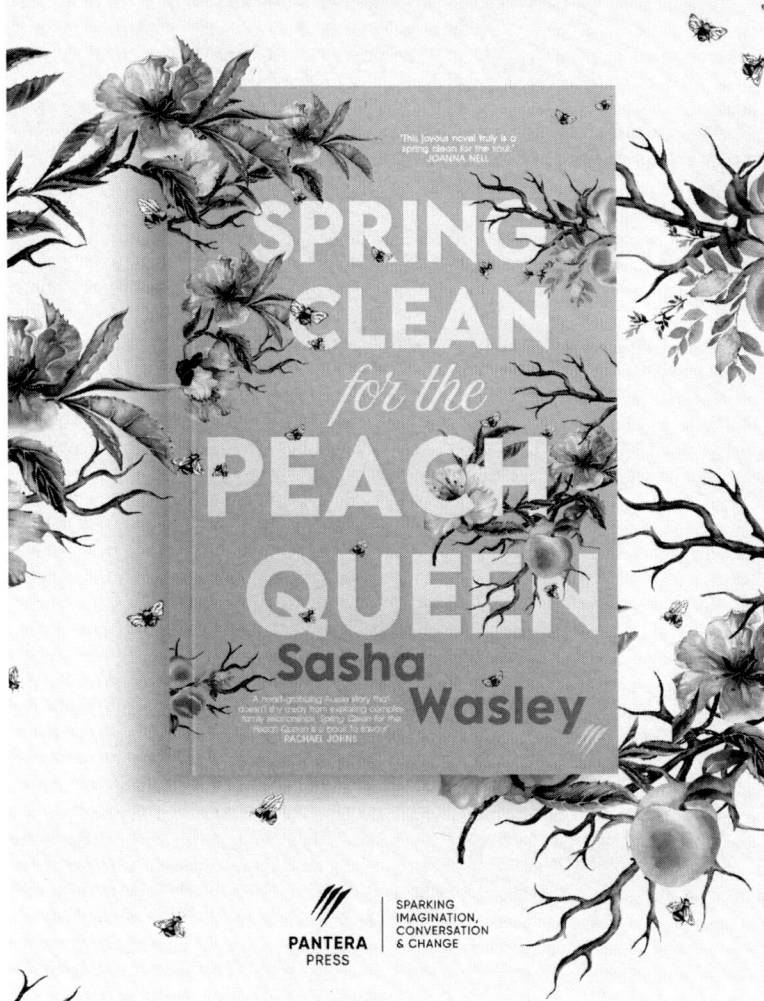

'A heart grabbing Aussie story'
RACHAEL JOHNS

A dazzling literary debut, Everyone and Everything will make you laugh, cry and call your sister.

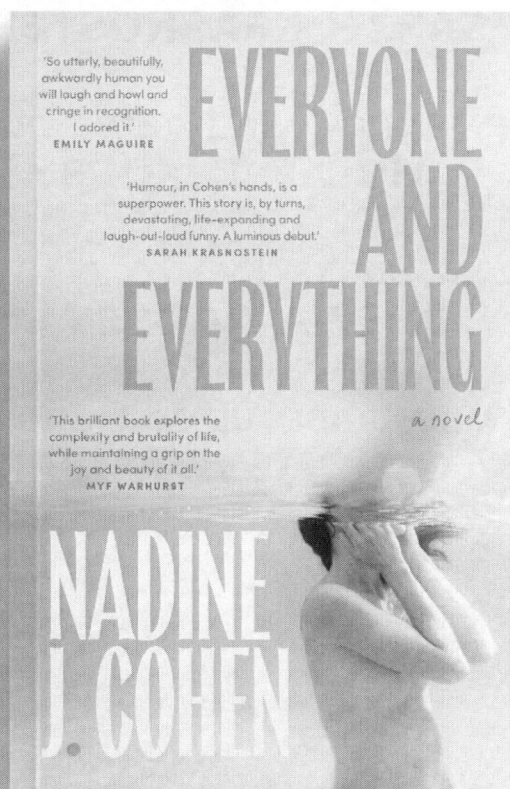

'So utterly, beautifully, awkwardly human you will laugh and howl and cringe in recognition.'
EMILY MAGUIRE

'This novel is melancholy, funny and unpredictable – just like its protagonist. A great read.'
ALLEE RICHARDS

'I couldn't put it down. Humour, in Cohen's hands, is a super power. Sh uses it so deftly to tell a story that is, by turns, devastating, life-expanding and laugh-out-loud funny.'
SARAH KRASNOSTEIN

'A clever, funny, and very warm novel.'
HOLLY THROSBY

'One of the best books I've read in ages and ages.'
EWA RAMSEY

'tender, honest and utterly unputdownable.'
GENEVIEVE NOVAK

PANTERA PRESS

SPARKING IMAGINATION, CONVERSATION & CHANGE

Back Cover Material

A heartwarming, hilarious, quintessentially Australian novel about young love, small towns and underdogs overcoming the odds

.

NORM has lived in Norman his whole life. It's where he grew up, where he went to school and met his best friend Ella. But the town is dying: the river has dried up, and with it all the jobs.

One night at the pub, Norm announces a plan. He's going to build a Big Thing – like Coffs Harbour's Big Banana or Ballina's Big Prawn – to drive tourism to the town and give it a future. And to show Ella that she could have a future here too, maybe even with him.

ELLA, meanwhile, plans to leave Norman for the big smoke. She's tired of being a big fish in a small pond, especially when that pond is running out of water.

Ella encourages Norm's big idea nonetheless. If it works, Norm will have a larger-than-life reminder of her. And if not, at least they'll have one last perfect summer together.

342

Will Norm from Norman build a Big Thing in time to save his town, and convince the girl of his dreams she belongs here – or is it too late?

'*The Next Big Thing* is absurd and moving, ridiculous and sublime ... It's soaringly silly and it'll steal your heart.'
Clare Fletcher, author of Five Bush Weddings

Manufactured by Amazon.ca
Acheson, AB